THE
LIBRARIAN

A.J. RIVERS

PROLOGUE

C ARLOTTA OPENED HER EYES AND SAT BOLT UPRIGHT. THE COLD OF the concrete had seeped into her bones and they ached.

Two other women and a man were in the room with her. She knew none of them. Fear flowed through her like a tidal wave, threatening to make her pass out again.

Had she passed out, or had she been knocked out? She couldn't remember. It had been a hard night of partying; lots of drinking, lots of powder up her nose, pills down her throat, and dancing. There had been dancing. Loud music. The pop-synth kind that paired well with laser lights.

Memories came back in snaps and snips, but none were complete. Just flashing images.

The man stirred and coughed.

"Hey," Carlotta said sharply. "Who the hell are you?" She struggled to stand, using one hand against the bare brick wall to pull upward.

The man's lank dark hair tumbled over his face as he jerked in her direction. He wore skin-tight pants and no shirt. His bare back and arm raked over the rough surface and he cursed as he sat upright. "Who the hell are *you*? Where are we?" He scrubbed at his face with his palms.

"That's what I was going to ask you. Where—"

A shrill scream pierced through the dank air. Carlotta clamped her hands over her ears and stumbled. The debris on the floor bit into her knees and she yelled indignantly.

"Shut up," the man bellowed.

"Who are you? What did you do to me?" the other woman asked, scuttling back toward a wall on her butt.

The woman beside her stood slowly, like someone waking from anesthesia. She turned to the panicked blonde and held one hand in a shushing gesture and pressed the other to her own temple. "Please, don't scream again."

"Screw you, dumbass. Look around. Did you sign up for a night in the dungeon? Because I didn't."

Carlotta gained her feet again. "I don't know any of you, and I don't know where we are. Do any of you know any more than I do?"

A resounding no was her answer. She nodded. "I remember being at a party last night. It was for artists in the area. Our... uhm... fall break, I guess you could call it. What's the last thing you remember?"

The man cleared his throat lightly. "Aren't you the artist Lotta Love?"

Carlotta blinked dumbly at him for a moment. It always took her off-guard when someone recognized her. The semi-fame was a new thing over the last couple of years, and people recognizing her still felt weird. She finally nodded.

He grinned and ran a hand through his shoulder-length hair to push it away from his forehead. "Cool. I'm Sylvester Stratford. I was in Connor Aldridge's Rising Star Artist Program last year. I think I started the program just a few months after you were out."

His grin seemed stupid in light of their situation. Carlotta nodded again and looked to the women.

The blonde against the wall stepped forward. "I'm Gabby Sloan. I'm in that program right now." She cast a furtive glance around and shrugged. "Or, I *was* in the program. This isn't part of it, right?"

"Damn, what drug are you on?" Sylvester asked sarcastically.

"No," Carlotta said, giving Sylvester a dark look. Her senses were returning, and so were more vivid memories from the previous night. She closed her eyes and braced against the wall.

THE LIBRARIAN

She sniffed coke from the back of a man's hand. He smiled and handed her a drink as he led her to a dark corner next to a small door. A placard on the door read: EXIT ONLY. Someone had drawn a smiley face in the O. Carlotta laughed and pointed at it.

The man opened the door and they stepped out into an abandoned parking lot surrounded by high, rusted, vine-laden fencing.

"That's right. Just this way," the man said, urging her forward.

Carlotta looked at the mover's box-truck and then at the man by her side. He was still smiling, but it didn't feel as friendly as when she had snorted the coke from his hand. She drank from the cup he had given her. It was bitter. She gagged and dropped it. Liquid splashed her foot. The man laughed, but it didn't sound good-natured. It sounded dark, menacing, and his arm tightened around her waist.

Carlotta tried to jerk free, but the world turned into a merry-go-round intent on slinging her off the edge.

Someone had hold of her as the memory faded. The dirty, dank room spun into sharp focus, and she swung wildly at the man holding onto her. Her fist slammed into the side of his face. Hair flew forward like stage curtains closing as his head jerked backward. They stumbled away from each other; him holding his face and cursing, and Carlotta squaring up to punch again.

"Whoa," the brunette said, intervening. She stepped between them and faced Carlotta. "What the hell just happened? You looked totally spaced-out."

Carlotta told them what she had remembered. "I'm sorry," she said to Sylvester.

Wiping blood from under his nose where a small steady trickle had started up, he nodded. "No problem." He tossed up his hands. "I'd say a busted nose is the least of my worries."

Gabby pounded at the metal door. "Hello?!" she yelled with her face an inch from the corrosion-crusted surface.

"I don't think that'll do any good," the brunette said. "I'm guessing we're somewhere that no one can hear us scream."

"Oh, and you're the authority on Club Dungeon now? Who the hell are you to tell me what to do, anyway?" Gabby snarked.

"Lila Briggs, the woman who's about to kick your ass if you don't shut up."

Gabby spun on her, fire in her eyes as she bared her teeth and clenched her fists.

Carlotta stepped between them and turned to look at Gabby. "She's right. We all need to stay calm and look for a way out."

"Oh, you mean like the freaking door right here?" Gabby kicked it and yelled for help twice more. The echo of her own voice was the only answer, and she screamed wordlessly as she ran her hands into her long hair.

Carlotta ignored her and looked around for the source of the weak light filtering down on them. It was a hole in the ceiling. The very high ceiling that was completely out of reach without a second story floor. "Well, that's useless."

They all looked up.

"That's at least twenty feet high," the brunette said.

"Does this feel like an abandoned warehouse to anyone else?" Sylvester asked.

"How the hell would I know what a warehouse *feels* like?" Gabby said, kicking the door and yelling again. She rubbed her arms and backed away a few steps. "This whole thing is too much. I just want to go home and wake up and believe I'm not in a *Saw* movie."

"That's not helping," Carlotta said sharply, still looking around for any possible way out. No windows, only one door with no door handle, and a pristine, shiny deadbolt that had been installed backward. They were screwed. "Were any of you at that party last night?"

"I was at a bar downtown trying to drink myself blind," Sylvester said.

"I was at home," the brunette said. "I had a glass of wine while I was working on a piece for submission at Monday's meeting."

"Meeting?" Gabby asked. "With who?"

"Connor Aldridge."

"You're in an Aldridge program?" Gabby moved closer.

"Yeah. Got accepted just last week."

"So, not *your* home, but one set up for you by the program, which means you either live with a group, or totally alone," Gabby persisted.

"Yeah, whatever. That's where I was, and I live totally alone. Hell of a way to celebrate a birthday, huh?" Her eyes widened, and she snapped her fingers. "Someone drugged the wine." She pointed to Carlotta. "And the coke you sniffed, or your drink." She pointed to Sylvester. "And probably one of your drinks at the bar. You said it was downtown. Downtown *where*? What city?" The panic on her face was mirrored on Sylvester and Gabby's faces.

"Duh, New York," he replied. "Isn't that where all of you were?"

"Yes," they answered simultaneously.

"And it was definitely my drink," Carlotta said, remembering the bitter taste of it and how the world spun after only a single sip.

Movement outside the door drew their attention. Gabby flew to the door and began yelling again. Carlotta shushed her, and Gabby shoved her away to continue yelling and pounding.

"Help us!" she screamed. "We can't get out. Open the door from your side; there's no handle in here. Who's out there? Hello? I can hear you. Please, help us. We can't open the door."

"That's the whole point," a man's dignified, calm voice replied.

Gabby stepped back as if she had been gut-punched, wrapped her arms around her waist, and shook her head. "No." Her voice was barely audible. Tears streamed down her face. "No," she said a little louder.

"Hey, whoever you are, you best let us out," Sylvester said. He postured at the door and thumbed his chest. "My family will be looking for me, and I'm sure the other families will be looking for these girls, too."

The man outside the door chuckled. "No, they won't. You, Sylvester, have no family. Not here, anyway, and the family you do have hasn't heard from you in nearly three years."

"What do you want from us?" Carlotta asked, her mind racing as she tried to figure out who the voice belonged to.

"Entertaining art. Merely that, and nothing more."

Gabby had retreated to the corner where she sank to the floor and pulled her knees up. Her sobs grew louder. "He's going to kill us, or traffic us," she said through hitching breaths.

"Shut up," Lila snapped. "He wants art; we'll give him art, then, right?" She looked to Carlotta and Sylvester for confirmation.

"Seriously?" Carlotta moved closer to the door as she lowered her voice, shocked at Lila's naivety. She put a palm against the door. Her heartbeat thundered through her entire body, and dizziness washed over her. "I know you're lying. What do you really want?"

Metal clanked and echoed from his side of the door. Something sloshed in a container, and the man began to hum. He stood close to the door; too close to be making the noises.

Carlotta put an ear to the door, listened intently for a moment, and raised her eyes to Sylvester. She was certain the horror in her core showed in her expression.

"What?" Sylvester whispered, closing the distance between them. "What did you hear?"

"There are other people." Her voice came out scratchy and hoarse. She spun to Lila. "Who was in your place earlier in the day? Who came in? That's who drugged you, and probably who drugged us."

Lila's mouth worked but no words came out. She shook her head. Her eyes flitted back and forth, back and forth as she pushed her memory.

5

"A delivery man came and dropped off art supplies. He came inside, but I was with him the entire…" Her eyes widened. "Lawrence," she gasped. "Lawrence," she said, stepping to the door. "The deliveryman, Lawrence? Are you—"

The man chuckled again. "Indeed. And it's almost time for you to perform, little artists. This is the day each of you will create your *tour de force*. It will be a collaboration, of sorts."

The scraping and clanging stopped and laughter filled the air.

A chainsaw's guttural attempt at starting silenced everything.

Carlotta saw reality set in on Sylvester's face. The transformation was sudden and the complete opposite of the laid-back, carefree, and snide artist he had been earlier.

The chainsaw started, and the wielder revved it.

Carlotta slammed her hands over her ears. Sylvester began to scream wordlessly as he pounded his fists and feet against the cinderblock walls opposite the door. Gabby buried her head under her arms and put her face to her knees. Lila's chest heaved, and her mouth opened in a silent scream. Fury mixed with fear in her eyes.

Carlotta looked up to the broken roof as the metal door opened. All went silent, and all sensations vanished.

She was dreaming. There was no other explanation. Too much booze. Too many pills and powders. She was having a bad trip. That was all.

She turned to face the open door.

A man stood there with the small chainsaw held in front of his thick mechanic's coveralls. She locked eyes with him through the clear shield he wore.

Such grand detail for a dream, she thought. *His eyes are the brightest blue I've ever seen. So blue, they seem unreal.*

She knew what his hands looked like under the blue gloves. She also knew he had a scar on his neck; a ragged nasty scar that had made him seem sexy as hell the night before.

Lila rushed toward him, arms batting the air in the direction of the shield.

There should have been sound, but it was like watching a movie with the volume muted.

Carlotta watched in stunned silence, wondering when she would shake the bad trip. As she sent up the addict's perpetual repentant prayer of: *If you get me through this, I swear I'll never do it again*—something warm showered her face, neck, arms, and pelted against her clothes.

Confused, Carlotta looked at the red goop covering her arms and shirt, and then she raised her eyes to the scene unfolding in front of her.

CHAPTER ONE

The Dead Librarian

Wednesday

WHO WAS DR. BRAN TO BE TELLING ANY AGENT WHETHER THEY were fit for duty? With her reputation of working fourteen-hour days, wasn't she the poster child for running from some internal conflict? Or, at the very least, wasn't she a workaholic?

Ava sat in her office with the door closed, seething over the latest update from the doctor. It didn't say she needed to be off work, or that she was unfit, but Dr. Bran had alluded that if Ava didn't get a handle on her inner conflict over Jason Ellis, that's what she would inevitably have to put in the reports and updates.

Why couldn't she understand the situation for what it really was? Ava believed she had explained it clearly enough that a child could understand. It wasn't so easy to get over the fact that she had fallen in love, and trusted completely, a man—a fellow special agent, by the way, not just some rando off the street—who turned out to be a very prolific serial killer.

Working to the point of exhaustion was the only way she could fall asleep at night. And that was usually slumped facedown in a pile of work at her kitchen table, or sagged onto the arm of the couch with the files in her lap.

"Get a dog or a cat," Dr. Bran suggested with her maddeningly measured Mona Lisa smile.

"I'm single. I don't have time for a pet. I couldn't care for it properly."

"Then get a damn plant. Get something in your life to care for and nurture. Something besides your worries, your guilt, and that anger you keep bottled-up inside."

"If I had ten dogs and a whole damn garden of plants, it would not change what Jason turned out to be. It wouldn't change that I was played for a fool."

"Or that he broke your heart." That smile faded. "That's most of the problem here, isn't it?"

"Well, aren't you just Ivy League smart? Maybe you should come join the team and put those laser-focused insights to work for the Bureau." Ava stood and moved toward the door. "Now, if we're done with this charade, I have work to do and lives to save." She turned and glared at the doctor. "But only if your ass is covered enough to call this session short of the forty-five-minute hour."

Dr. Bran frowned and pulled off her glasses, but she remained seated with her legs crossed. "Next week. Same day; same time; right here."

"Dog, cat, plant." Ava scoffed and closed the file.

In the bullpen, Ava motioned for the team to follow her. "Taking this one to the conference room, everybody." She turned and walked out the door, down the hall, and into the conference room.

Metford was the first in the room behind her. "Hey, is everything okay? You've been—"

She pulled the white screen into place. "Everything's just peachy, Metford. How's it going with you? Life treating you right?" She smiled brightly and thumped his arm. "How are the wife and kids? Growing like weeds, I bet." She dropped the smile and moved to the head of the table where she jerked a chair out.

"Okay," he said, stretching the word out long. He took a step back as the others entered the room. "Not sure what that's about, but yeah, life's okay. Except for the wife and kids thing."

Ava clicked her tongue and shook her head. "You know, you should really think about getting something in your life to take care of besides yourself and all those useless worries and all that bottled-up anger." She clenched a fist for emphasis before sitting.

"Ooh, I know this one," Dane said with a grin. "What is… Dr. Bran's favorite self-help suggestion?" She pulled out her chair. "Did I get it right?"

"Gold star to Dane." Ava opened the casefile and turned on her tablet to access all the digital files. She put up a photo of Teagan Reese.

"I've seen her around," Dane said. "Isn't she a librarian-slash-artist-slash-curator, or something like that?"

"Librarian?" Metford asked with a dubious expression.

"That's right," Ava said. "This is Teagan Reese. She's twenty-eight, and she was the librarian at Fairhaven Library and Center for Art Culture right here in Fairhaven."

"We're investigating a *librarian*? What did she do to get on our screen?" Metford scoffed. "Was she skimming off the top of the late fees account?"

Ava tapped on the crime scene photo, and it replaced the posed, pretty picture of Teagan. "She's dead. Murdered in the library, night before last. She was married to Brad Reese. They had two small children. Penny and Thomas, ages six and four. Brad and the kids are missing. No one can seem to locate them since her death."

"Seen this a million times. It was the husband," Dane said. "They argued, he killed her, and then he took off with the kids."

Ava raised her shoulders. "The police requested our help because that's the assumption. They noted that Thomas has asthma. We need to figure out who killed Mrs. Reese, and where her husband and kids are. Are they safe? Are they victims of whoever killed her? Is there more than meets the eye to this case. We must keep an open mind to any possibility." She tapped another photo, and a picture of Penny and Thomas' smiling faces filled the screen. "They need to be found."

Each team member shifted in their seat and sat a little straighter. Dane ran a hand over her face, and she couldn't keep a steady gaze on the picture. Ashton couldn't take his eyes off the kids.

Metford motioned at the screen but didn't make eye contact with Ava. "Can you go back to the crime scene?"

Ava obliged.

"How was she killed?" Dane asked.

"Shot twice. Once in the head; once in the heart. She was put back in her chair, and someone placed a sweater jacket over her head."

"The crime scene was manipulated," Ashton said. "But there is blood on the shelves, books, and floor where she was shot out in front of her desk. Why move the body if it does nothing to change how the crime appears?"

"A bullet in the head and one in the chest sounds like an execution," Dane said.

"Execution for what, though?" Metford asked. "She's a librarian, for God's sake."

"She is a person," Ava corrected. "A person who became a victim. Get rid of the stereotype in your head about librarians. She wasn't just shot. There was bruising on the right side of her face, and she had a split lip. Somebody left-handed worked her over pretty good before they shot her."

"Beating and shooting," Metford said. "I'd say that's overkill on a woman her size. She weighs what, a buck-ten?"

Ava nodded. "Close to it, I'd say."

"The sweater over her head usually indicates remorse." He leaned his elbows on the table and squinted up at the screen. "Maybe that's why she was put back in her chair. Maybe it wasn't to manipulate the scene and change how it seemed. The killer just couldn't stand seeing her on the floor like that."

"Then why shoot her in the first place?" Ashton asked.

"Maybe she and Brad got into an argument, things got out of hand, and he hit her. I could see her being a spitfire," Metford said, nodding. "Maybe she fought back, and in the heat of anger, he used the gun."

"And afterward, he was ashamed and regretted it," Dane added. "He couldn't let her stay on the floor, and he couldn't leave her face uncovered."

"People cover the faces of their loved ones for different reasons, but some of the most popular are: as a sign of respect, religious reasons, and to protect the living—to make it easier to see their loved one and accept the death without having to look at their face or see their eyes," Ava said.

"Did they find the murder weapon yet?" Ashton asked.

"No," Ava said. "They're running tests, but the investigator said he thought it was probably a nine-millimeter."

"What evidence did they gather?" Metford asked.

Ava tapped another picture, and the evidence log lit up the screen. "As you can see, they collected over a hundred sets of fingerprints from the library—it's a public space, so that was to be expected. There were twenty-seven sets found in a ten-foot radius of Teagan's desk. They're hoping they get a hit from that pool of prints. The killer had to get close enough to leave prints somewhere in that ten-foot circle when he put her back in the chair."

"Unless he was wearing gloves," Metford pointed out.

Ava nodded agreement. "This wasn't a robbery. At least, the police don't think so. Nothing was stolen from the library, or from Mrs. Reese's personal effects. Her cell was on the desk inches from her right hand; her purse was under her desk and, turned on its side, but all her effects were there.

There was no sign of sexual assault, so this wasn't a rape turned deadly, though there is no way to know if her attacker meant to rape her, and she fought so hard that he never got the chance. Most likely, rape was not the motive here."

"What about Brad, Penny, and Thomas?" Dane asked. "Any evidence of them being there?"

"Not that I have come across in the reports from Detective Reinhold. The only thing I know for sure is that no one has been able to get into contact with them since Mrs. Reese's murder. He's not answering his work phone, cellphone, or the house phone. The police have been to the house a couple of times, but no one ever comes to the door, and they haven't seen any sign that Brad or the kids are in the house. Dead quiet and dead still, as they put it."

"Did they force the door and go inside, or just look through windows on the ground floor?" Dane asked.

"They did not force the door yet because there was no sign of anyone being inside, although his car is still in the garage. I don't know if he only had the one, but that seems logical. Mrs. Reese's car was parked at the library. It's unlikely they owned a third car, but it will be looked into."

From what she had seen in the files, things were adding up and pointing toward Brad Reese. If he killed his wife and ran with the kids, those kids could be in danger. Guilt, remorse, and fear could make a man lose his grip on his emotions, and he could snap without warning.

CHAPTER TWO

Crime Scene Analysis

AVA PUT UP A HEADSHOT OF TEAGAN SMILING. IT WAS HER ID photo. "This is the victim," she said. "Teagan Reese, twenty-eight. This photo was taken back in January when she renewed her driver's license. She was the librarian at Fairhaven Library and Center for Art Culture in town. Her position at the library is the result of a promotion three months ago. She, as you already know, was married to Brad Reese for eight years, and they have two small children together, Penny and Thomas. Thomas has asthma.

"What we know from the police is that Teagan has no relatives. No family. Her parents lived in Massachusetts, where her father died of a heart attack, and her mother was killed in an automobile accident two months later. That was in 2010."

Ava put up another picture. "This is how Teagan was found Tuesday morning by Suri Nyquist, her coworker and friend."

The photo belied the brutality of the murder. An observer would never know whose head and upper body lay under the red and white sweater if they weren't told. But the next photo showed the possible scene of a struggle and the spot in front of the shelves where Teagan had been shot.

Blood spatter and smears were quite evident in the distance shot. Ava flipped to the next picture in the series. It was a close-up of the floor and shelves where Teagan had perished.

"Were any shoeprints recovered from the blood on the floor?" Metford asked.

"No," Ava answered. "Whoever killed her and then moved her body was very aware of not leaving any evidence." She flipped to the next image. It was a shot of Teagan slumped on her desk, but focused more on the wall and floor shelves behind it.

"I bet the picture on the pin board behind her desk is from one of her kids," Dane said.

"That wasn't noted, but probably so."

The next image was a closeup of Teagan's bruised face and split lip. Ava left it up for a moment. The next shot was of Teagan's right palm. "Her nails are in good condition, her hand isn't broken, but something made this irregular bruising pattern on her palm."

"She wasn't holding anything when she was found," Dane said, referring back to the previous photos.

"That's right, but we should try to figure it out. It seems insignificant, but it could give us more clues as to what happened."

She flipped to another image. It was a close-up of Teagan's desk after her body had been removed. "What we're looking at here is the state of the items on her desk. Everything seems to be relatively neat and in proper order."

"And there's very little blood on anything," Dane said, grimacing.

"Considering she was shot in the head," Ashton added.

Ava shook her head. "It just means that Mrs. Reese was dead before the killer moved her to the chair. Maybe dead for several minutes; maybe for several hours. We don't have the reports back on the exact time of death yet." She turned off the tablet. "We need to go to the crime scene. I want to be quick but thorough with this. Those two kids' safety, maybe their lives, depend on us. The library is large. Main floor, upstairs, basement, and a separate building on-site for activities and events, so we're all going. Metford, you're with me on the main floor. Dane, you take the basement and upstairs, and Ashton, I want you in that event building. We need to look for anything that could be evidence of those kids or Brad being there at the time of Mrs. Reese's murder, or any evidence of how the killer entered or left the building. Look for security cameras on nearby houses and businesses; ATMs, traffic cameras, look everywhere and make notes."

Everybody stood to exit. Instead of the usual talk and noise, they were silent, and their faces grim. It was easy to understand how knowing that two kids' lives might depend on how they performed their duties over the next several hours could make them tense and withdrawn into their own thoughts.

At the library, Ava walked in. The team followed, and they all stood in the entryway.

"Teagan's workspace is visible from the entrance," Dane said, moving straight ahead.

"Which means she could have seen anyone who entered through the front here," Metford said.

"And look at the size of these windows," Dane commented, pointing. "I didn't realize how much glass this place has. Those go right down to the floor almost. Could the killer have gone through one of them?"

The team walked to the nearest set of windows and looked over them. Ava leaned in close and looked up. She pointed to the top right corner. Hidden between the base of the blinds and the wall was a silver circle and a thin wire that ran to the top of the bottom pane. "Security alarms. Check all the other windows for the same thing."

A few moments later, the team reassembled at the entryway.

"Every single window is wired," Ashton said.

"So, the window theory is unlikely," Dane said. She turned and pointed out several doors with push-bars. "All those lead outside, and I didn't see any wires on them."

Ashton shook his head. "Alarms are wired straight into the library's electrical system. If the door opens, an alarm goes off."

"All right, you all know where to go. Get it wrapped up quickly and then meet us in Teagan's office."

Ava and Metford went to the office, taking in the seemingly endless shelves of books as they went.

"Ever notice how quiet it is in a library?" Metford asked.

"Maybe because it's closed and we're the only people in it."

"No, I mean all the time. There could be a group of people in here right now, and I could almost guarantee that the only sound you'd hear would be the turning of pages, and maybe a chair scraping the floor every now and then. They're creepy buildings. Like tombs and mausoleums."

"Libraries are supposed to be quiet, Metford. Otherwise, how would anyone ever be able to concentrate on what they're reading?"

"Never bothers me. But I don't really read too much."

"Shocking." She stepped around some short shelves and stopped. It was the spot where Teagan had been shot.

"Pictures didn't really do it justice, did they?" Metford asked, scanning the blood along the entire length of the shoulder-high shelves.

"Shelves must be eighteen or twenty feet long," Ava said. "And there's even spatter on the wall." She pointed to the markings left by forensics on the slim portion of wall that separated Teagan's desk from the rest of the library.

"Most of the spatter is on the floor." Metford moved, aimed his finger at a downward angle, eyed the spatter, and shook his head. "He would have blowback on him if he was that close to her when he pulled the trigger."

Ava turned to scan the books behind Metford for signs of a shadow. If the gunman was close to any wall, or similar surface—such as a shelf packed with books—when he pulled the trigger, the blowback blood spatter would leave an outline on the wall behind the gunman. It would look like a shadow, and could offer some details about the shooter: approximate height, build, which hand the gun was in, and sometimes it could even help investigators determine whether the shooter was male or female and how they likely wore their hair. It all depended on the type of gun used, the shooter's distance from the victim, and his distance from the wall. But there was no blowback shadow on the books.

"He shot her from far enough away that there's no shadow, just the even spray of blood." She gestured toward the shelf.

She moved to Teagan's workspace. It was called an office, but the last time Ava checked, an office implied a room that had a door, and Teagan's office did not. It was more like a corner of the main floor with a single wall separating it from the check-out counter. There was a large window behind the desk, but if she were working, Teagan would not have seen anyone approaching via the window.

A hardback edition of *Jane Eyre* clung precariously to the edge of the desk. The papers underneath it hung limply by a corner caught between the book and the desk. As Ava stepped around the edge to the blood-stained chair, the papers shifted enough to cascade to the floor. She picked them up and saw that they were notes for an upcoming young artist event. For the sake of leaving the scene as it was in the photos, she lifted the book to put the papers underneath. The book opened as she dropped it back into place. In the split-second it was open, it revealed a folded piece of notebook paper.

Ava took out the piece of paper. Teagan's name was written on it in big balloon-style letters and encased in a crudely drawn heart. It reminded Ava of the 'love letters' kids wrote to one another when she was in middle school.

Teagan,

You are so beautiful. Pretty and kind and you have nice kids. They are cute. You help me and you are nice to me when nobody else will be. I do not think you know who is writing this but I love you. I have for a very long time and I can not keep it to myself any more. I have to tell you but I am too scared you will laugh so leaving this note is the only way I can say it. Maybe one day you will know who I am.

"Find something?" Dane asked as she and the others entered the area.

"Weird love note from an anonymous admirer." Ava handed it to Dane.

The others leaned in to see the letter.

"Looks like it's from a kid," Dane said, handing it back.

"Pre-teen with a crush on the librarian?" Metford asked.

"There's something else about it," Ava said, reading for the tenth time. "There are no contractions at all." She turned it toward them. "Even pre-teens use contractions: You're, I'm, they're, don't, you'll. Most people write the same way they speak, and using contractions is a normal part of our speech patterns."

"Unless you don't use them when you talk," Ashton said.

"Yeah, I went to school with a kid who had a mental problem, and she talked like that even when she was seventeen," Dane said. "She was slow; took the Special-Ed classes. People made fun of her, but she was a sweet person—even to the ones who teased her the worst."

Ava read the note again, nodded. She slid it into a large plastic evidence bag. "Put it in evidence," she told Ashton.

"Okay," she said. "Did anyone find anything?"

No one had.

She nodded again. "Let's go over this. The murder must have taken place between eight at night and eight in the morning." She pointed to the desk lamp. "Teagan's desk light was on and so were the overheads that were always left on overnight."

"Yeah, as a precaution to prevent crimes," Dane scoffed.

"Look around. How could this murder happen without anyone witnessing it? The blinds are left halfway up every night. That's a bunch of windows; a bunch of places where passersby could have seen what was going on."

After several different run-throughs of what might have taken place, Metford, who had been portraying the gunman, tossed up his hands and spun in a circle. "There's no way. They are in the wide open from all angles." He pointed to spatters on a shelf about four feet above a large puddle of blood on the floor. "This was the first shot." He pointed to his chest. Pointing to the spatter on lower shelves and the wall, he said, "And that's shot number two." He pointed to his head, indicating just above and between his eyes where Teagan had been shot. "She was standing at the first shot, fell to her knees, and the gunman shot her a second time."

Ava nudged him away from the shelves and the mess on the floor. "Her right palm had bruising consistent with her holding something very tightly. Perhaps something she was using as a weapon." She pulled up the picture on a tablet and held it out for them to see. "Look around and see if we can find what might have made these marks on her palm."

Ashton stood at a small shelf and table combo that sat in the left back corner of the room. He bent and lifted a cord that had an attachment like a cellphone charger. "This has been pulled out of something." Moving the shelf from the wall, he lifted the end with the plug still intact. "USB isn't damaged, and the adapter plug for the wall outlet is fine, too."

"Isn't that just a cellphone charger?" Ava asked.

"Nope. Cellphones use a different size on this end." He held up the smaller of the two ends. He looked back at the table. "What was sitting here?"

Ava consulted the police reports. "That's where the small salt lamp was sitting. The one Suri Nyquist spoke about in her statement. But it belonged to Teagan, and Suri couldn't recall the last time she had seen it for sure."

"If Mrs. Reese used it as a weapon, it could leave an irregular pattern of bruises on her hand."

"He's right," Dane said. "I have one, and their surface is bumpy and rough."

"You have a salt light?" Metford asked.

"Yeah, I heard they were supposed to help with stress headaches."

"Did it help?" he asked.

She shrugged. "Not really."

"If Mrs. Reese used the lamp to defend herself, that's why it's missing," Ava said, ignoring Metford and Dane's conversation. She walked to the bookshelves again. "If she hit him, his DNA would be on it. The killer took it to protect himself."

"If she did hit him with it, his blood could be on her or her clothes," Ashton offered.

Ava made the call and gave orders for all the blood on Teagan's body and clothes to be tested. "And if it comes up as someone else's blood, run it through the database and see if you get any hits. Okay. Thanks." She motioned toward the main doors. "We need to plan our next move."

CHAPTER THREE

The Reese World

"SOMEONE SHOULD GO TO THE REESE HOME AND CHECK THINGS out," Dane said.

Ashton nodded. "If Mr. Reese's car is there, but no one answers the phone or door, I say we force entry."

Ava agreed. "The door should have been forced after the first attempt. Even if they're not home, something in there might give us an idea where they went. We need to speak with Mr. Reese's parents, too. They live a few miles away, and it'll take about forty-five minutes to get there."

Metford moved closer. "I say we go to the parents' house." He gestured to indicate Ava and himself.

"Right, Ashton would be more useful at the Reese home with Dane where the electronics might still be," Ava said. "Search the house, garage, and any other building on the property."

Dane and Ashton confirmed their assignment and walked out.

"Okay, let's get this moving. We have a murder to solve and two missing kids. No time to spare." Ava headed out to the vehicle and climbed into the driver seat.

Metford got in. "Are you sure you're okay?"

She finished punching the address into the GPS. "Why wouldn't I be, Metford? I'm fine." She pulled into traffic.

"You're tight. Tense. Prickly, even."

"Oh, because I was such a peach to be around before, huh?"

"You were more relaxed, yeah."

"I'm *prickly* because someone murdered a mother of two and those two are now missing. I don't want a couple of kids getting murdered if I can help it."

They turned onto a rough-paved road with no center line. The shoulders weren't marked, and if she misjudged, she'd just be in a ditch, or stuck in a livestock fence. A mile down the road, an older model Chevy pickup appeared in the rearview. Ava checked the posted speed as the truck steadily gained on them. Thirty-five felt unsafe on the unlined road. However fast the truck was moving, it was above the posted limit and definitely unsafe.

"Cows and barns," Metford said. "Definitely outside city limits. How far did you say Brad's parents lived?"

The pickup had closed the distance between them and was tailgating.

"GPS is a wonderful invention, isn't it? I mean, it's got a big screen right there on the dash. Easy for the driver and passengers to see." She tapped the edge with her finger. "And right there's the ETA. Technology is amazing." Even to her own ears, the comments were tainted with bad attitude and sarcasm. Metford didn't really deserve all the flak she had been doling out; he just happened to be the closest target when the agitation began to leak out.

"See? That's what I was talking about. That right there. I was just trying to—"

The truck sped forward even closer to her bumper with an angry roar.

"What the hell?" she asked, watching the erratic driver in the rearview. The tint on its windows was above the legal percentage. It was so dark that even with the sun shining directly on the windshield, she could only make out the slightest silhouette of the driver. "Can't he see the government tag?"

Metford turned to look out the back. "Maybe doesn't realize he could catch a charge for it. Wanna take care of it?"

"No, we have higher priorities right now." Stepping on the gas, Ava pulled away from the truck, noting that it was an '80s model Chevrolet. The hood was covered in black primer and the rest that she could see was covered in gray primer.

The truck slowed and Ava pulled far ahead. She breathed a sigh of relief. "Finally. Must've seen the tag and decided to back off."

"Good, but you probably should slow down. Tight curve ahead." Metford pointed ahead.

Ava let off the accelerator and gripped the wheel tighter. The curve was steeper than it looked, and she had to touch the brake as she neared the center. The road straightened on the other side. Glancing into the rearview, Ava gasped. "Brace," she said loudly, taking her own advice and gripping the wheel again.

"Wha—"

The truck rammed her, jolting the whole SUV toward the right-hand ditch. Ava fought the wheel and got back on the road. She stepped on the gas and reached for the mic to call in the incident, but the truck rammed her again, and the SUV skittered toward the ditch, its passenger side tires dropping off the asphalt. Jerking the wheel, she managed to get back on the pavement. As her rearend fish-tailed, the driver of the truck hit her yet again, catching Ava's back bumper perfectly to send her careening out of control as she stepped on the brake and twisted the wheel.

"Jesus!" Metford had undone his seatbelt to lean out the window with his gun. He fired twice, and the truck hit them a final time. The brakes caught just as they were hit, and it sent the SUV nose-first into the deep ditch.

Glass shattered, metal screamed, and every loose item flew toward Ava's face. She squeezed her eyes tight and waited for the car to stop. It came to rest with the grill embedded in dirt. The whole thing had shifted onto the passenger side.

"Get the plate!" Ava barked.

But as the truck passed by, Ava saw that it was a short-wheel base— and the license plate was missing.

"I think my arm is broken," Metford said, holding his right arm gingerly.

"Is that all your injuries?"

"Yeah. How about you? You have blood on your face. How bad is it?"

Ava touched her face above her left eyebrow. The sting let her know it was a good-size cut, but nothing major. There were other scratches on her face, and her arm and side would be bruised from slamming into the console. "It's nothing serious. I'm fine."

She strained to push open the door. The angle of the car made the door open at an uptilt. She had to jump a couple of feet to the ground. She opened the hatch. "Can you get out?"

"Yeah. Going for the door now."

"Come out this way." She released the catches and shoved the backseat down. "I'm calling it in."

Ava called in the incident and put a BOLO for the pickup truck. The ambulance and tow trucks arrived shortly. Metford's right arm was put in a sling for a shoulder injury. Nothing was broken. The EMT bandaged Ava's eyebrow and a cut on her forearm.

A uniform gave them a ride back to headquarters.

"You two should go home and rest," Sal said, coming out of her office as soon as she spotted Ava and Metford. "Just go home. You're both injured."

"What happened?" Dane asked, rushing toward them from the entrance hall.

Ashton was right behind her.

Ava quickly told them the story. "We still need to speak with Mr. Reese's parents. Today."

"We can all go," Ashton said. "There was no one at Brad's house, so we had the door forced. Forensics is there scouring for evidence. They already gave us the heads-up that it would be a while before they finished. It's a pretty big house."

"Plus they have the garage and one outbuilding to work, too," Dane added.

"I say we go. I'm fine," Ava said, glancing over at Sal with bated breath.

Sal took a moment, then sighed. "Fine. But any more incidents out there, I want you two to retreat immediately. That's an order."

At the Reese home, Ava stepped out of the car and rubbed her right side. The swelling was coming on fast, and the soreness wasn't being shy.

Mr. Reese opened the door and let them in. Mrs. Reese stood in the kitchen with her arms crossed. A woman with dark hair sat on the sofa in front of the kitchen. She held a yapping Yorkie that she stroked and shushed as if it were a child.

"This is Millie, Brad's older sister," Mr. Reese said.

Millie looked at Ava and then eyed the others with what could only be interpreted as disdain.

"Do you live here, Millie?" Ava asked.

"It's Mrs. Young, and no, I do not live here."

"Mrs. Young?"

"That's right."

"Where's your husband? Is he with you?"

"You can visit him, if you want to. He's over at Green Hills Cemetery. Been there since last year." Millie's expression was cold, hard, emotionless except for the anger that showed through in small glimpses.

"Millie," Mr. Reese said. "They're here to help."

"That's right," Ava said as she stepped past the woman and into the kitchen with the parents. She asked them about the last time they had seen Brad and the kids, and if they had any idea where Brad might have taken the kids if he wanted to avoid law enforcement.

Mrs. Reese immediately scowled and backed away to stand propped against the cookstove. "Brad has no reason to avoid law enforcement because my son is not a murderer."

"I didn't mean to imply that. We just need to be able to check everywhere he might have gone with the kids," Ava said, taking a step toward the woman.

"Why don't you stop wasting time and effort looking *at* him and start looking *for* him? He didn't kill Teagan, and he's not on the run. He's missing, and you're treating him as if he were a criminal!" Mrs. Reese yelled.

"This might seem less like an accusation if he hadn't run off with the kids right after his wife was murdered," Ava responded coldly. "I don't have time for shoulder-gripping and back-patting here. All I want is to find Penny and Thomas. Remember them? Your grandkids? They could be in danger."

The Yorkie started barking again. The shrill sound tap-danced up and down Ava's spine.

Mrs. Reese crossed her arms and looked at the floor.

"Do you know something?" Ava asked her.

Mrs. Reese shook her head but didn't make eye contact.

"Mrs. Reese, I'm giving you a chance to help your son and your grandchildren. If you know something you're not telling me, I'll have you charged with interfering with an investigation. Not to mention, if something happens to those babies, how the hell are you going to sleep knowing you had a chance to save them and did nothing?"

Mrs. Reese broke into tears. Her husband went to comfort her.

"We've told you all we know," he said.

"She hasn't. She knows something, and if you love your son and grandchildren—"

Mrs. Reese jerked away from her husband, fire in her eyes. She jabbed a finger at Ava as she advanced. "You get out of my house this instant! You know nothing about us!" she screamed.

Millie stepped between the two women and glared at Ava. "You heard her. Get out. You cannot and *will* not come into her home and speak to her this way." The Yorkie, still perched on Millie's arm, growled and yapped at Ava.

Metford took Ava's arm and turned her toward the door. "I need to speak with you," he said.

Ava pulled her arm out of his grasp and halted in the living room. "What about? I'm in the middle of questioning her."

"Dane and Ashton can handle it from here." He looked to Dane for confirmation.

"We got it. Go ahead," Dane assured them.

Ava jerked the door open and exited the house. "What, Metford? Did someone find Brad and the kids?"

"No. You know why I brought you out here. What was that back there? And don't give me the crap about you just want to find the kids. Now, what's up with you lately?"

She put her hands in her hair and blew air out as she walked in a large circle.

"Come on, Ava. You haven't been right since that Housewife case."

She stopped pacing and threw up her hands roughly, ignoring the soreness. "If I was the same, then maybe you should worry. I fell in love with a serial killer, Metford. How did anyone think that was going to affect me? Lighten my appetite for a few weeks, maybe I wouldn't sleep too well for a week or two?" She walked up to him. "The foundation of my life and work crumbled that day. All a good detective has sometimes is her gut instinct. We all trust that gut instinct. But, unlike you and everyone else at work, I can't say mine has never led me wrong because it sure as shit did." She scoffed and turned away in frustration and disgust at her lack of good judgment. "Some of the deaths are on my hands, Metford. If I had just—"

"Hey, nope. We're not playing that game. You know better. It's BS and it will make you crazy. What happened was not your fault, and I'm sure if he duped you, he was well-seasoned at his schtick. He knew exactly how to manipulate you."

With tears choking her, she chuckled. "Yeah, just pile on the compliments. He implied he was interested in a romantic relationship with me.

I should have known better, but I was stupid. I don't want to talk about this anymore. Not today; not ever." She inhaled deeply and put her hands on her hips.

"That's your call, but if you change your mind and ever need anyone to talk to about it, or just someone to listen while you talk, I'm here. In the meantime, you can't let that incident cause you to act like you did in there. It's interfering with work. That's a problem. Talk to me before you get to that point again. Talk to Sal, talk to the therapist, talk to *someone*. I don't care who."

Dane and Ashton came outside. Dane held up her notepad.

"What's that?" Metford asked.

"Information about Brad's work and his friends that his parents knew about. They gave us the address of their beach house in Fairhaven, too."

Ashton dangled a set of housekeys. "They gave us the keys so we could check the place out."

"Good work," Ava said. "Actually, no. You know what? That was great work, guys."

"I thought we could go check the house on our way back to HQ," Dane said.

"Good call," Ava said, getting in the car.

Maybe all the decisions didn't have to be on her. The team was working very well without her micro-managing; maybe working better than she was at the moment. Of course, none of them been in love with a serial killer.

CHAPTER FOUR

Teagan's World

AFTER TURNING UP NOTHING AT THE BEACH HOUSE, AVA AND THE team went back to the office to do a deep dive into Teagan Reese's life. The quickest way to find Penny and Thomas was to find out everything they could about the victim. There was a reason she was murdered, and until they discovered the motive, they might not ever figure out who did it. If the kids were to be found safe, Ava and the team needed to know why Teagan was chosen as the victim.

"What do we know about the Fairhaven Library and Center for Art Culture other than it's a public library?" Metford asked.

"The library does a lot of good for the town," Ava said. "They offer after-school activities for kids, artistic classes for all ages, host Angel Tree every Christmas, and even have a charity for underprivileged kids."

"Yes, I've heard of that," Dane said. "Upward Arc, isn't it?"

"Yeah, that's it," Ashton said. "They donate electronics to the schools, too."

"And the library has the art appreciation center, the gallery, and the event building," Ava said. "A lot of big-name artists visit to give speeches, hold charity dinners, and lend their work to draw people into the library. It's not just painting, but all kinds of art from the canvas to the stage, though the focus is on painting, sketching, and the like. The art side of the library runs on donations from high profile sponsors, from what I'm reading."

"And many of them are from pretty big places—New York or DC or Chicago," Dane said. "The New York art world is a scene I have a little experience with."

"As an agent or just pedestrian?" Metford asked.

"Agent. I don't know how much experience you've had with the artistic side of the world, but sometimes artists can be… unstable at best," Dane answered.

"That's what makes their work so in-your-face and stand-out, is what I've always heard," Metford said. "We thinking an unstable artist killed Teagan Reese?"

"No," Ava said, shutting it down before the brainstorming session could go completely off the rails. "We need to look into this without any biases, and we need to follow solid leads; no conjecture." She pulled up the financials for the library. "There are three main donors that keep the art and culture side of the library running. Looks like they practically funded it themselves for the past two years."

"What are their names?" Dane asked.

"One is from Fairhaven. Connor Aldridge."

"I've heard of him," Ashton said. "He's kind of a big deal around here. He used to be a local photographer and painter who hit the big time with some of his shots from the time of the Iraq War."

"He was in the war?" Metford asked.

"No, he took shots of soldiers who returned during that time. Got some of President George W. Bush that were in top magazines and run on primetime newscasts."

"And I thought he was going to be an artist I could actually admire," Metford said, shaking his head.

"Why can't you still?" Dane asked.

"The only shots he fired for his country were with a camera."

"Okay," Ava said, pushing the team back from derailing again. She didn't want the session to turn into a political debate. "So, we know Connor Aldridge is a local. Ash, why don't you find out what you can about him, Karl Harmon, and George Bosworth III? All the pertinent information."

"On it," Ashton said, pulling the laptop toward him.

"Other than charity dinners and ten-dollar donations from regular locals, that's it for the financials," Ava said.

"What about the interviews and statements collected by PD?" Dane asked.

Ava opened the file and pulled the precious few papers from it. "Detective Reinhold gave these to me. That's all he got." She passed the papers to Dane.

"Shanna Preston, fifty," Dane read aloud as she scanned the interviews. "Regular patron. Del Washburn. Twenty-one. Patron. Suri Nyquist, twenty-four. She's the one who found Teagan and called 911. She was a library aide. And then we have Rita Mae Leonard, fifty-three. Teagan's boss at the library... oh, this is interesting." She pushed the paper back to Ava. "Looks like there was something going on with Solomon Furlong."

Ava read it. "We need to find Mr. Furlong and ask him some questions."

"Were they having an affair, or what?" Metford asked.

"If the boss' statement is true," Dane said. "Looks like there was some jealousy on Solomon Furlong's part because Teagan beat him out for the job. He wanted to be the librarian in Fairhaven, and he was pissed because she got the position."

"Ms. Leonard says she saw them arguing Monday, one day before Teagan was found murdered," Ava said. She put the paper back into the file. "He works there part-time, and Ms. Leonard gave his address but said he was away on an extended vacation in Mexico and had been since sometime Tuesday morning, the day Teagan's body was discovered."

"Dang," Metford exclaimed. "There's that much rivalry for a *librarian* job?" He stood.

"Teagan Reese got a substantial salary when she took that position," Ava said. "Everyone else, with the exception of Ms. Leonard and Suri Nyquist, make just a little over minimum wage."

"Sounds like Solomon Furlong is our guy, if you ask me," Metford said.

"Seems too obvious," Dane said. "If you execute your coworker, whom you had an argument with the day before—in public, no less— and then you disappear on a vacation to Mexico..." She shook her head. "Too obvious, isn't it?"

"No way. He works in a library. It's not like he's Ted Bundy. He probably freaked out and ran."

Dane grumbled. "Where are we headed?" she asked Ava.

"Let's go to the library and get some more details in these statements. I know we have these, but we need our own, and now that we better know what to ask, maybe we can get something that will turn into a sure lead."

Rita Mae Leonard was a composed, smartly dressed woman. Her level of composure was what Ava thought of as high-class composure. It was the type that bordered on cold and uncaring. But then she began to talk, and Ava's opinion of the woman changed.

"Teagan was a lovely woman. Not just physically. She carried herself in a way that drew people to her. She was sweet, responsible, took her job at the library very seriously, got along famously with all the artists and sponsors…" Ms. Leonard sighed heavily. "I just don't understand who could have done such a horrible thing to her. She never hurt anyone that I know of."

Ava nodded sympathetically and kept eye contact while she took notes. "And what about her duties here? What was she in charge of?"

"That's a long list, Agent. She took care of so much that wasn't in her list of duties that it's almost impossible to tell you everything she did."

"I just need to know what was in her job description, and even whatever is in the fine print."

Ms. Leonard chuckled lightly. "There's nothing in the fine print, Agent James. We're a center for culture and art, not a fast-food restaurant or chain retailer."

"Very well," Ava said, smiling.

"Teagan was, of course, our librarian. But she was also in charge of the art and culture center. That's why our choice for librarian must be checked so thoroughly—they are in charge of almost everything. I am… *was*… the only person Teagan reported to. She ran almost everything by me, but I didn't spend much time re-doing what I knew she was perfectly capable of handling on her own. There were the regular librarian duties, many of which she assigned to Suri Nyquist. Suri was her assistant, but Teagan didn't like to call her that. She called Suri her partner. She said they ran the place in tandem with one another."

"So, Teagan made the activity lists?" Ava held up a paper that listed the different events that were scheduled on a calendar page.

"Yes. The activities for the kids, I think, were her favorite. She would spend her own money to add to the supplies for those classes. She even taught one of the painting classes. She used to be an artist. Did you know that?"

"I do. Is that why she was a better fit for the job than anyone else?"

Ms. Leonard looked down and cleared her throat before nodding. "That's part of the reason, yes. She also has the proper connections. High-profile connections are important for our establishment. She understood that." She looked down again. "Mr. Furlong did not have those connections, and he did not understand their importance."

"You are talking about Solomon Furlong, correct?"

"Yes. Teagan was also over him. He was simply a part-time employee. Not that he is unappreciated here, because he is very appreciated. He's been with us for more than a decade now, and he does a fabulous job. He simply is not, and never will be, of Teagan's caliber. She was in New York, and she made some very powerful friends; loyal friends who were more than eager to help fund whatever she asked them to fund. The donations poured in when she took charge in that department, and I've no doubt they would've doubled when she took the librarian position if she had lived long enough." She dabbed a tear from the corner of one eye.

"You told Detective Reinhold that Mr. Furlong and Teagan argued the day before she was found. Tell me about that."

"It was very heated. Mr. Furlong was furious that she had gotten the job. He confronted her right out there in the middle of the lobby. Thankfully, the only patrons were over in the culture center and in the events building. She told him that she won the position fair and square against him. That made him angrier, and he accused her of not being qualified to put together events, let alone run the entire center. He said she got the job solely based on who she knew and … and …" Ms. Leonard blushed crimson. "Must I really repeat exactly what he said to her?"

"I'm sorry, Ms. Leonard, but I need to hear it in your own words. I can't infer what you're meaning. You have to tell me."

"He said she got the job based on who she knew and who she… *blew*," she whispered the last word. "Vulgar. Obscene. And wholly untrue. Teagan slapped him." She pursed her lips and sat straighter. "And I don't blame her. Had I been in her shoes, I might have slapped him with a book in my hand. Mr. Furlong told her that she didn't deserve the job and that he wished she would just die; that she deserved to die. By then, I had made it to where they were, and I told him to apologize immediately and then go home for the day."

"Did he? Apologize, I mean."

"Teagan said she didn't need an insincerity such as that from a low-brow like him, and that she didn't mind if he stayed the rest of the day because right there working part-time for minimum wage under her was right where he deserved to be, and he'd never be more than a minimum-wage loser. I'd never heard her speak like that to anyone, but I knew something had been wrong for the last week. I think Mr. Furlong was the proverbial straw that broke the camel's back."

Ava asked more questions and learned that Teagan had been a ball of nerves for a week. She had overlooked things at work, made silly mistakes that she had never made, and was a little short-tempered. Ava had to wonder why. What was happening that made the normally cool, collected Teagan act so out of character?

Suri Nyquist was next. She was a quiet young woman. Thin as a whip with bright eyes and a quick smile. *If her looks wouldn't disarm a man, her charm and wit would*, Ava thought.

Suri went over finding Teagan that morning. Several times, she used a tissue to dab tears away. Her eyes were puffy, indicating she had cried harder before arriving at work.

"Was Teagan your boss first, or your friend, would you say?" Ava asked.

"Friend," Suri answered without hesitation. "Definitely, we were friends and then coworkers. And just so you know, she never treated anyone like they were her underling. Nobody. She treated everybody equally. Just like me; she always made me feel as if I were doing just as much good for the library and community as she was. She made sure all the employees, and even the patrons, knew she truly appreciated them."

"So, she was a golden boss," Ava said, writing it down.

"A damn unicorn, if you ask me."

"And everyone here liked her, got along with her?"

"Everybody except Solomon. He was always a jerk to her, and she just let him treat her that way. Said she only worked with him; wasn't like she was married to him, or anything."

"Did they often argue?"

"No, only a couple of times that I ever saw. The other argument was because she charged him late fees on some books and DVDs. He lost his mind, but she wouldn't back down. Told him that he wasn't above the rules that everyone else in the world had to live by and he could pay up, or he couldn't check out any more books or DVDs. He paid but was mad for weeks over it."

After a few more questions, Ava asked if there had been any patrons present on Monday.

"The library and center were open as usual, so yeah, there were patrons all the way up until we closed that night at eight. Teagan was staying late to get ahead on a budgeting plan that would allow for more children's classes during winter and summer breaks from school. Said she could get more done if she just stayed an hour over at work instead of trying to work at her kitchen table with Brad and the kids all vying for attention."

"There weren't any patrons when you found Teagan?"

"God, no," she exclaimed. "I was here early. We always come in a few minutes early to get the coffee started and set up whatever displays are needed in the lobby to advertise the newest activity. I was completely alone. I felt like something was wrong when I saw her car, but she was nowhere to be seen. I thought maybe she just went in ahead of me." Her face scrunched and she covered it with her hand. She whimpered and then drew a hitching breath, which she held.

Ava knew Suri was reliving the terrible moment when she walked in and realized her friend was dead, and that she had been murdered. She also knew Suri would continue to fight for control over her emotions until she allowed herself at least one hard ugly-cry session about it. For whatever reason, the emotions never seemed so raw after an ugly-cry session.

Then you know that's what you need to do about a certain handsome agent who stole your heart. It was her grandmother's wizened voice playing through her mind. Ava shook her head and took a deep breath. If she could answer that voice, she would tell it that after Jason stole her heart, he intended to put a knife through it.

No time to think about crying over a serial killer who manipulated her.

"Thank you, Suri. You can go whenever you're ready," Ava said in a low voice.

CHAPTER FIVE

Whatever Goes Up…

T HE TEAM MET UP WITH AVA IN THE EVENTS BUILDING AFTER COM-
pleting their interviews. She told them what she had learned and felt
as if she were closer to knowing Teagan Reese, but no closer to knowing why she'd been murdered.

The other interviews had yielded even less than Ava's.

Ashton worked with the laptop while everyone else hashed out and
pieced together the precious little information they had.

"She had to have had more friends than this," Dane said. "We need to
talk to someone who really knew her."

"I want to speak with Solomon Furlong. He and Teagan argued the
day before she was murdered. They both said some very harsh things,
but Solomon told her he wished she would die and that she deserved to
die," Ava said.

"Jealousy is a motive, but really? A librarian's title is worth killing over? I think that was said in the heat of an argument," Metford countered.

"I think it could be motive," Dane said. "It wasn't just about the title or the raise in pay. Nothing like that, maybe. There's some prestige that comes along with being the librarian at this particular establishment because of the celebrity nature of the artists who come to the functions."

"I got some more information about our victim," Ashton said.

"What is it?" Ava asked.

"A bio of sorts. I stitched it together from records on the internet, but I think it's useful."

"Are you reading it out to us?" Ava asked.

"I just sent it to each of you in a file, but the gist of it is that she was born in 1996, and she was an aspiring artist all through her childhood. She was good. Won awards everywhere she entered her artwork, no matter what medium she used for the piece. When she was sixteen, her mother moved to New York City so Teagan could get exposure for her art, make a name for herself. Her mother was killed in a mugging as she walked back from a convenience store one night in 2014. Teagan was eighteen and alone in the city, but she didn't leave. She stuck it out, worked several part-time jobs, held to her artist schedule for showings, struggled to keep an apartment, she called it her skinny life in the Big Apple. In 2016, she met and married Brad Reese."

"In the same year?" Dane asked.

"Yep. He was older than her by fourteen years."

"Hm," said Ava.

"They had Penny in 2018, when Teagan was twenty-two, and that's when she just sort of backed out of the art scene. Came here, got a job at the library, and that's where she's been since."

"When did she get the job here?" Ava asked, pulling up the file on her tablet.

"She had Thomas in 2020 and came to work here about three months later, from what I read."

Ava nodded. "It says she was a real rising star in New York City even before she turned eighteen, and after her mother's death, she had sponsors, people backing her, and she rose to the top."

"Can you imagine being eighteen, alone in New York City, scrambling to keep a place to live and food enough to keep from starving, and then, all of a sudden, you're at the top of the art world and being paraded around like a prized show horse, and you have everything you need in spades?" Dane asked. "It's gotta be confusing and stressful for an adult, but for a kid?"

"Where's her dad in all this? I'm seeing nothing about him," Metford said, scrolling through the file on his tablet.

"I never found any mention of her father in any of the articles," Ashton said. "He could be dead."

"Or she didn't know who he was. Maybe she didn't want anything to do with him," Dane opined.

"That would explain her daddy issues," Metford said.

"Daddy issues?" Ava asked.

"Yeah, the man she married was fourteen years older than her. That screams daddy issues to me." He raised his shoulders and looked around. "Anyone else get that from it?"

"Maybe," Dane hedged. "I think she was looking for safety and security, myself. Her mother was gone, she was only what, nineteen, twenty? She had been on her own since she was a teenager. She wanted someone to help her keep it all together."

"Exactly what a dad would do, right?" Metford asked.

Dane shook her head. "I don't think it was any sort of issue. He offered something that maybe she had never had, or at least not since her mom died. Could have been as simple as non-judgmental companionship. New York City is a hard city even for seasoned adults."

"Or he could have been a creep looking for a meal ticket on the way to the top. He finds a young, vulnerable girl, all alone…"

"Then why would he kill her, Metford?" Dane countered.

Ava cleared her throat to cut off the speculation before it began. "Either way, she ended up married to a way older guy and then had a kid when she was twenty-two. By then, she was on her way back here, and it seems that she made a good life for herself here," she said. "Ms. Leonard, Teagan's boss, said that Teagan had the right connections in the art world; that's why she got the job over Solomon Furlong."

"He had the experience, she had only the connections," Metford said. "That's why he was so angry. That's probably why they argued. Basically, what I'm hearing is that she got the job by name-dropping."

"No," Ashton said. "She might not have had the years of experience that Furlong had, but she had a love for artwork and children that she took every opportunity to showcase. She had her first kid and started slipping from the art world. It's obvious that having kids changed her worldview and priorities."

"Right," Dane said. "After having the kids, she realized they were more important than making a big name for herself in the city. Or she figured she had already made a big enough name for herself and it was time to focus on family."

Ava pulled up a photo of the letter she had found in Teagan's office. She turned the tablet around so the team could see it. "Then what about this? If she was so family-focused, family-centered, then why would this be hidden in her office here?"

"She might not have found it yet," Dane said. "It does say that leaving the note was the only way the writer could tell her about their feelings."

"Still looks like a kid did that," Metford said.

"Or an adult who has a low IQ," Ashton said.

"She worked with a lot of kids," Dane said. "I would say it's probably from a pre-teen boy who just had a crush on Teagan like we discussed before."

Ava nodded and turned the tablet off. "Is there anyone left on the interviewee list who hasn't been interviewed besides Solomon Furlong?"

A knock came at the side door. Ava opened it. Rita Leonard stood there, glancing nervously over her shoulder. "Yes?"

"I need to tell you something, but I don't want anyone else to hear it," Ms. Leonard said, glancing over her shoulder again. "It's about Teagan and Connor Aldridge."

Ava stepped aside. "Please, come in."

Ms. Leonard stepped inside quickly, looked at the team, and then handed Ava a cellphone.

There was a long message displayed in tiny font on the screen. "What's this?" Ava asked.

"It's a text Solomon sent after he left for his vacation." She glanced over at the team and then out a nearby window as if expecting to see someone spying.

I know why Mrs. Reese is in the position for which I am clearly the more-qualified candidate. Her connections in NYC are a boon to the center, but ask her how she acquires such tremendous donations from Mr. Connor Aldridge. His celebrity shields him from so much, and I don't expect you to make a scandal of this, but you should question their 'platonic' relationship. I happen to know it's not strictly platonic. Not a good look for the library.

"Why didn't you turn this over before, Ms. Leonard?"

"I had forgotten all about it, to be honest. With her murder, and the upheaval it caused, I can hardly think straight." She reached for the phone.

Ava pulled it back. "I'm going to need this. It should have been turned over for evidence at the beginning of this murder investigation."

Ms. Leonard recoiled. "I'm sorry, Agent James. As I said, I forgot about it. I hate cellphones. They're abhorrent, beastly things, and I rarely even turn it on. That's the truth."

"Did you reply to his message?"

"No. I refuse to send text messages even to my own family. I call them instead."

"Did you *call* Mr. Furlong after this message?"

Ms. Leonard shook her head. "No."

"Why not? I would have. Immediately, in fact."

"I didn't think I needed to. That was Solomon lashing out in an effort to smear Teagan's name so she might be removed from the position that he so longed for." She pointed to the phone. "That he obviously believed should have been his. Am I correct? Isn't that what you would think?"

Ava took the phone to Ashton. "Extract everything you can from it as soon as you can."

"What?" Ms. Leonard exclaimed. "That is my personal property." She stepped forward.

Ava blocked her path. "I'm sorry. You'll get it back once it has been searched and released."

"How long?"

Ash looked from the screen to Ms. Leonard. "Are there any security lock codes, passwords, anything of that nature?"

"I have no idea. I simply use the damn thing for emergencies."

Ava's eyed her, surprised to see a crack in that austere, pompous façade she wore.

Ashton cleared his throat and put the phone on the table. "If there are passcodes of any kind that I have to figure out on my own, that will slow the whole process and it could be weeks, or even months before you get it back."

"Nineteen-oh-one," Ms. Leonard said, scowling at him and then at Ava. "Do I need to repeat it?"

"No, ma'am," Ashton said, entering it into a file on the laptop. "Thank you."

"Is there anything else you might have forgotten about?" Dane asked with an accusatory lift of one eyebrow.

"No. Absolutely not." Ms. Leonard went back to the door. "I could have left that alone. I could have kept it to myself to prevent Teagan's good name from being needlessly besmirched, but I didn't. I brought it to you, and I ask that you use discretion when using that information. Teagan was a good woman, no matter if she was having illicit dealings with a donor. Please don't smear Mr. Aldridge's name unnecessarily, either. This center does a lot of good for the community. Without his donations, his loyalty, much of it would never happen at all."

"You have my word, Ms. Leonard," Ava said, opening the door for her. "If I need any further information, I'll let you know."

After a sour glare at Ashton, Ms. Leonard stepped out and walked briskly back to the library.

"Okay, what do we know about Connor Aldridge?" Ava asked, going back to the table.

"I'm on it," Ashton said.

"Whoever wrote the love letter might be a suspect," Ava said. "We need to find out who wrote it for sure. If it was a kid, great. If not..." She sighed. "Unrequited love can make people do crazy things." She hated having first-hand knowledge in that area. Hated that she had fallen for someone she thought loved her when he was just manipulating her so he could add her to his collection of kills. Serial killers sucked.

"Connor Aldridge is married to Margueritte, and they have a home here in Fairhaven. He's fifty, and she's forty-one. They are, of course, very rich and prestigious. Lots of influence in New York City's art world and in the lower orders of city politics."

"We have all this," Metford said. "Anything we don't know yet?"

"Looks like she manages his appointments... she seems to be his personal assistant and assists by overseeing some of the sponsorship recruits in New York City. That's about it," Ashton said.

"Is she French?" Dane asked.

"Why does that matter?" Ava asked.

"I'm just thinking about the art scene in France. Maybe she's connected there, and that could lead to another avenue of necessary investigation, if so."

"She's not," Ashton said. "Her maiden name is Arrowood, and she was born in New Orleans, from what I can find in the birth records."

"How do you do that?" Dane asked.

"What?"

"Get information so fast on the internet when it takes me an hour to find a good lobster bisque recipe."

"By accessing the network arms of any database—"

"Nope," Dane said, throwing up one hand. "You lost me at network arms. I don't wanna know. Not really. That's your area of expertise." She chuckled.

"Amen to that," Metford said.

"Okay, from here, we need to figure out the next move," Ava said. "Metford, you're with me. We're going to canvass the area around the library. Dane, you and Ashton canvass around the Reese home. Back to the office when you finish."

"We're on it," Ashton said, putting his various electronics into carrying cases.

CHAPTER SIX

The Canvass

AVA EXITED THE EVENTS BUILDING BY THE SIDE DOOR AND STOPPED on the neatly manicured grass to scan the area nearby for cameras. She pointed to the strip mall. "There would be people there until when, eight or nine at night, at least?"

"Maybe. We'll walk over and check the business hours at each place."

As they headed for the road, Ava noted that the entire north side of the library and center would not have secondary security cameras anywhere. Along that entire side was only the main, four-lane thoroughfare.

Even in the daytime, there was scarce traffic on the side road they crossed to get to the strip mall. North of the strip mall, at the end of the road, sat a large church.

"That might have a camera that looks across to the north side of the library," she said.

Metford held up his hand and rocked it back and forth. "Eh. It would be so far away that we wouldn't be able to identify anyone unless they went through the church parking lot."

"Maybe they did. We're not leaving anything to chance."

They inquired at all seven businesses about their hours and security cameras. Only Randy's Hardware at the southernmost end of the strip mall had outside security cameras.

"The cameras look new," Ava told Ben Randall as he retrieved footage from Monday and Tuesday. "Have you had recent break-ins?"

The gruff man shook his head and adjusted his hat. "Damn kids spraypainted up my window and tried to pry open the delivery door on the parking lot side. Who knows what they woulda took if they got in?"

"When did that happen?" Metford asked.

"Last week. Thursday night or Friday morning." He cursed and shoved the mouse around harshly in a circle on the table. "Damn computers. Not worth a hoot in a hailstorm when you need them to be."

"I could have someone come by later and retrieve the footage from all three cameras," Ava offered.

"No. It's not going to outdo me. I gotta learn it sometime. Might as well be now." He tried to access the storage again. "Oh, and two of them cameras are dummies. Only one really records anything."

Metford and Ava looked at each other, and he rolled his eyes.

"Which one would that be, Mr. Randall?" Ava asked, hoping it wasn't the one pointed down at the delivery door.

"One at the very end of the building. It's looking right down the outside wall." He pointed toward the road and the library beyond. "Picks up part of the library, too. That's what you're wanting, right?" He looked up from under bushy eyebrows that had lodged over the bridge of his nose, giving him a permanent look of being annoyed.

"Yes, that's perfect," she said. "Thank you."

She and Metford took the footage twenty minutes later and left Randy's Hardware.

There was only one other camera on the entire block with useable footage, and that was at an apartment building across the road on the west side of the library. Exactly one external camera was in the correct position to pick up anything beyond the entrances and exits.

"At least Mr. Allen knew how to work the security system," Metford said.

"One camera to cover the whole parking lot, though? We'll be lucky if we can see anything on the footage. Did you see how high that camera was?" They turned left out of the apartment complex and walked north, toward the main road.

"Ashton always works his magic on that stuff. He'll get us clear images, if there's anything on there to use at all."

"Turning right at the main road, Ava sighed. "There is nothing on this side at all. Just the road." She pointed east. "Let's go that way.""

"It's just the church. We already spoke to the preacher; no one was there to see anything and their cameras are dummies. Let's take the footage back and watch it."

"No, past the church." She walked faster. "Looks like maybe a homeless encampment. Maybe someone from there saw someone suspicious."

"You mean besides the other homeless people?" He trotted to catch up to her. "Come on, Ava. I know you have a soft spot for the homeless, but now is really not the time—"

She shot him a hard look, turned away, and walked even faster. On the other side of the church, she stopped. There was an abandoned store, an empty tax prep office, a barber shop, and a nail salon. Two cars were present. Probably the people running the barber shop and the nail salon. Adjacent to the abandoned store and in the same lot, there were three tents with shopping carts filled to overflowing with what most people considered junk. Ava knew it was the belongings of whoever lived in the tents.

A skinny, shirtless man swiped at the pavement with a worn-out broom. He looked up at their approach but didn't stop sweeping.

"I help you?" he asked when they were close enough.

Ava held up her badge. "Yes. We're Special Agents James and Metford. We just need to ask you a few questions."

The man gripped the broom with both hands, and his eyes widened. He glanced toward a tent guiltily. "I ain't hurting anything. None of us are. We even keep the place clean." He pointed at the ground. "See?"

"None of you are in any sort of trouble. We're investigating a murder at the library that happened Monday night or early Tuesday morning, and we were wondering if you recall seeing anyone acting suspicious around here then."

"We can't even see the library from here, and there ain't been nobody come through here in weeks."

"Did you happen to see anyone anywhere around here during the last few days?" Metford asked. He pointed toward the church and then swooped his hand around to indicate the whole block. "Anywhere."

"No. We keep to ourselves as much as we can."

A woman poked her head out of one of the tents, and an older man stepped out of the other.

"Hello," Ava said. She repeated her questions to them, but they shook their heads. They all stayed in their little area most of the time.

"Except when they open the food pantry across the road," the woman said. "Or when we go on up the road to Mama and Papa's Restaurant." She pointed east toward the small restaurant.

There was a convenience store in the same lot with the restaurant. Across the road, an ancient sign pointed to an old Salvation Army.

"Where is the food pantry?" Metford asked.

"In front of these businesses," the man said. "Straight across the road. Can't miss it."

Ava thanked them and walked to the alleyway behind the church. They turned left on the side road and were immediately faced with the burned remnants of a large restaurant. Far behind it, blue, brown, and gray tarps had been strung up around a plot. The tarps were tattered at the bottom and flapped noisily in the gusts of wind that churned up ash and dust and trash. The Grace Food Pantry sat across a wide lot marked with faded lines indicating parking slots.

"Says it's a shelter, too," Metford mentioned, pointing at a sign on the side of the pantry building.

"They're in the right place. I wonder what's back behind those tarps and the fence behind it?"

"We'll find out soon enough." Metford opened the door to Grace Food Pantry and Shelter.

"Hello, friends," a woman in her mid-fifties said. A nametag pinned to her shirt read 'Janice'. She smiled gently as she approached. Looking them up and down quickly, she clasped her hands. "Are you in need?"

Ava held up her badge. "Of answers only, ma'am." She introduced herself and Metford, and then put the same questions to the woman that had been asked of the homeless people across the street.

Janice shook her head. "I heard about the murder. Terrible thing, but I can assure you that no one here saw anything. We close at five in the evening."

"What about the shelter?" Ava asked, pointing to the interior entrance to that section of the building.

"I don't know, but you're welcome to go ask, provided that you don't agitate them. Many of our residents have a history with law enforcement."

Ava nodded. "I promise we're just here regarding the case at the library, ma'am."

That seemed to mollify her. "Well, as I said, you're welcome to ask, but I don't know how helpful they'll be. We've only had five people staying lately, and only two are here today."

"Where are the other three?" Metford asked, walking to the door.

"It's hard to say, but they've been returning every night. Maybe they're out looking for work. They don't own cars, so they can't have gone too awfully far."

Metford and Ava stepped into a short hallway. At the end of it, there was another door.

Janice hurried past him, took a key from her pocket, and unlocked it. "We keep it locked," she said looking sheepish. "Safety protocol. You understand."

Neither of the people there had seen anyone suspicious, but Janice motioned for Ava to come back before leaving again.

"Yes?" Ava asked.

Janice looked nervously at Metford. It was plain that she didn't trust him. She leaned close and whispered, "Mac Norrie. That's who you wanna talk to. He sees everything in a two-block radius somehow."

"Who is Mac Norrie? Where does he live?"

She snickered. "Nowhere and everywhere, I guess. Right now, he's staying down at the fenced section in back of this lot. If anyone suspicious was around that library, he'll know about it."

"Thank you," Ava said, taking her leave.

She and Metford spoke to the people at the Salvation Army, the Corner Convenience, Mama and Papa's Restaurant, Top Nails, and Hi-Res Barber Shop. No one had seen a suspicious person or activity. No more suspicious than usual, anyway.

"Okay, nothing," Metford said. He glanced at his watch. "I'm starving, and the restaurant smelled like a big plate of fresh burgers and fries to me." He chucked his thumb in that direction. "Grab something?"

"Not yet. We don't have time." She looked both ways at the street and trotted across.

Metford followed, groaning as he stepped beside her. "The fence and Mac Norrie?"

"Yep."

As they neared the fence, a ruckus broke out on the other side. People yelled, cheered, jeered, and something shattered. A man screamed.

Without a word, Ava and Metford drew their guns and ran for the partially open gate, slipping inside. At the opposite end of the abandoned warehouse, a group of people made a ring around two men fighting.

"Hey!" Ava yelled as she ran toward them, gun held high. One man turned, saw her, and bolted.

Metford yelled, and everyone turned toward him. "FBI, stay where you are!" he bellowed, gun leveled at them.

The two fighting men slowly stepped back from each other and kept their hands high.

"Everybody on the ground," Ava said, stepping closer. "Legs out straight, crossed at the ankles."

They all obeyed. A man in a wheelchair with only one leg laughed. "Can I borrow an ankle?" He laughed again. "Matter of fact, let me borrow a leg to go with it."

With everyone settled, Ava moved the two men who had been locked in battle away from each other. It had been a fight over who owned a Coleman camping stove. One had bought the stove, the other bought the little fuel tank, and they both claimed ownership.

"Mac Norrie?" Ava asked, tiring of the squabble.

"Ole Mac stays over in the construction trailer. Ya walked right past his place getting here." The man pointed through the gate toward the tarps.

Ava nodded. She asked them about the murder and if anyone suspicious had been around. Again, a huge resounding no was her answer.

She and Metford left through the gate and walked to the flapping tarps. He lifted the corner of one. A tiny construction company trailer sat in the center of a thirty-by-thirty square lot of pavement. To one side, a barrel obviously used for burning trash and a big charcoal grill. To the other side, two plastic barrels full of water, and one of those medium-sized, hard plastic, blue wading pools with the cartoonish prints of turtles and fish all over it.

The door slammed open and a man with frizzy gray hair and beard stepped out, glaring at them. "Who are you? Can't you see you're trespassing?" He pointed to the tarps. "This is my property, and you need to get off it."

Ava and Metford showed their badges and introduced themselves.

The man blanched. "I didn't steal anything, and I didn't hurt anything." He crossed his arms and looked defiantly at them.

"We're not here about any of... this," Ava said. She repeated the same questions for him.

Twenty minutes into talking with Mac Norrie, Ava was beginning to believe he was the eyes of Fairhaven; especially the area they were in. He seemed to know the comings and goings of every homeless person around, the businesses that came and went, who owned them, who frequented them, and he seemed to be very fond of the library, though he said it was the park on the other side of the street he was most interested in.

"There's a park there?" Metford asked.

"Yes. The entrance from that side is small; not easily spotted if you don't already know about it. It's between the two houses and that awful, ugly apartment complex. The park is little, too. That's why I like it. I stay there a lot during the days."

"We walked right by it," Ava said. "There are signs posted on either side of the entrance."

"I was more focused on looking for security cameras at the apartment," Metford said defensively.

"Mr. Norrie, did you see anyone suspicious around the library on Monday?"

He shook his head and looked at his feet.

"What is it? Do you know something about the librarian's murder?" Metford asked.

"No, nothing like that, but ..." he let his words fade out.

"But what? It might seem inconsequential to you, but it might be the one thing we need to know about," Ava urged.

"It's just that I know someone who hung around the library a lot. Maybe too much. But it was because that pretty librarian was nice to him."

Ava brightened. "That's exactly the kind of thing we need to know about. Who is this man, Mr. Norrie?"

"Rusty. Not sure about his last name, but he's a good guy. He is." Mr. Norrie looked down and ran a hand over his long gray beard. "I tried to get him to leave her alone. Told him she wasn't going to give him the time of day, but he wouldn't let up. Always swooning and mooning over her like a teenager in love."

Ava looked to Metford. "The love note."

"What love note?" Mr. Norrie asked. "Did he write one to her?"

"We're not sure who wrote it, but it's possible."

Mr. Norrie turned away and wrung his hands.

"What else, Mr. Norrie? What do you want to tell us?"

"It's just that Rusty... He's been different since coming home from the war. He has a bad temper, and it made him a little off up here." He put a finger to his temple. "It's his problem with women that has me worried. He gets too attached too fast, and he thinks they're falling in love with him when they're not. They're only being nice because he's a homeless veteran with an obvious mental problem. Nobody will tell him that.

Nobody wants to hurt his feelings." He groaned and ran a hand idly over his beard again.

"He has a history of getting attached to women?" Ava asked.

Mr. Norrie nodded. "And when he figures out they're not in love with him, he gets mad. Really mad." He sighed and turned to face them again. "You might want to talk to Cara Marks. She's a homeless woman a couple blocks from here. She had trouble with Rusty a while back, but I don't want to retell the story. It's hers to tell."

Ava's phone vibrated with a notification. "Thank you, Mr. Norrie." She walked away with Metford as she checked her phone. "We got a file. Looks like Mr. Randall figured out the security system well enough to send... *links?*"

"To the cloud storage." Metford reached for her phone. They continued to walk as he tried to pull up the video. At the main road, he shook his head and handed the phone back to her. "The store is right there. Let's just go watch it on his computer. We can't access the link without a password."

"Where's Ashton when you need him?"

They reached the hardware store and went inside. Mr. Randall smiled sheepishly and held up both hands. "Wasn't me. My son sent the link because he said the disc I gave you was probably unusable."

"You can't record from the screen like you did with a VHS player, Pops." The younger version of Mr. Randall walked to the front of the store.

"And we can't access the link you sent us without the password," Metford said.

The younger Randall guffawed and motioned for them to follow him to the office. "Give me that disc and I can make you a readable copy." He took the disc and went into the room. "The password was in the message, by the way. I thought the FBI would be clever enough to figure that out. Big Way Camera 24. That was the password, just take out the spaces."

"Can we just watch the footage from your computer? That would make our jobs go more smoothly today," Ava said, giving Metford the cue not to engage with the snark about the password or the FBI being less than clever.

"Sure. I still have it pulled up here." He pointed at the screen. "Just hit the spacebar when you're ready." He leaned forward and touched the spacebar. "It's that long one right there. Use it to pause the video, too." He grinned and stepped back.

"I know where the spacebar is, Mr. Randall, thank you," Metford said.

A figure appeared on the screen and walked toward the side of the library, and then he was out of view. Ava played it again.

"Look at the way he turns his head as he walks," she said.

"Just enough to keep the camera from seeing his face," Metford agreed.

"He turns to avoid the other camera, too," Younger Randall said. "Like he knew they were there."

"Exactly," Ava said. "That means…" She thanked Randall, took the newly burned disc, and left the store. She turned to Metford. "This guy, whoever he is, might not be new to killing if he knew where the cameras were beforehand and avoided them like that."

"Damn, you're probably right, but I really hope not."

"Yeah, me too." But she didn't think she was wrong. She had seen the differences between amateur and seasoned killers to think this was the first kill, or even the third or fourth kill, for their perpetrator.

CHAPTER SEVEN

From the Neighborhood

ASHTON LOOKED UP AND DOWN THE STREET SEVERAL TIMES. Dane walked to the driveway of 325 Sysco Street. The front door of the Reese home still had the unbroken police seal. "Front, back, both side doors are still sealed. No one's been here," she called to Ashton, who was still looking back and forth along the street. He looked as though he were watching a tennis match. She walked to the sidewalk and down to him. "What are you looking at?" She tried to follow his gaze, but all she saw were houses.

"I don't see any cameras on any of these houses except for these three." He pointed to the two houses across the street and facing the Reese home, and the one beside it.

"The others have privacy fences," Dane said, nodding. "Well, you want to split up or team up to do this?"

"I don't want to do it at all. I hate this part of the job," he said. "But split up and meet back here when we're done. We'll team up for the last three here."

"Hour-and-a-half, two tops," she confirmed and headed to one of the other houses.

Two hours later, Dane came back to the car. Ashton sat in the driver's seat drumming the steering wheel with his thumbs. She motioned for him to get out.

"What's up?" he asked.

"I got nothing from the other houses; what about you?"

"Zilch."

They went to the house beside Reese's first, and then the one straight across from it. No one saw anything other than the police and forensic search at the Reese home, but both had Ring doorbell footage, which they handed over readily.

As Dane and Ashton walked to the house directly across from the Reese home, a teenage girl was walking down the driveway from the garage. She eyed them suspiciously.

Dane presented her badge. "Hi, we're Special Agents Dane and Ashton. Do you live here?"

She nodded. "You're here about Mrs. Reese, aren't you?"

"Yes, we are. Did you know her?"

"I knew who she was. Everybody knows everybody in this neighborhood. Side effect of living in the suburbs." She rolled her eyes, crossed her arms, and cocked a hip.

"What's your name?" Ashton asked.

"Jerri Mondale, and I'm only seventeen, in case that matters."

"We're just trying to find anyone who has any information about where Brad, Penny, and Thomas might be," Dane said.

Jerri shook her head.

"Have you seen anybody who looks suspicious wandering around the neighborhood?" Ashton asked.

Jerri dropped her arms to her sides, looked over her shoulder toward her house, and then back to them as she shifted her weight from one foot to the other. "Maybe." She looked over her shoulder nervously again.

"Jerri, we need to know what you saw, when, and where," Dane said, looking up at the house. There was no movement, but Jerri sure acted worried that someone was watching her, or perhaps that someone in there would see or hear her.

"Over there." Jerri pointed to the Reese house. "Back near that privacy patio on the left."

"Good, good," Ashton said. "When was this?"

"Tuesday morning," she said curtly as she cast another glance at her own house.

"But no one else saw anything that morning," Dane said. "Monday morning, everyone would have been going in and out of the house to go to work or school."

Jerri stepped forward and dropped her voice a little. "It was before sunrise, okay? It was still really dark out. I only saw him because he coughed, and when I looked over, I saw him looking through the bottom window there. It's a basement window, and there was a light on in there for a few seconds, and then it went out. I kept walking, but I was quiet. I didn't want to draw his attention."

"Where did he go after the light in the basement went out?" Ashton asked.

Jerri shrugged. "He was walking around the front of the house. That's the last I saw, and then I went inside."

"What time was it? Do you remember?" Ashton asked.

Jerri tucked hair behind her ear and flipped her foot onto its side, then put it flat. She repeated the movement several times.

"Jerri?" Dane prompted.

"About four, or four-thirty, I guess."

"What were you doing outside at that time?" Ashton asked, looking puzzled.

Jerri lowered her voice to a whisper and shrunk in on herself. "Coming home."

"From where? Where would a seventeen-year-old girl be coming home from at that time of morning? Were you alone?" The pitch of his voice rose.

She flared up. "Yes, I was alone. I had sneaked out the night before to go see my boyfriend, okay? I had to get back in here before Mom got up to get ready for work."

"Okay," Ashton said, looking like an upset father learning that his kid was sneaking out.

"Why didn't you tell anyone about this until now?" Dane asked gently. If there was one thing she understood, it was teenage girls who felt like women and resented the fact that adults were still telling them what to do. New York City had been full of them, and her sister's girls had taught her many life lessons in teenage girls' lives. Some she never wanted to learn.

"I didn't want to get into trouble was one reason, but also, I just didn't think much about it because there have been some homeless people trickling into the neighborhood over the last year or so. I just thought it might have been one of them looking for somewhere safe to sleep for the night. This place might be boring, but it's a lot safer than the public parks or the beach."

"All right," Dane said. "Are your parents home now?"

"Just my mom. They're divorced." She motioned toward the front door. "I have to go. I have an appointment."

"Thank you." Dane watched as Jerri hurried down the sidewalk toward Barker Street.

"An appointment?" Ashton asked, looking doubtful.

"Probably with the boyfriend. Let's go." Dane knocked on the door and showed her badge when Ms. Mondale opened it.

"The FBI?" She motioned to see both their badges.

"Yes, ma'am," Ashton said. "We're just trying to get some information about your neighbors, the Reeses."

"About the Reeses? I knew something was wrong when I saw the police over there Tuesday."

"If you don't mind, we need to speak about it."

"Sure, come on in. I thought they were on vacation or something. Haven't seen anyone over there in days, and usually the kids are outside, and I see Mrs. Reese coming in from work late in the evenings—usually after dinner when I'm in here reading or watching TV for the evening."

"Are you Jerri's mother?" Dane asked. Something about the way the teenager acted made her want to be sure and cover all her bases.

"Yes, why? What does she have to do with this?"

"We just spoke with her—"

Ms. Mondale's eyes went wide and she held up her hands to stop Dane. "Wait, you spoke to my daughter without permission? I didn't think that was even legal. She's only seventeen."

"We were just gathering information. She isn't a suspect," Dane said. "And there's nothing to worry about, unless you know something about what happened to the Reeses."

Ms. Mondale shook her head and turned toward the living room. "I have no idea what's going on. As I said, I knew something was wrong when I saw the police over there."

"Ms. Mondale, Jerri saw someone outside the Reese residence on Tuesday morning before sunrise," Dane said.

"Call me Sherri, please. Okay, she saw someone outside in the dark. It could have been Brad."

"She would have recognized him, but she didn't, and there's something else."

"She might have recognized him even in the dark. I don't know. Her room is at the end of the house on the second floor; it's not the best view, and there aren't a lot of streetlights here. You said there was something else?"

Dane nodded and glanced at Ashton. "Jerri wasn't in her room when she saw the man at Brad Reese's house."

"Okay. Where was she?"

"Outside."

"Before sunrise?"

"Yes, ma'am. She, uh, said she had sneaked out the night before and was returning before you got up for work. She said she didn't say anything because she didn't want to get into trouble, but also because she thought the man might have been homeless and looking for a place to sleep for the night. Is that something that happens here regularly?"

Sherri's face was red. Her lips had turned into thin white pressure lines. Her knuckles burned white and purple as she tried to contain her anger. Dane understood the reaction. Her sister had looked that way many times over the years, but mainly when one of her daughters had done something that they were going to be in big trouble over.

"Ms. Mondale?" Ashton prompted. "Are there normally homeless people wandering the neighborhood?"

"What time did she say it was when she saw that man?"

"Around four in the morning," Dane replied.

"I told her to stop seeing that boy," she exclaimed through clenched teeth. She took a deep breath. "I'll deal with that later."

"She's a teenager," Dane said. "Don't be too hard on her."

"I think I'm not hard enough on her. Ever since the divorce…" She exhaled deeply and let her eyes close for a moment. Then she looked at Dane and smiled, seemingly recovered. "Now, what did you need to ask me? I really have to go to the supermarket."

"What about the homeless in the area?" Ashton asked again.

"No, they're not a problem, but we have seen more than usual over the last year, maybe two. Do you think that's who Jerri saw?"

"We don't know," Dane said. "That's what we're trying to find out. So far, your daughter is the only one who saw anything out of the ordinary."

"God," Sherri said, looking past them and out the window toward the Reese residence. "If I had seen someone, I would have called the police, but I wasn't up then. I don't get up until quarter-til-six most mornings, and never as early as four-thirty." She grinned. "Lately, it's been more like quarter-after-six. I have no energy anymore. Being a single parent to a rebellious teenage daughter is not for the faint of heart."

"No, ma'am," Dane said, thinking again of her sister and nieces.

"Do you have surveillance footage from your security camera? I saw that it points toward the Reese house," Ashton said.

"Yes. It automatically gets stored in the cloud. I haven't had time to even look at any of it for weeks. It's such a hassle to log in, and the computer runs slow." She shook her head and stood. "But I can make you a copy. Just tell me the dates you need."

"From midnight Sunday through today would be great," Dane responded.

"Do you mind if I come with you?" Ashton asked. "I'm the resident tech geek on the team. I could retrieve the footage and speed up your computer while I'm in there. Won't take but a few minutes."

"I don't know; I'm really busy," she said.

"Up to you," Ashton said, sitting again.

Sherri walked to the hallway and looked back to them. "I'll just be a minute."

It took ten, but she returned with a thumb drive and handed it to Ashton. "I hope the drive is okay. I didn't have any discs. They clutter up everything, in my opinion. Thumb drives are just easier."

"This is fine," Ashton said. "Thank you."

Dane stood. "Yes, thank you. If we need anything else, we'll be in touch."

Sherri followed them to the door and shut it behind them.

"Jerri is in serious trouble," Ashton said once they had crossed the street and stood at the car again. "You could have left out the part about the boyfriend."

"She needed to know, Ashton. Did you see the dark circles under her eyes? The way she tensed up at the mention of the boyfriend? My bet is that she hasn't been divorced long, and she is having a hell of a time trying to keep her daughter under control and reconcile her working life with her home life."

"Telling her about the boyfriend added tension they probably didn't need right now." He got in the car and put the key in the ignition. "It's not our job to play hall monitor with people's kids."

Dane got in and buckled her seatbelt. "Maybe. But if my nieces were sneaking out, I would be glad for someone to play hall monitor and tell their mother. Or me, for that matter. I'm calling Ava to see what she wants us to do. This took us longer than expected."

"I didn't know you had nieces."

Dane put the phone to her ear. "I like keeping my family separate from my work. Being an agent isn't the safest profession." Ava answered, and Dane explained the situation. She hung up. "Beach house. We need to search for Brad and the kids there again, just to make sure they haven't shown up."

"The beach house it is."

CHAPTER EIGHT

Witness Interviews and Timelines

Thursday

Cara Marks

CARA WAS A WHIP-THIN WOMAN WITH STRINGY BROWN HAIR AND scared-rabbit eyes. Living on the streets had done the twenty-nine-year-old no favors and had made her hyper-alert. It wasn't the side effects of something she was pushing into her veins or smoking. It was survival instinct. Something she had learned through years of tri-al-and-error on the streets of several cities.

"Cara, what can you tell me about Rusty Moore?" Ava asked.

She sniffed and shifted restlessly in the seat. Her gaze moved and darted. "He's a jerk, ya know, just a weirdo."

"What do you mean 'he was a jerk'?" Metford asked.

"He's got a bad temper. Likes to resolve conflict with his fists and feet." She looked toward the door. "How long's this gonna take?"

"Not long," Ava assured her. "We heard that you and Rusty had a… *relationship* that soured."

Cara shook her head. "No. No, there was no relationship. He got a crush, or something, on me, and he followed me around everywhere I went. He was like a puppy begging for attention. I told him he was being too weird and that he needed to leave me alone. He told me how beautiful I was, how he wanted to take care of me, yada-yada-yada. But there was no relationship."

"You're speaking in past tense," Ava said. "That implies that he stopped following you around and begging for attention."

Cara nodded, pulled her hair into a ponytail using the elastic she wore on her wrist. "Yeah, but it cost me, too." She bared her teeth and pointed out the empty space in the bottom. "That. Bastard beat me almost unconscious. And that was after he broke everything in my tent."

"Was the attack unprovoked?" Metford asked. "Or did something set him off?"

Scoffing, Cara pulled the ponytail into a messy bun. "You could say that something set him off. I'd had enough of his crap, and I wanted him to leave me alone, so I told him that. Maybe not so nicely, but I had to get my point across. He was starting to leave love notes and poems that looked like they were written by a second-grader. I'd wake up in the mornings, and he would be there, outside my tent, just hovering with that scary, stupid grin on his face. I had a job at a diner for a couple of months, but he kept coming around, and the owner fired me. So, yeah, maybe I was rude and maybe that set him off." She bobbed her shoulders and moved to the edge of the seat. "Can I go now? I don't like it here; the walls… they make me feel like I'm in a coffin."

"Sure," Ava said, standing. "I'll walk you out." She opened the door and waited for Cara. "Do you know if Rusty owns a gun, Cara?"

"Not a clue, but I know he don't need one. He's dangerous enough without a weapon. If he'd had one that day, I wouldn't be here."

Ava thanked her and went back to the interview room. "Who's next on the list?"

Suri Nyquist

"Suri Nyquist. Teagan's coworker and friend," Metford said. "She's already here. Been waiting in the bullpen."

"I'll get her." Ava returned with Suri in front of her.

Suri was very still and very calm compared to Cara. The interview was shorter than the one with Cara. Suri had already spoken with them once and only needed to repeat what she had told them so it could be recorded in an official statement.

"Do you know anyone who might have had a grudge against Teagan? Someone who might have wanted to hurt her?" Metford asked.

"I told you about Solomon Furlong. Haven't you questioned him yet?"

"We've not been able to get in touch with Mr. Furlong," Ava said.

"Maybe you should try harder. Send someone to talk to him instead of being so passive about it."

"Ms. Nyquist, we can't send anyone. We don't know where he is, and besides, we have no evidence that he's the killer," Ava said in a calm tone even though she wanted to yell at the woman for suggesting they were being too passive. There were still laws to abide by. Even the worst of the worst had rights that were protected. The FBI couldn't hunt down a man without a reason, and so far, they did not have a solid reason.

Suri grimaced and shook her head. "It's disappointing how the law does so much to uphold and protect murderers."

"Everyone says that until it's their rights that are being put at risk. Then they're glad the laws are in place to protect them," Metford said.

Ava shot him a warning look. If she had to keep her cool, he was going to.

"I'm sorry, Agent Metford, but my rights aren't at risk because I'm not going around making myself seem like a murderer. I'm following all the rules. I try to be a good, kind, considerate human being—unlike Solomon Furlong. Now, since my liberties are still intact due to my own behavior, I think we're done. You asked who might have reason to hurt Teagan, and I've told you. You have my statement, and you know where to find me if you need anything further. Goodbye, Agents."

"I'll walk you out," Ava said, standing.

Suri turned a cold look to her. "No need. I can find my own way out just like I found my way in." With a flip of her hair, she was gone and the door was swinging shut behind her.

"Wow, that was a one-eighty from when we spoke to her last time," Metford commented.

"Her friend was brutally murdered at their workplace and she was the one who found her. She has a right to be upset."

"But not at us. We're doing our job."

Ava raised an eyebrow. "You want hazard pay for hurt feelings?"

"Okay, I see your mood hasn't improved much." He pulled the clipboard with the list of interviewees toward him and checked the box next to Suri Nyquist's name.

"Sorry, but that's how easy it is to lash out at the closest person."

"Right. And that just proves your point about Ms. Nyquist."

"It should."

Manny Dierks

Ava took the list of interviewees and pointed to a name. "Who's Manny Dierks?"

"He saw the police at the library and spoke to an officer outside. The officer told him to speak with the detective in charge, but the guy didn't hang around."

"Is he here now?"

"Not sure, but he was earlier. Out by the vending machines getting coffee, last I heard."

Ava waited a few seconds. Metford didn't offer to go get Dierks. She motioned as if for him to stay seated. "By all means, don't get up. I'll go."

"We've had ten interviews already, and you've insisted on bringing each one in here. If you want me to go, just—"

Ava walked out. Having a temper wasn't a bad thing; not being able to control it was. Her fuse had been short for months and seeing the lauded Dr. Bran only seemed to make it worse.

Get a plant. Get a pet.

The advice kept looping through her mind, angering her further. "I don't need a pet; I have murder cases. I don't need a plant, I have Metford," she mumbled under her breath. Maybe she should tell Dr. Bran that at their next appointment.

A man in a polo shirt stood next to the door that looked out over street.

"Mr. Dierks?" she asked.

The man turned and smiled. "Last time I checked."

Great, he's got jokes, she thought, motioning him to follow.

"I'm Special Agent James. Thank you for coming in today."

"You bet. I told that cop what I saw the other day. It's probably no big deal, but it might be." He chuckled.

Was it a nervous chuckle or did he find something about Teagan's murder comical? She pointed to the interview room. "In there."

Grinning broadly, he stuck his hand out to Metford across the table. Metford looked at it with confusion.

"Manny Dierks, man, here to help." He pushed his hand closer.

Metford looked from the hand to the man. "Mr. Dierks, if you could take a seat, please. This shouldn't take long."

Manny's smile dissipated slowly and he withdrew his hand. "Right. So much for camaraderie, huh?"

"We just need to know what you saw at the library, Mr. Dierks," Ava said, taking a seat.

"Well, which day? I go by there four times a day, at least." He held up a finger. "Monday through Friday, anyway."

"You don't go by the library four times a day on the weekends?" Metford asked.

There was an uptilt to his voice and the corners of his mouth that signaled he was being facetious. Ava cleared her throat and cocked an eyebrow at him.

"No, I don't work the weekends," Manny said.

"Right," Metford said, putting on a serious face again. "So, which day do you think we want to know about?"

Manny's grin returned briefly. "Well, I would say you want to know what I saw the night before that pretty librarian was found dead at work, right?"

Ava nudged Metford's foot to keep his sarcasm at bay with another warning look. "That would be great. What did you see the night before the librarian's murder?"

"Well, I was just going past the library to get back to work. I had been at Little Joe's, the all-night convenience store with the deli?"

Ava nodded.

"Yeah, I went there on my lunch break to grab a burrito, and I was on my way back to work when I saw this man leaving the library by one of the back doors. He had on a dark hood and long sleeves. I didn't get a look at his face or anything like that, but he was carrying a messenger bag."

"Was he carrying anything else?" Metford asked.

"Not that I saw, but the messenger bag was bulged in the middle. Not like it just had books in it."

"Mr. Dierks, can you show me on these photos which door you saw him come out of?" Ava slid several pictures of the library toward him.

He looked at the shots of the back. "That one, I think. It could have been the one right beside it, but I think it was this one. I was walking along the sidewalk on the other side of Higgins Street. I walk to the intersection, take a left, and Soderquist Fulfillment Center is half a block down on the left."

"You work third shift there?" Metford asked.

"Yeah, why else would I have been going for lunch at three in the morning?"

"And you're certain the man came out of the library? He wasn't just walking past the building?" Ava asked.

"What am I, blind now? Of course, I'm sure he came out of it. I heard the door shut and everything. He noticed me and I noticed him. I went back to work, and he went wherever he went, I guess."

"You didn't think it was odd that someone was there in the middle of the night?" Ava asked.

"That's why I stopped and told that officer what I saw; that's why I'm here now when I should be home in bed getting ready for my shift tonight. Didn't he show up on the security cameras at the library or something? I see on TV all the time about how security cameras help solve crimes."

"There were none that recorded on that side of the building, and none facing that direction either," Metford said.

"Thank you for stopping by, Mr. Dierks. You've been a big help," Ava said, standing and opening the door for him. "I can walk you out; I know you need to be going."

"Oh, thanks. Yeah, if I think of anything else, I'll call." He held out his hand as if waiting for an offering. "Your card?" he asked when she didn't respond readily.

"Oh, sorry." Ava grabbed one of her cards and gave it to him. "Let's get you on your way, Mr. Dierks."

"Call me Manny. I'm helping you solve a murder, so I think we can be on a first-name basis, Special Agent?"

She clamped her mouth shut and walked to the exit door. "Thanks again, Mr. Dierks."

"What's your first name, Agent James?"

She shook his hand and guided him out the door. "It's Special Agent James, Mr. Dierks. You have a good day now." She retreated down the hallway and into the interview room.

"Can we be on a first-name basis?" Metford asked. "Did you see the way his face lit up when you offered to walk him out?" He laughed.

Timeline

Dane knocked on the partially open door. "We're finished with our interviews. What now?"

"We need to establish a timeline. Bullpen," Ava said, leading the way.

"Okay, from what we know, Teagan was murdered Monday night, or early Tuesday morning," Metford said.

"Was there anything in your interviews that contradicted that?" Ava asked.

"No," Dane said. She handed Ava a stack of papers. "Everyone we interviewed had seen Teagan on Monday. A few had been at the library when it was closing time. None of them reported seeing or hearing anything out of the ordinary."

"But would they have noticed if someone was acting just a bit off, or if something was slightly out of the ordinary?" Ava asked.

"I think so," Ashton said. "They were regular patrons. One said she was there faithfully on Monday, Wednesday, and Friday, and that she spent the afternoons there."

"That was Shanna Preston," Dane supplied. "Fifty, retired early, AKA she's got more money than she can spend. She's old money, and she has donated around twenty thousand over the last few years."

"Right. We have Manny Dierks. He saw a man leaving the library through this back door, possibly the one right beside it, at three in the morning. He's calling it Monday night, but it would technically be Tuesday morning."

"About four hours before Suri went to work and found Teagan dead," Dane noted.

"The man he saw was carrying a messenger bag with something bulky inside," Metford said.

"The salt lamp?" Ashton asked.

"Could be," Ava answered. "Bad news is that none of the security cameras around the area have a view behind the library, but..." Ava turned on the footage she had acquired from Randy's Hardware.

"This is the footage from the single camera that might have caught our perp," Metford said. "Hardware store on the east side of the library, in the strip mall there."

Ashton held up a thumb drive excitedly. "Play this next; I think we got the same guy on this footage from the Reeses' neighborhood. But just like around the library, there was only one camera with a good view."

"That looks a lot like the same man," Dane said.

Ava put up the video and played the file. "I think you're right. Their gait is the same, and he looks to be about the right height."

"The weight is even comparable to the man on the other video," Ashton said. "And look at the way he moves his arms and hands when he walks."

Ava played the video again and then switched to the hardware store footage.

"I see it," Metford said. "Ashton, can you enhance the footage from either source to get us even a halfway decent look at his face?"

"I can try. At the very least, I think I'll be able to sync up the two videos so we can see how closely the gait, arc of his arms, weight, and height line up."

Ava removed the drives and handed them to Ashton. "You're on it. Quick as possible, we need to find those kids and their father."

"Right."

"I need to confirm witness statements," Dane said.

"So do we. Get started and let me know what you find."

"On it." Dane went to her desk and picked up the phone.

"Metford, I need you to work on confirming the stories from our interviewees while I work on putting the timeline on the board."

Over an hour later, Dane had finished. "I have three of the twelve who lied about where they were Monday evening. The rest told the truth."

"Okay, go see where Metford's at with his confirmations." She hadn't kept up with where he had vanished to.

A few minutes later, Ava finished with the timeline and started reading over Detective Reinhold's report again. It was better to check and not need the information than the other way around. Her father and uncle used to say, 'Measure three times, cut once.' Same theory, different analogy.

"We ended up with an even dozen truth-tellers, eleven liars," Metford said as he walked into the bullpen.

Dane and Ashton followed him in.

"How many of the witnesses who lied were doing so to cover up the fact that they have more information about Teagan's death or that they had something to do with it?"

"None," Metford said. "They were all where they said they were by the time the library closed. It was the stuff about where they were Monday before the library closed that they lied about. Two lied because they're cheating on their spouses and had said they were at the library to cover their butts."

"But they weren't at the library?" Ava asked.

"Right. They were both with their girlfriends in different parts of the city, and then they were at home with their wives later."

"And you checked to make sure they were with their girlfriends? You spoke to people who saw them, got video footage of them that had a timestamp?"

"I spoke with one motel manager and one apartment landlady. They have both agreed to send us timestamped footage from their security system that shows the men in question."

"Good. I want to see it when it arrives. We need to go over suspects."

"Manny Dierks definitely needs to be up there," Metford said. "He gave off all the wrong types of vibes."

"He did seem a little too excited about all this." She put his name up underneath Solomon Furlong's. "And he was in the right vicinity, but if he's a suspect, we need a motive."

"He had opportunity," Metford said. "And I already checked... he owns a gun. I'm with Meatloaf on this one. Two outta three ain't bad."

"Motive could have been anything," Dane pointed out.

"Especially if he happens to be a serial killer," Ashton said.

He was right. Jason Ellis didn't have clearcut motives for each of his victims other than the twisted need to kill young women who had little kids, or women who got in his way.

"So far, we have Teagan's husband Brad; the jealous coworker, Solomon Furlong; the homeless man with a bad temper toward women, Rusty Moore; Teagan's possible lover and town celebrity, Connor Aldridge; and Manny Dierks. Do we have anyone else to add to the suspect list?"

No one did.

"Want me to try to get in contact with Solomon Furlong again?" Metford asked.

"Definitely. I'm going to keep working through the interviewees' statements and try piece more of this together. Solomon argued with Teagan before the library closed Monday evening. The video from the hardware store shows a man approaching the library around eight-thirty Monday night. Everyone was gone from the library at that time except for Teagan Reese. Dierks saw someone leaving by the library's back door at three in the morning on Tuesday morning. Jerri Mondale, Teagan and Brad's teenage neighbor saw someone lurking around their house around four or four-thirty in the morning on Tuesday morning. The security footage from the Mondale house shows what seems to be the same man as in the hardware video. Then, Suri Nyquist, the coworker and friend, goes to work, finds her friend murdered, calls 911, and Fairhaven's finest show up." She held up Detective Reinhold's report.

"We just need to figure out who the man in the videos is," Dane said. "Are we in agreement that it is a man in the videos?"

"Yes," they answered in unison.

"Not a man disguised as a woman?"

"No," Ashton said. "I did the build analysis while I was syncing the videos. It's a man. Ninety-percent chance it's a man, according to the measurements and movements."

"I'm not even going to ask how that works, but okay," Dane said.

"Let us see the synced videos, Ash," Ava said.

The videos ran on the screen side by side. If not for the different backgrounds, Ava would have thought they were the same video, just duplicated.

"I mirrored the images from the neighborhood so he would be walking in the same direction in both clips, but as you can see, it's the same man. Five steps synced up perfectly, and that's what you see at the very beginning. The rest of it is not so perfect because he turns away in one and is disappearing around a corner in the other."

"That is the same man. I wish we had some footage of Solomon Furlong and Brad Reese to compare," Dane said. "Maybe if I go back to Sherri Mondale, she can find footage of Brad and we could compare them."

"That's a possibility and a good idea. See if she'll turn over all her footage so Ashton can scour it for anyone else lurking around. Maybe he can find our anonymous guy in daylight if it's not Brad Reese."

"Are we calling it tonight, Ava?" Dane asked.

"I'm not. I'm not going home until I find those kids," Ava said.

"I've not been home since Tuesday morning," she said.

"None of us have," Ashton added.

Metford hung up his phone. "Furlong isn't answering his cellphone or his home phone."

"What do you expect? It's almost midnight now," Dane said. "We're not going to get anywhere again until morning, and I don't know about you, but I need time to process all of this and then maybe I can come up with some connection we're missing."

Ava pursed her lips and looked at the floor. "You know what? Call it. All of you. Go home and get some rest. But I want all of you back in here early tomorrow."

"What time is early?" Metford asked.

"Six."

Dane and Ashton left in a hurry.

"I think they wanted to get out of here before you changed your mind," Metford said.

"You better follow suit because I'm on the brink of changing it now."

"I'll be here earlier than six. Coffee and breakfast from Pete's?" he asked as he moved toward the door.

"Just be here, Metford."

"I'll take that as a yes." He turned and left.

The office was quiet in a way that sent chills over Ava's back. Some places weren't meant to stand empty, devoid of the ruckus of the everyday business and life for which they were built. Jails, schools, and hospitals were at the top of that list, followed by FBI buildings and government buildings. But it would be good to be left alone in an empty quiet space for a while so she could think without distraction.

CHAPTER NINE

Forensic Insights

THE NEXT MORNING, AVA SAT AT HER DESK RUBBING HER EYES, WON-dering how long she had been asleep. A cup of coffee and an individ-ual box of donuts stood on the corner of her desk.

"Metford," she said, reaching for the coffee and standing at the same time. She peered out of her doorway toward the bullpen and saw him sitting at his desk working. She took the donuts and went to his desk. Offering him a donut, she said, "Why didn't you wake me?"

He took a donut. "Thanks, Metford. I really needed a few minutes of sleep. Oh, and thanks for the coffee and donuts, too," he said cheekily.

"Thanks for the coffee and donuts, but I wish you had woken me."

"You know if you say something nice and it's followed by 'but', you didn't really mean it, right?"

"No, that's not how that goes. The 'but' negates everything before it." She grinned and drank from the lukewarm coffee.

"So, you're not really thankful for the coffee, donuts, or the few minutes of sleep." He turned to his computer.

"I am, but—"

"There it is again." He laughed. "I'm just giving you a hard time. I said your name, but you didn't budge, and from the look of that red patch on your forehead and the dried saliva at the corner of your mouth, it seemed you coulda used more sleep. You're fine; it's just now six. Nobody saw you snoozing at your desk but me."

She rubbed a hand down the side of her face. "Great. That makes me feel so much better. I'm going to go clean up."

By ten-to-seven, the office was in full swing. Ava and the team had been going over paperwork and making calls for an hour. At seven, everyone gathered for the morning briefing. Before Ava could start, Santos walked in.

"You're back," Ava said, smiling despite the headache and fog-brain.

Santos smiled and set her things on the closest desk as everyone turned to her. "Looks like, and about time, too."

It took a few minutes for everyone to welcome her back, shake her hand, ask how she was, and then settle again.

"Are you riding the desk, or back in the field?" Ava asked from the front.

"I don't see a desk with a saddle," Santos said, her face glowing.

"I got the doctor's report on my desk," Sal said. "She's been released to full duty."

"And not a minute too soon," Santos said. She turned to Metford as she sat in the chair nearest him. "Miss me?"

"It's been … *peaceful* in the office. I was just starting to get used to it."

They grinned at each other. Ava couldn't help but think they acted like siblings, forever teasing each other and arguing, but still there was a connection there. An unbreakable bond forged while learning to work together and to trust each other with their lives. It was a moment in which Ava found herself envious of them. Her bond with Molly had been lifelong, and nothing could completely sever it, but she hardly had time to even speak with Molly on the phone anymore. And she couldn't talk to her about the job, or what they had both been through while Molly was being held captive. It was like they had no common ground anymore, and Ava had no anchor. She could be tossed at the whim of her turbulent career. That was an unpleasant thought with even more unpleasant imagery.

"Ava, we're ready when you are," Sal said with a concerned look. "Santos is joining on the case, so be sure to get her up to date today, as well."

Ava nodded and cleared her throat before going over the case and what was in the works for the day concerning it.

"Okay, you have your assignments for the day," she said. "Be flexible in case anything else comes up. Santos, go with Dane and she'll get you caught up while you're with her today."

Santos nodded. "Sounds great."

Ava's phone rang. It was the lab. She hung up. "Ashton, Metford, we need to go to the lab. The results are in on our evidence."

"One car or two?" Metford asked.

"Ashton is going to a different lab for the digital evidence. You're with me."

Ava finally felt the rush of wakefulness and hurried to the car with Metford in-tow.

At the lab, Ava and Metford were shown all the evidence collected from the library and the Reese residence. Vincent Zhang was new to the team, and Ava liked his down-to-earth personality and his attention to detail. As with most of the lab workers, he was reserved and quiet.

"This is what we found of importance to the case," Zhang said, pointing to a smaller table with a handful of items displayed.

"What about all that?" Ava asked, motioning to the hundreds of items sitting on tables and carts.

Zhang looked at it, then back to her. "Useless. This is it. We lifted a set of prints from Penny Reese's dresser as noted in the picture there. We got a clean set from the table in the victim's office, also noted in the accompanying photo. And then we had this." He picked up a bag and held it under a light. "It was found at the library as well."

Ava took it. "What is it?"

Zhang smiled and picked up the papers that had been under the bag. "It's a piece of deer bone." He flipped a few pages.

"Deer bone? In a library?" Metford asked, taking the bag to have a look.

"Yeah. I know. Weird, right?" Zhang asked as he handed the paper to Ava. "But it isn't new by any means. It's old."

Ava looked at the paperwork but didn't see anything of use. "Okay, but what was it doing in the library, and why is it important?"

Zhang nodded and grinned wider. "Because I found out it was part of a knife handle. It could belong to the killer."

"But the victim was shot twice, not stabbed," Metford said.

"Right," Zhang said, crestfallen. "There was a speck of blood on it that matched the victim's blood anyway."

"Thanks, Zhang," Ava said. "What about these prints? Did you find a match for them?"

"Not yet, but they do match each other. Whoever left the prints on the library table left them on the dresser at the Reese residence. Forefinger and middle finger of the right hand."

"In six-year-old Penny's room," Metford said.

"They aren't her father's prints?" Ava asked.

"Assuming his were part of the mass of prints taken from the house, no. These two sets were unique."

"Run them through AFIS; run them through all the databases. We need to know who they belong to." She turned to leave and stopped. "Actually, Zhang, run all the prints through the system. If you get any hits, call me."

Zhang looked forlorn and pointed to a box that contained what was possibly thousands of individual prints that had been pulled from the scenes. There was no trace of a smile. "Right. I'm on it. Possibly until my retirement, but I'm on it."

Metford laughed and went out the door behind Ava.

"That was a lot of nothing," he said.

"No, sometimes even the smallest, most inconsequential thing can break a case wide open. You know that. We need to stay positive for the kids' sake."

"You keep saying that, but the truth is that their mother was murdered at work, and now they, and their father, are missing without a trace. It's kinda hard to stay positive when you're a realist."

She spun on him. "Don't think like that. If I had thought that way, where would Molly be? I kept my hope when there was none to be had; when it seemed that she should be long dead, I kept hope." She turned and stalked to the car. "And now she's home with her mother making a recovery."

Metford got in. "Molly was a unique case, Ava. How many of the women survived as many years as she did with that ring?"

"That's not the point," she said, pulling into traffic with a heavy foot on the accelerator.

She wanted nothing to do with being a realist when it came to kids. If there was a sliver of hope, she would keep it alive no matter what she had to do.

"All I'm saying…" He sighed. "It's been four days, Ava. You need to—"

"No, Metford. They're alive. We're going to find them. Maybe their dad, too. That's that. Drop it."

"Okay." He turned to look out the window and remained silent on the ride back to the office.

CHAPTER TEN

Building a Case

AFTER ASHTON RETURNED, AVA CALLED A MEETING. "WE NEED TO put the evidence together in a way that makes sense." She shared what she had learned at the lab, and then asked Ashton to share what he had found.

"I discovered deleted texts between Teagan Reese and an unknown person. They seemed to be of a romantic nature."

"And you know romantic texts when you see them?" Metford asked.

"They were discussing a previous… *ahem*… interaction, if you will. In detail. And they were planning another meeting."

"They were sexting?" Dane asked bluntly.

Ashton tilted his head. "It was very detailed."

"Were there pictures?" Metford asked.

"Metford," Ava warned.

"No, if there were pictures, we could use them to identify the guy," he said defensively.

"There were no pictures." Ashton handed Ava papers. "That's the printouts of the messages."

"And you don't know who the man is?" Ava read over them quickly.

"No. The phone number is from a burner phone," Ashton said.

"Cheaters love burner phones," Metford said.

"Leave it to you to know that," Santos sniped.

"All right," Ava said, passing the papers to Metford. "Does anyone have any theories? Viable theories."

"We should widen our search area around the library," Dane said. "Go to businesses farther away in the general direction the man was seen taking when he left the library at three on Tuesday morning. He would have become more confident the farther away from the library he got, and maybe he lowered that damn hood enough to be caught on a camera somewhere."

"And there are traffic cams starting just a couple of blocks from there," Santos added.

"Okay, that's on you two. Check for footage where you think it's possible, but keep it within a reasonable distance. While you're out there, go by Penny's school and speak with her teachers to see if they might have any idea where Brad would have taken them. Did they say anything about a trip they were going on? Were they excited about a surprise he had told them about? Did they act afraid, excited, or normal during the days leading up to Teagan's murder?"

"Got it," Dane said.

"What if the perp's main goal was to kidnap the kids?" Santos asked. "Schools always have great security camera angles outside. I could ask to go over the footage from the last week and see if anyone stands out."

"Great idea," Ava said. It was good to see Santos getting back into the groove of work so quickly. "I'm going to check with local pharmacies to see if Brad has picked up an inhaler for Thomas yet."

"We should check those little doc-in-a-box stations, too. He could take him to one of them in an emergency situation. They would've prescribed an inhaler, and probably had some on-hand," Metford said.

"If he was desperate enough, he could have stolen inhalers," Ashton said.

"Especially if it wasn't Brad," Santos said. "Just saying. If a kidnapper wanted the kids, he could've stolen what he needed to keep the kid from dying."

"If someone killed Teagan just to kidnap the kids, it doesn't make sense," Metford said. "I mean, Brad was with the kids at home. Why not just kill him and take the kids? Besides, if it happened the way you suggest, then where is Brad?"

"He could be dead, too. The kidnapper could've coerced him into leaving with him and the kids. That would keep the kids quiet and calmer; easier to handle. Then he could've killed Brad when they reached the perp's destination and dumped the body somewhere."

"We'll look at it from several angles for now," Ava said. "I don't see that we have any choice."

"Could have been anyone on that suspect list," Ashton said. "Jealousy is just as much a motivator as love, hate, revenge, money…"

A terrible thought hit Ava. What if the kids were to be sold into the sex trade? Her gaze drifted to the pictures of them on the board and her gut knotted. That would be motive enough to kill the parents.

"How does the deer bone fit into this?" Ashton asked.

"We're not sure," Ava said.

"If it was a dagger-type knife with the bone handle, do you think that might have left the bruising in Teagan's palm?" Santos asked.

"We're thinking that was from the salt lamp that's missing," Metford said.

"Yeah, but what if she had the knife? Or was it maybe a display in the library or art center that she grabbed to try and protect herself when she realized someone was in there?"

"It had her blood on it," Ava said.

"But if she had used it, wouldn't the perp's blood be on the scene, too?" Metford asked.

"He's right," Dane said. "Even if she just hit him with it, there would be some evidence of him on the scene."

"Okay, so maybe it was his. The piece of bone was broken off," Santos said. "That means there had to be some sort of impact. Maybe they fought more than what we're thinking."

"Yeah," Ashton said. "Men wear that type of knife in a sheath attached to their belt or strapped around a leg as a concealed backup."

"Good thinking," Ava said. "If they fought, maybe there's a piece of furniture in there that has his DNA on it. We need to check with the director and make sure she's not found anything missing from either the library or the art center."

"Even the storage areas that might have been overlooked," Santos said. "Teagan might have been in one of them when the perp attacked her, and then he went back during the hours after he killed her and straightened up, cleaned up behind himself."

"She was beaten," Metford said. "Did the scene where she was shot indicate any sort of blood spatter or smears from the beating?"

"I don't think so," Ava said. "But that's something to look into."

Why hadn't she thought of the kidnapping theory before? Was she so focused on Brad being the guilty party that she had missed such a significant possibility?

CHAPTER ELEVEN

Initial Profile

"CONSIDERING THE EVIDENCE WE HAVE SO FAR, AND ONLY THE evidence, I have a profile," Ava said. "I think we're looking for a man between the ages of thirty and fifty. He's fit but not so much that he stands out in a crowd. He's good at blending in, and he doesn't care to get his hands dirty. He probably works with his hands, and it's likely that he has very few attachments to people."

"From what we saw on the footage, he doesn't seem too muscular," Ashton said.

"But he was wearing a baggy hoodie that probably hid a lot," Ava said.

"He was wearing jeans that showed his legs were muscular," Dane said. "And I would peg his age at the thirty mark from the way he moved."

"I agree with that," Santos said. "And remember, a man doesn't have to be very muscular to overpower a woman her size."

"Men are inherently stronger," Metford said.

Everyone looked at him.

"It's a proven fact. That's scientific," he said. "Ashton."

Everyone turned to Ashton, who shrugged.

"He's right."

"Is either video clear enough that we can tell whether he has a knife strapped to his leg under those jeans or maybe on his belt?" Santos asked.

"No," Ava said.

"He had to have planned this for a while," Dane added. "No way this was a crime of opportunity."

"So, that probably rules out Manny Dierks," Metford said.

"It could have been Furlong," Ashton said. "He works with her. He knows the library's hours, layout, and Teagan's habit of staying late. He might even know what time she usually left for home when she worked late like that."

"But why would he go after the husband and kids?" Metford asked.

"Maybe he knew Brad would immediately think of him as a suspect," Ashton offered.

"And the kids?" Ava asked. "Why take them?"

"I don't know," Ashton said. "Maybe he didn't take them any farther than he took Brad."

"He might have killed them, is what you're saying?" Ava asked.

Ashton nodded.

"Whoever he was, he would be cold, calculating, and would strike without hesitation," Santos said, her hand moving to her side. "Without training of any kind to protect herself, Teagan would not have stood a chance."

"We don't know that she didn't have training," Ava pointed out.

"Yeah, we do," Santos said. "She didn't have enough defensive wounds to indicate any sort of training."

"It's hard to train to defend yourself from bullets," Metford pointed out.

"But she was beaten before she was shot," Santos countered. "If she'd had any decent training, she would have scratched, bit, kicked, gone for his eyes, throat, groin, whatever she could to get away."

"We think she probably hit him with the salt lamp," Ava said.

"That's another reason I don't believe this is his first time killing someone," Dane said. "It just smacks of someone who knows what to clean up afterward, like they've done it before and have practice."

"He was seen heading for the library at eight-thirty Monday night," Ava said. "He didn't leave until three Tuesday morning. What was he doing in there all that time?"

"Cleaning up and staging the scene," Dane said.

Metford nodded. "Unless he didn't kill her until later. Might have been beating on her for some time before she was able to get hold of the lamp. She hits him, runs around her desk and toward the end of the short shelves so she could put something between her and him, and that's when he shot her."

"Makes sense, but wouldn't somebody have heard her if he was beating on her?" Ashton asked. "She would probably scream, right? And even though it's late, it's not so late that he doesn't have to worry about a passerby hearing and reporting the screams."

"Or seeing him," Dane reminded them. "Those windows show the entire library, and he would have been hard-pressed to remain unseen while beating her even in the office. It was very open, she probably still had the lights on, and all it would take is someone glancing up in that direction if they were walking by."

"So, it was probably later when he got hold of her," Santos said. "And we don't know for sure he didn't hold her in one of the storage rooms before she was shot. Like Metford said, maybe she hit him with the lamp and made a break for it and that's why he shot her."

"Why shoot her at all if he was worried about the noise or being seen through a window?" Ashton asked.

"Self-preservation," Ava said.

"Exactly. He couldn't let her go without risking arrest." Santos smiled.

"That's where the knife comes in," Metford said. "Maybe he was worried about the noise and being seen. Maybe he intended to use the knife in whatever room he was holding her out of sight, but the situation got out of control. She panicked and fought for her life when she saw the knife, broke free, ran to the office to get her phone maybe, and they fought there. Salt lamp for defense. She ran. He shot because he panicked."

"No, he didn't panic," Santos said. "People like that don't usually panic. He shot her in the chest and then in the head. That's an execution. He was angry. Pissed that things had gone out of his control, and he reacted…" She looked wide-eyed at Dane and then Ava.

"In the way he was accustomed to reacting when similar situations had gotten out of control in the past," Dane said, finishing Santos' thought.

"You mean there might really be a serial killer on the loose here?" Ashton asked.

CHAPTER TWELVE

The Chase Begins

A VA HELD UP A HAND TO QUIET THEM. "LET'S NOT MAKE THIS ANY worse than it already is. I agree with what you're all saying, but let's leave out the part about him being a serial killer. We have no basis for that in the evidence."

"Except in the way he killed Teagan Reese," Metford said.

"We need to focus here," Ava said loudly. "The kids, remember? Figuring out who the man in the videos is will lead us to the kids." She exhaled deeply. "Can we do that?" Why were tears lingering at the backs of her eyeballs just waiting for any reason to fall? What was going on with her emotions lately? She turned her back to the team and stared at the timeline on the board to keep them from seeing how upset she was. Dr. Bran was already reading her emotions, she didn't need the whole team trying to diagnose her even if it was just during their lunch breaks and at the bar after work.

"Yeah, we can do that," Metford said.

"Good. Thank you." She turned to face them. "Manny Dierks is the low man on our totem pole of suspects, but he is still on the list. Solomon Furlong. Dane, you and Santos try tracking him down again today. Ashton, stay here and get to those traffic cameras around the library. Scour them for any sign of our perp. Metford, you're with me again. We need to go back to the library and do another walkthrough with the director Ms. Leonard."

"If you want the camera search done by the end of the day, I'm going to need help," Ashton said.

"Call in whoever you need. As many as you need. Just get it done." Ava walked out knowing Metford would catch up before she made it to the car.

At the library, they walked in and were shocked to find out that someone else had already been hired to fill Teagan's spot temporarily.

"That was fast, wasn't it?" Ava asked Ms. Leonard.

"This is vital public service, Agent James. I would have thought if anyone could understand that, it would be you and your partner. After all, if you were, God forbid, killed in the line of duty, aren't there multiple people waiting in line for your spot in the Bureau?"

"That's… different."

"Not at all. When a necessary position is vacated suddenly, there is a need to fill it as soon as possible so that the whole enterprise runs smoothly. Miss Vickers is only temporary until Solomon gets back to work."

"So, he was next in line for the job?" Metford asked.

"Not my choice, but there are people over me who think he is the next suitable candidate. There's nothing I can do about it unless he does something to warrant demotion or termination."

"It doesn't matter to your superiors that he is a suspect in the murder of the former librarian?" Ava asked.

"He hasn't been formally charged with anything. You haven't even spoken to him yet, have you?"

"That would be easier to do if we knew how to reach him. We can find records of him leaving for his vacation, and then it's a blank slate. He's not at home, doesn't answer his phone."

"He hasn't reached out to me again, either, but I suppose he wouldn't. He was very angry when he didn't get the job. I have sent him a letter to inform him of his pending promotion. Procedure." Her eyes darted upward as she scoffed. She stepped into Teagan's old office and announced Ava and Metford.

"Miss Vickers," Ava said. "We need you to step out until we're finished. Thank you."

The temp stood. She was a slender, tall woman with perfect posture. She looked as if she and Ms. Leonard had gone to the same school. One that teaches the students how to look naturally aloof, cold, and austere all at the same time.

Ava and Metford went over the office again, checking for signs of damage to any hard surface that might have caused the break on the knife handle. They came up with nothing.

Miss Vickers sat in a chair at the back of the library where the room connected to the hallway leading to the art center. She stood when she saw them.

"You can go back to your office," Metford said. "We're done."

"Thank you," she said, walking by them.

"Friendly, isn't she?" Metford asked.

"I wouldn't be happy if I knew I was working where a woman was very recently attacked and killed," Ava said.

"You have a point."

"Storage rooms and the art center," she said, feeling heavy.

Was it lack of sleep or burnout causing her to feel so unenthused about the investigative process? Could it have anything to do with the fact that she felt the whole case was hopeless? She couldn't voice that feeling. Not after browbeating the rest of the team about holding onto hope for the sake of those two kids.

The storage areas could have been used for any number of nefarious deeds, and no one would be the wiser unless blatant evidence was left behind. There were boxes, bags, shelves to the ceiling, drawers packed full of items that were for display and some in need of repair, and they were so cluttered that it was difficult to move around and search for clues.

"This is useless," Metford said, shoving a box to the side. Something glass inside cracked. "I'm not paying for that," he said.

"This is the last room. If the killer had Teagan in here, we wouldn't know even if we cleaned it out, and we don't have time for that."

"I've not seen anything that suggests she was ever back in any of these rooms that night."

They made their way out of the library, and for good measure, they walked along the back of the building and to the hardware store. Turning back, they walked the path again.

"He definitely wasn't worried about being seen walking to the library," Metford said, pointing out how exposed he would have been.

"No one would have thought boo about a man walking in this direction. He went behind the building. If anyone were out on either of these three sides, they wouldn't be able to see him enter through the back or exit there later."

Metford stopped at the doors and looked around. "If someone drove by on Main, they could have seen him."

"And do you think about it when you see someone go into or come out of a building when you're driving by?"

"Not really."

"Exactly. You're on your way somewhere else."

He turned toward the strip mall and the church again. "What about that homeless camp behind the abandoned store? The one behind the church? I have a straight line of vision between the church and strip mall. I can even see part of the tax prep store."

"We already talked to the homeless living there. They didn't see anything." Ava pulled a door open.

"With that food pantry and shelter behind the church, what are the chances that there were no homeless people on that side road or the alley there? If anyone was there, they had an unobstructed view all along the back here."

"And we ran that lead right into the ground already." She stepped inside.

Metford caught up. "What's going on? You were all about different angles and keeping hope earlier, and now you act like it's impossible that someone was around that we haven't talked to yet. That would be our best lead; finding someone who saw the perp well enough to identify him."

"The homeless people out there just want to be left alone. They're not going to talk to us, and if someone out there did see the perp, they are probably afraid to come forward. They aren't stupid. They've put it together by now that he killed Teagan. Might have even seen the whole thing go down through one of those windows."

"That's right. There could be a witness out there. What if one of them had seen that Teagan was working late and was waiting on her. She wasn't mean to them like the others; Suri Nyquist even said so. Maybe someone waiting to ask for money, or food, or something. They could've seen her murder," he said excitedly.

"And there has been a police and FBI presence here since Tuesday morning. Plenty of time for a good Samaritan to come forward or call in an anonymous tip." She walked out the front door.

"All right, but I'm not going to let this go for long. If something doesn't pan out today, I'm following this."

"No argument here, but I still think it's a waste of time." She got in and started the car.

Back at the office, there was no relief from the letdowns. Ashton and the other tech had found nothing on the traffic cams. Dane and Santos didn't get hold of Furlong, and Penny's teachers had no clue where Brad might take them.

"And the kids hadn't spoken about a trip or anything of that nature in the past week or so?" Ava asked.

"No, not at all, according to the teachers," Santos said.

"They gave us permission to search the girl's desk and her locker," Dane added.

"The girl has a name. Penny. Did you find anything pertinent in her locker or desk?"

"Nothing. And I know she has a name. I didn't mean to sound indifferent."

"It's fine. We came up empty, too. This guy is like a ghost. We caught a couple of useless videos of him, and nothing after that. It's time to start at the beginning again." She went to her office to gather her thoughts, and then went to the timeline board where she looked over paperwork, hoping something would stand out to her.

CHAPTER THIRTEEN

A Break?

AVA SPOTTED THE LIST OF DONORS TO THE LIBRARY AND READ OVER it.

George Bosworth III was the number one donor on the list, but it was not by a wide margin. Connor Aldrige and Karl Harmon came in a close second and third place.

"Connor Aldridge," Ava said aloud. "Were you really having an affair with Teagan? Would you kill to hide it?"

"What?" Metford asked, walking up behind her.

Ava showed him the list. "I'm thinking we need to go over these names again." She pointed to Connor's name. "That's the man Solomon Furlong said Teagan was having an affair with."

"Yeah, we knew that, but we don't know if it's true. That was an angry text from Solomon to his boss, and he was furious about the job ordeal."

"It's time to figure out if it is true. And these other men; we'll check into them, too. Anyone who donates that much money to a library-slash-art center might be into something less than legal. Who knows? Maybe Teagan wasn't in-the-know about it yet. Or maybe she just didn't agree with whatever was going on, and she refused to play by their rules."

"And you think one of them would kill her for it?"

Ava considered it. "Didn't Ms. Leonard say that her superiors are the ones who wanted Furlong instated as librarian against her wishes?"

"Yeah. You think she knows if something illegal is going on?"

"That woman doesn't miss anything. Have you met her?"

"Let's nail her down and see what we can get, then."

"She won't tell us anything at all. Look what happened to Teagan. Do you really think Ms. Leonard would put her own life at stake by telling us what's really going on?"

"She let us read the text from Solomon that implied Teagan and Connor were more than friends."

"That was inevitable. She knew that would be found sooner or later, and she knew how guilty she would seem if she hadn't shown us in the beginning. She's smarter than that. Again, have you met her?"

"Right. Let's look into these super-rich old dudes instead." He plucked the paper from her hand.

"Instead of rattling a super-rich wannabe old dudette?"

Metford laughed. "I'm just going to act like I did not hear you use the word dudette. Where did you even hear that word?"

"Nope. You're acting like you didn't hear me say it, so I don't have to explain anything."

Ava called another impromptu meeting and presented the list of names to the team.

"The order of the donors has changed," Ashton said.

"How so?" Ava asked.

"Connor Aldridge is at the top, along with his wife Margueritte. Seems they made a huge donation to the library at the end of last month, and the list updates only on the fifteenth of every month." He held up the new list.

Ava took it and tossed the old one in the trash. "So, Connor and Margueritte are the top donors. Karl Harmon is second. George Bosworth III is last."

"Just like his name," Metford chuckled. "The third."

"Maybe that'll make it easier for you to remember," Santos said in a whisper.

"I'm thinking that maybe one of these men might be the killer," Ava said.

"No way," Dane said. "Sorry, but they're all fifty and older. I just don't think we're looking for anyone in their age range."

"In any event, these are the names we're working with," Ava said. "Dane, Santos, you locate George Bosworth III. Ash, you search for Connor; he seems to have a big presence online, and we all know you're the best when it comes to that. Metford, we'll look for Karl Harmon. He has a beach house here but a main residence in DC. If any of you need either of us, know that we might be in DC or on our way there if Harmon isn't at his beach house."

"Should I grab my go-bag?" Metford asked, standing.

"To be safe, yeah," Ava answered.

Sal stood by the door. "On your way to DC, did I hear?"

"Not unless we need to," Ava said.

"Check in as soon as you find him. If you don't find him at the beach house... We really can't spare you going to DC and being absent for hours on end, Ava."

"We won't stay, then. I'll drive us back no matter what time it is."

"And it's how many hours one-way?"

"Less than two."

"That's if traffic is cooperative. Don't go until you've exhausted all leads here first. Understood?"

"Understood," Ava said, moving past her.

Metford got in the car and buckled up. "How far to the beach house, and is it near the one Brad's parents own?"

"It's about forty minutes from here, and it is not near the other one. Completely different area farther south."

Harmon's beach house was secluded on a grassy hill with a short picket fence around the front and side yards.

"No one's outside," Metford said.

"Means nothing. He could be inside or down at the beach." Ava parked and turned off the engine.

As they walked up the path to the gate in the fence, the front door opened and a man stepped out. He wore Bahama shorts, a floppy sunhat, and a horrible Hawaiian flowered shirt that flapped open in the breeze revealing his pale torso.

"Mr. Harmon?" Ava said, holding up her badge. "Karl Harmon?"

"Yes, that's me. What's this about, officers?"

"Special Agents James and Metford," she corrected him.

"I'm sorry. I can't see your badges from here. What's this about?"

"Teagan Reese. Know her?" Ava asked.

"Yes. Terrible what happened to her. She was a lovely woman."

"Your name came up on the list of top donors to the library where she worked."

"Yes."

"Could we have five minutes to ask you some questions? We're just gathering information. I'm not sure if you're aware that her husband and children are missing."

The shock on his face was genuine. "No, I didn't realize they still hadn't been located. Come in, please."

They went through the gate and Karl held the front door for them.

"Kind of a quaint place for someone with your money, isn't it?" Metford asked.

"That's the way I prefer it. I don't want to be bothered by people when I come here; I come here to relax and enjoy the peace. Hard to do if you have a huge fancy house full of staff just to keep it clean and fix your meals."

"You cook for yourself?" Ava asked.

"And you act astonished that I can. I'm a simple man, Special Agent James." He smiled, tilted his head, and winked flirtatiously. "Now, what's this terrible business about Mrs. Reese's children and husband? They were a nice family, but I admit to only meeting them once. Briefly. At a showing in the Fairhaven Center."

"They went missing the same day she was found murdered. Did you know anyone that might have wanted to hurt Teagan?"

He thought about it, or acted as if he did, and then shook his head. "No. No one that I can think of." He cleared his throat and looked down. "There was some friction between her and someone at the library over a job. I remember she mentioned it in passing that day I was at the center and met her family."

"Yes, there was, and we're checking that aspect of the case thoroughly. When was this event at the center when you met the Reese family?"

"A few weeks ago. Maybe three. Four, perhaps."

"Did you see anyone who didn't belong? Someone who looked nervous or may have been lingering around close to Mrs. Reese?" Metford asked.

"No. Of course, I'm not at the center enough to know who would seem out of place there. Every town is different."

"Right," Metford agreed.

"What about the other donors? Were any of them present?" Ava asked.

Karl started to say something and then closed his mouth. "Yes. Connor Aldridge was there with his wife Margueritte. It was one of their former sponsored artists who was being showcased that night. He was proud of that." He opened his mouth again to say something, but decided against it and closed his mouth, opting instead to look at the floor in front of his feet.

"Mr. Harmon, what were you about to say?" Ava asked.

He shook his head.

"It might seem like it's nothing or not worth mentioning, but it is," Ava said. "We take everything into account, no matter how small."

"Connor was having an affair with Teagan, but I don't think he had anything to do with her death. I want to make that clear. Connor is a womanizer, but he's certainly not violent, and he would never hurt anyone."

"Then why would you tell us about the affair?" Metford asked.

"Because I don't want it coming back to bite me in the ass later. Connor is a close friend, but I have to look out for myself. I don't want to be dragged into the middle of this because you learn later that I knew about the affair and didn't say anything. I'm a public figure, and I don't need that kind of thing getting out." He turned away and stood at a window.

"How long was the affair going on? Do you know?" Ava asked.

"I'm not sure. Probably a year; maybe more, maybe less." He shrugged but didn't turn around.

"That's not a usual one- or two-time deal, Mr. Harmon," Metford said. "That's more like a commitment."

"I know, but they were crazy about each other, to hear him tell it. At one time, I think he was contemplating ending his marriage to Margueritte to be with Teagan."

"But she was married with two kids," Ava said.

"He wanted her to get a divorce and bring the kids with her. Or so he said. He and Margueritte didn't have kids. She said she couldn't get pregnant, but I think she didn't want kids, and after a while, Connor stopped mentioning it. Then he started up the affair with Teagan. I tried to talk sense into him. She was half his age, and she brought nothing to the table. We had a little falling out over it for a few weeks, and that's when I decided to let it go. It was his business if he derailed his life. Probably it was just a midlife crisis."

"Did the affair end?" Ava asked.

He shrugged again. "I didn't ask him about it, and he hadn't mentioned it in a couple of months, so I don't know."

Ava thanked him and left.

In the car, Metford said, "Connor Aldridge is definitely climbing the suspect list."

"I agree. Two mentions of the affair from two different people make it seem more viable. Connor might have killed her during a lover's quarrel."

"If she refused to divorce Brad and make Connor the new daddy, it might have infuriated him."

"Harmon said Aldridge isn't violent, but whoever killed Teagan was. She was beaten up pretty badly."

"Maybe he was trying to convince her to say yes to him. Men like Aldridge aren't used to not getting their way," Metford pointed out.

Ava pondered the possibilities on the drive back to the office. "If Connor wanted the kids, do you think it's possible that he killed Teagan and then went for the kids anyway?"

"At this point, anything is possible. If he'd already killed Teagan, he wouldn't think much of killing Brad, I'm sure."

CHAPTER FOURTEEN

Locating Connor Aldridge and Where's Rusty?

ASHTON GAVE AVA ADDRESSES AND PHONE NUMBERS LOCATED IN New York City and Fairhaven. "Those are the two addresses I found for Connor Aldridge. There are more on the back for New York. They are his properties, but they aren't listed as his residences."

"What are they?"

"Properties for his artist mentoring, artist sponsorships, and studios."

"Great. That didn't complicate the situation any at all," she said sarcastically. "If he killed Teagan, he has about twenty places that are possible hideouts. Did you make any calls?"

"I called all of them. No answer anywhere, but I left messages at each number."

"Thanks. I'll try them all again."

She went to her office and started at the top of the list. Calling a few numbers, she got assistants who took messages. For the rest, she left voicemails. The longer she sat there, the more it weighed on her that if he was the killer, he could be getting further and further from her reach.

She went to Ashton. "This is his personal cellphone number. I want you to put a trace on its location. You can do that, right?"

Ashton blinked stupidly for a moment. "Not without orders."

"Well," Ava said, lowering her voice and glancing around. "Consider it an order, then."

"Ava, I can't. You know we have to have probable cause and approval for that."

"Ashton, he might be the killer. The longer we sit here doing nothing, the better his chances for slipping right through our fingers. If he leaves the country…" She ran a hand over her hair and took a deep breath. He was right. That didn't make it any easier to deal with. "The kids."

"I'm sorry. I can't."

"Can't or won't?"

"I won't do it, Ava. We adhere to protocols for a reason. If we violate any of his rights, and he is the killer, he walks on a technicality. How is that good for the kids or any sort of justice for their murdered mother? Ask again when you have the approval." He turned to walk away.

She wanted to apologize for asking him to do something that would have landed them both in a world of trouble if it had been discovered, but she couldn't.

Can't or won't? she asked herself silently.

Angry with the laws that tied her hands behind her back and the ones that allowed a possible killer to go frolicking wherever he chose, she stormed into Sal's office.

"Ava," Sal said, pulling her glasses off.

Ava shut the door and brandished the paper with Connor Aldridge's cellphone number written on it. "I want a trace on this cellphone number. I need to find Connor Aldridge, and he's not answering any of his phones."

"So, go to his house and knock on the door. He lives in Fairhaven, right?"

"That's not his only address." She pulled out the other paper and put the list on Sal's desk. "There. Those are his *known* addresses, and he could be at any one of them right now. Even if the whole team flew up there and split up, it would take a couple days to visit each address, and he would get wind of it and just run. I want to track his phone to pinpoint where he is."

"So, the case has been solved and Connor Aldridge is the murderer?" Sal looked surprised.

"Not exactly, but it's very likely that he is the killer. He was having an affair with Teagan Reese. It has come to our attention that he wanted her to divorce Brad, take the kids, and marry Connor. He was going to divorce his wife to be with her and the kids."

"Then why would he kill her, Ava?"

"Maybe she changed her mind, and he snapped. Afterward, maybe he took Brad and the kids, killed Brad, and ran with the kids."

"That doesn't add up. Were the kids his motive all along?"

"I don't know. That's why I need to find him right now and question him."

Sal put on her glasses and looked at the number. "You know I can't get authorization for this without probable cause. What evidence do you have that he's the killer? Or the one who took the kids and their father?"

Ava sat heavily in the nearest chair. "I don't have definitive proof, but I have two men who talked about the affair between Mrs. Reese and Mr. Aldridge. It's the most viable lead I have right now."

Sal tapped her fingers against the desk for a moment. "What about Mrs. Aldridge? They are married. It's likely that she's with him. Have you tried calling her?"

The effect of that simple suggestion was like someone throwing a bucket of water over a campfire. Ava shrank into herself. Chagrined, she shook her head. "I hadn't even thought about it." She stood abruptly and reached for the paper. "Sorry. I don't know what's wrong with me lately." She left before Sal could respond.

Ashton looked at her suspiciously as she approached.

She held up a hand to stop him before he protested. "Different tack. I need you to find Margueritte's number. All of them."

He nodded and turned to his computer. A minute later, he handed her a paper with three numbers. "She has a private landline in their Fairhaven residence. The second one is her personal cell number, and the last one is also one of Connor's in New York City."

She took the paper and read the numbers. "Thanks."

"You're welcome." He had already turned away again.

"Ash," she said.

Keeping his fingers on the keys, he looked at her. "Yes?"

"I'm sorry. About earlier. I shouldn't have asked you to do that. It was wrong, and I'm glad you didn't give in."

He nodded and went back to work.

Ava went to her office and called the landline. There was no answer, but she left a message for Mrs. Aldridge.

"Here we go again," she muttered as she dialed the cellphone number.

"Margueritte Aldridge speaking," a woman's voice answered.

For a moment, Ava expected a beep.

"Hello?" the woman said.

"Yes, Mrs. Aldridge?"

"Speaking."

Ava introduced herself. "We need to speak to you and Mr. Aldridge concerning the death of Teagan Reese. When could you come by the office?"

"Teagan Reese was the lovely librarian in Fairhaven."

"Yes, ma'am. She was murdered earlier this week."

"I don't understand why you need to speak with us about it. We've been in New York City for days. We've had a new gallery opening."

"You're in New York?"

"Yes, since Wednesday."

"When will you be back here?"

"We were planning on returning home in the morning on an early flight. I still don't understand why you need to speak with us."

"We're just going down the list of donors to the library so we can clear people off our lists as soon as possible. I tried calling your husband, but he didn't answer. My colleague and I both left messages. We would appreciate you coming by as soon as possible. Or I could come to your house after you get back tomorrow. Would that be easier for you?"

"Oh, no, no. We'll come by there before we go home. Best to deal with business matters early."

"I'll see you at what time in the morning, Mrs. Aldridge?"

"Our flight is due to land at nine, so we should be there by ten-thirty, no later than eleven. It really depends on traffic."

"Thank you, Mrs. Aldridge."

Ava hung up and gathered the team. "We need to find out all we can about Connor and Margueritte Aldridge. They're coming for an interview in the morning between ten-thirty and eleven."

"You got him to answer a phone?" Metford asked.

"No, his wife answered her cellphone."

"Where are they? Why hasn't he been answering?"

"She says they're in New York City. Been there since Wednesday because they had a new gallery opening, but they're due home tomorrow."

"And she just agreed to the interview?" Metford looked doubtful.

"She did. Said she didn't know why we would even want to interview them in connection with the case."

"We had no luck contacting Mr. Bosworth," Dane said. "We left messages. Hopefully, he'll return the calls soon."

"Do you really think Connor is the killer?" Santos asked. She pointed to Metford. "We heard that was your working theory."

"It is my working theory. Did Metford tell you that we now have two different men saying that Connor and Teagan were having an affair?"

"He did," Santos replied. "But it might not be him."

"But it could be," Ava retorted. Why all the backlash at every turn? Why were they bucking her on this?

"What if it was his wife?" Santos raised an eyebrow.

Confused, Ava floundered. Had she missed some other important angle? Did she have such tunnel-vision that she kept missing things that should have been obvious?

"If Mrs. Aldridge found out about the affair, maybe she killed Teagan in a fit of jealous rage," Santos said.

"But it was a man on the videos," Ava said.

"We don't know that for sure. We couldn't see the face. Do we even know Mrs. Aldridge's build? Who knows? Maybe she's the one in the videos."

Ava looked to Ashton. "Can you get pictures of her off the internet? Full body shots, preferably a few that will give us a good idea of her build."

"I can try."

"I don't think it was a rage killing," Dane said. "The crime scene doesn't entirely indicate a rage killing."

"It doesn't entirely indicate a murder of opportunity, either," Ava said. "But we can't rule it out yet."

"It doesn't completely comply with the textbook version of a cold, methodical murder, however," Ashton said, not looking away from the computer.

"So, what does the crime scene show? What kind of murder was it?" Metford asked.

"That's just it," Dane said. "It's not any of these, but it seems possible that it could have been any of them, too."

"Is it possible that the staging caused the confusing scene reading?" Santos asked.

"That's something we'll have to come back to. For now, Connor must be kept on as a suspect until something is found that proves he had nothing to do with the murder beyond a doubt," Ava said. "There are too many possibilities still up the air to take him off the list."

"We should add his wife to that list," Santos said.

"Agreed," Metford said. "Though I don't think we should bring up anything about the affair in the interview."

"Why not?" Santos asked, looking agitated.

"Give him an opportunity to come clean on his own. That way we can judge whether his wife already knew, and if not, we can still tell how much he was worried about her finding out."

"And we'll be able to gauge her reaction to it," Ava said.

"*If* he comes clean about it," Dane added.

"Bingo," said Metford.

"Here's the only full body picture of Margueritte Aldridge I could find in a quick sweep of the internet." Ashton took the paper from the printer and gave it to Ava. "There are folding chairs close by to give an idea of her size."

Ava studied it. She wanted to be able to dismiss that Mrs. Aldridge could be the person on the footage, but she could do no such thing. Margueritte was tall and athletically built. With a hoodie and jeans, she could very well be the person on the footage.

"That's her husband beside her," Ashton said. "But I guess most of you already knew that." He looked directly at Metford. "Or maybe not."

"I didn't." Metford took the photo. "Either one of them could be our perp if you put them in a baggy hoodie and jeans."

So much for removing Margueritte from the suspect list.

"Has anyone spoken to Rusty Moore yet?" Ava asked, recalling that he wasn't included in their last discussion over the suspect list.

"We haven't been able to locate him," Dane said.

"He's still on the list, right?" Santos asked.

Ava turned to the board and added his name. "Yes. Double your efforts to find him."

"Apparently he moves around a lot," Dane said. "We talked to a lot of people who have seen him, and most of them actively avoid him."

"Got a nasty temper, and everybody we've talked to says they never know what's going to set him off," Santos added. "But nobody's sure where he's been this week."

"That's suspicious, isn't it?" Ashton asked.

"Yes," Ava said.

It was more than suspicious since he was the person who was always hanging around the library and pining for Teagan's attention. She decided to deal with finding him after the next morning's interview.

CHAPTER FIFTEEN

The Pressure is On

S AL WALKED TO THE FRONT OF THE ROOM. "I KNOW YOU'RE ALL working very hard on this case, and I'm sure you're aware of how high profile it is. It's making front page news here in Fairhaven and the surrounding areas." She held up a newspaper to prove her words. "This is the fourth day, and it's still on the front page. And so far, we've given no updates to the public, and I haven't had one for my superiors, either. They're on my back about it. I need something I can give my bosses." She looked directly at Ava. "Today."

Ava nodded. "Yes, ma'am. I'll work on it right away, but the Aldridge interview is happening in the morning, so…" She looked at Sal questioningly.

"What, Ava?"

"Would you rather wait until after that interview when we might have an actual update to give?"

"No. Today. I need it to be on my desk by the time you leave so I can have it on their desk when they come to work in the morning. And if anything comes from the interview, that will be another update." She looked to the team. "We need this case resolved. Starting tomorrow when you report to work, no one is going home until it is. Make appropriate arrangements."

"We've barely had a break since the case started," Ava said.

"I know, but now it's mandatory. The Fairhaven Library and Center for Art Culture is very important to this city and to the officials that run this city. They want those children found and the culprit held accountable for this atrocity just as much as all of you do."

"For completely different reasons, I bet," Metford said.

Sal pinned him with a sharp gaze. "That's unfair, Special Agent Metford. Unfair and unwarranted. We are responsible for bringing this case to a swift and just end. And that's what's going to happen. Do all of you understand?"

Everyone agreed and kept quiet.

Sal motioned for Ava to follow her as she left and turned to go into her office.

"What's going on, Sal?"

"I want you to give the update to the public."

"You mean a press update, like in front of cameras and with mics in my face." Ava frowned.

"That would be the idea, yes. You're lead on this case. It will look good for your career and for the department."

"But I've never done that, and I don't want to. Dealing with the press has always been your deal, or the press liaison's. Why change up now on such a high-profile case?"

"Because it's a necessary step in furthering your career. It's time. You need to move forward and learn more about how the Bureau works besides just paperwork and fieldwork. I have meetings and don't have time to do the press update."

Would it land her in trouble if she called BS on that? "Then hand it off to the liaison. I need to be working the case, not holding a press conference."

"If you don't give them something, it will bring the suits down on the whole department, but mostly on your team and us." Sal pointed at Ava and then herself. "Go figure out what questions you'll answer, and stick to that template. If they ask for something you can't give, just tell them 'No comment.' You'll do fine. I have faith in you, Ava. Now, go."

Suppressing the urge to argue her point, Ava left and stepped into her office. She needed to be alone for a while so she could think. As she paced the room, she imagined it must be how a caged lion felt. Everything he was comfortable with, everything he knew and loved was in sight but unattainable because of the bars. He could even stick a paw out between the bars, but he could never get hold of the one thing he truly wanted: freedom from the cage.

Was that what the office was? A cage, that once she was in, she could never be truly free from?

No, she thought. *I can walk through that door and be right back in the field, back with the team, back where I'm comfortable, and doing what I love.*

She opened the door and went back to the team. "I know this sucks, but I need all of you to be very careful about what information you give about this case. As a matter of fact, let's make this simple. Do not give any information to anyone outside this team. No one. We can't risk the media getting any details and running with them, or this case could blow up in our faces."

"Was she serious about mandatory OT?" Metford asked.

"Yes. Very serious."

"What's going on with this case that makes it so different than any other we've worked?" Santos asked.

"To be honest, I'm not sure, but we have orders and we're going to follow them. I have a press conference to get ready for. You have your assignments?"

Everyone did.

"Let's get to it, then. I want to get this over with and get back to the case." She walked to her office again.

The press conference was set up quickly, and the scene was chaotic when Ava stepped to the podium. Her heart thundered and her lungs tightened. Sweat prickled at the back of her neck and in her underarms as the media clamored to get their mics in the best positions.

The whole thing was over in a matter of minutes, and Ava rushed away, eager to get out of sight of the cameras and to leave the journalists behind.

Sal met her walking into the office. "So, how was it?"

"Awful. I need a shower. I sweated more in front of those cameras than I do in my morning workouts."

"I'm sure you did fine."

"Did you know that rumors have already started to fly that there is some drug and sex scandal connected to Teagan's death and that it involves some of the public officials in Fairhaven?"

"Rumors always get started when the public isn't updated often enough on cases that catch their interest."

"And the questions about the murder… If those journalists actually got to see a bloody crime scene once, I don't think they'd be so relentless in their pursuit of details about them."

Sal let out a silent laugh. "You'd be surprised."

"The press thing is done. Does this mean I can get back to working the case? Doing something that makes a difference."

"This was an important part of the casework, Ava, and it did make a difference. Didn't you just hear yourself?"

"About?"

"The rumors that you squashed about public officials. And you didn't give them any of the juicy details they were screaming for. You quashed all that. You put it into perspective for a lot of people. What you just did instills a bit more respect in the public's mind for us, for the case, for the deceased, and her missing family." Sal patted Ava's shoulder and walked past her to disappear into the recess of the elevator bank.

Maybe Ava had done all those things, but it hadn't felt like it when the lights were blinding her and people were rapid-firing questions at her. A sense of accomplishment settled in her chest as she rejoined the team.

CHAPTER SIXTEEN

Alibis

VERIFYING ALIBIS COULD BE VERY SIMPLE OR VERY DIFFICULT. IT was tedium that could not be overlooked or taken lightly, and it was usually mentally exhausting.

"How many alibis are unconfirmed?" Ava asked.

"Two," Metford said glumly. "I need coffee." He scrubbed at his face with both palms and then stretched.

"I think jumper cables might work for me," Santos said. "So, what now? We're here for the long haul unless you want us to call it a night and start the mandatory in the morning."

"It's not mandatory until then, so if you want to go, you can."

"I'm staying," Metford said.

"Me, too," Dane added.

"Three," Ashton called from the doorway.

"I'm not going to be the only one leaving," Santos said.

"It's okay if you need to go," Ava said. "You're just getting back to work, and—"

"I'm fine. Seriously." Santos stood to stretch. "All my alibis checked out within minutes."

"Yeah, all of them did except Rusty Moore and Brad Reese," Metford said.

"We haven't located either of them yet, so we don't have alibis to confirm. And make that three because we haven't talked to Connor to get his alibi straight yet. His wife says they were in New York by Wednesday, but that doesn't account for where they were when Teagan was murdered."

"What about Mac Norrie, the homeless guy you talked to?" Santos asked.

"What about him? He's the one who gave us the tip about Rusty Moore and pointed us in Cara Marks' direction."

"Should we put him on the suspect list?"

Ava thought about it for a moment. "No, why would we?"

"We don't know for sure where he was the night Teagan was killed, and he was awful quick to point you in a different direction."

"Hold up," Ashton said. "I found something when I was going through the traffic cameras. I think it's Mac Norrie."

"Can you pull it up? I can confirm if it's him or not," Ava said.

Ashton worked for several seconds and then pushed away from the computer. "Right there."

Ava leaned to see the picture better. Metford stood beside her.

"That's him," Metford said. "Mac Norrie."

Ava stood and stared at the background a moment longer. "That's a twenty-four-hour convenience store up in North Fairhaven, Ashton."

He moved back to the keyboard and took the picture off the screen. "Yeah, but he was there at midnight that night. He's stealing food. So, that means he wasn't at the library when Teagan was murdered."

"Right, he couldn't have walked up there and back in that time," Metford said. "He's not that athletic, if you remember."

Ignoring Metford, she stepped to the side to eye Ashton again. "Why were you searching traffic cams that far out of the area? I thought I said to stay within a reasonable distance. Nothing from up there would have been any use to us because we wouldn't be able to prove it was the same person who's on the footage at the library. There's no continuity of path to follow."

Ashton cleared his throat and looked at the computer again. "But it was of use. It eliminated Mac Norrie as a suspect. That's a plus, right?"

"But it was a waste of time and resources to go that far out."

"Sorry. It won't happen again," he said.

"We can't afford to waste resources on things that will do no good," she reiterated.

Metford put a hand on her shoulder. "Being upset about it won't do any good, either. He's right; at least it cleared the old man."

"Okay, but don't do that."

Ashton nodded.

"Why don't you track the digital trails of Brad, Teagan, Connor, Solomon, and anyone else pertinent to the case? We could use that to maybe get a lead on what was really going on before she was killed."

"How long do I have to come up with something?"

"Not very. We need this done fast. You heard Rossi; the assistant directors are on her back to close this case."

"I can get digital tracks on all of them at once if I can recruit a team to help. Some of the people over in Cyber Forensics owe me a favor…" He raised his eyebrows in question.

"That's between you and Rossi. If she says okay, I'm fine with it."

Ashton shot from his seat and headed for Sal's office, returning a few minutes later. He grabbed a folder from his desk. "Rossi approved it, but it means that the team I'm bringing will have access to the whole of the case, and for the duration."

"That's fine, but be sure they know that before they agree."

"Will do." He was out the door and headed for the elevator before she could say more.

CHAPTER SEVENTEEN

Geek Squad Extraordinaire

I T WAS THE FIRST TIME ASHTON HAD PERMISSION TO RECRUIT A
team to help him. He was accustomed to being the guru of his team,
but he had longed to head his own team for a while. Walking into their
lab, he felt like he was coming home. The electronic beeps and whirs, the
clacking of fingers flying over keyboards, and even the sound of several
CPU fans humming in the background made up the symphony of his
happy place.

"Dwight Ashton," a man exclaimed as Ashton walked deeper into
the large room. "The man, the legend." He turned in the opposite direction. "Hey, come meet Special Agent Dwight Ashton, guys."

"Hi, Daniel. Could we turn the dial back on the pomp and circum-
stance here?" Ashton asked. "I just came to ask a favor."

Another man and a woman appeared from around a corner.

"Sure, sure, but first, I'd like to introduce you to Heath Statham and Chandra Davis. Guys, this is Special Agent Dwight Ashton."

"You mean the computer whiz you talk about all the time?" Heath asked.

"Not computer whiz, he's a tech god," Chandra said, sticking her hand out to Ashton. "It's nice to meet you after everything Daniel has told us about you."

Ashton's face burned as he shook Chandra's hand. "Thanks. Nice to meet you, too." He stepped back and lifted the folder awkwardly. "I just need some extra hands on this, if you've got the time."

"We will make the time for you, Special Agent—"

"Just Ashton is fine. Or Dwight. Whichever..." Ashton let out a pent-up breath. "And I'm not as good as you are with the tech, Daniel, so stop filling their heads with nonsense about me. It's going to make me look bad when they see the real me at work."

He sort of meant that, but then again, he sort of didn't. Daniel had been trying to recruit him to Cyber Forensics since he had been in the Fairhaven field office, but Ashton couldn't bring himself to leave his team.

"He's modest to a fault," Daniel said to Chandra and Heath.

Ashton lifted the file again. "Really, I need help with this, and my supervisory agent cleared me to recruit help from you guys." He looked at the empty chairs across the room. "Where are the others?"

"Why? Are you afraid we won't be enough help?" Daniel asked.

"No, it's just..." He looked at the three of them standing there with wide smiles and expectant eyes. "I can't ask you to help if you're all that's in the unit."

"We're not. The other guys are in the lab upstairs. Another case." Daniel clapped his hands once and stepped forward for the file.

Ashton held it tight. "I have to tell you that if you agree to help with this case, you're stuck on it for the duration, and we can't tell anyone outside the team anything about it. Not a single detail leaves the team."

"I'm okay with that. Beats the hell out of what we've been doing," Daniel said.

"Which is nothing much at all. I've been working on a new firewall for the telecommunication system for a field office in North Carolina," Heath said.

"Yeah, for the last month," Chandra added.

Ashton gave Daniel the file and a brief overview of what they knew so far.

"This is an order to retrieve data from multiple tech gadgets at different locations and all the computers at the Fairhaven Library and Center for Art Culture," he said, sounding amazed.

"Now you see why I need help. My equipment's great, but there's just not enough of it or of me to get this done."

Daniel shook his hand. "We got you on this. When do we start and where?"

"I'll go through the city's traffic cams and surveillance cams in public areas to see if I can locate Brad or his kids. I'll also gather any personal security footage from residences and businesses. I need you to figure out who can do which job the fastest with the rest of it. We'll all go to the library and work on several computers at once so we're not there when it's open for normal business, but that will be later tonight after they're closed."

"My man, we don't need to go to the library to do that." Daniel waved to indicate the massive amount of tech at their disposal. "We can get into any public network from right here. All we need is approval, and it looks like you've got that." He patted the folder.

After only ninety minutes of work, Chandra brought Ashton a stack of printouts. "I thought you would want these as soon as possible so you can take them to your team. I already sent the file over to Special Agent James's email, but it's been half an hour and she still hasn't opened the file."

"Thank you."

Ashton saw the printouts were emails between Teagan Reese and Connor Aldridge.

The affair had been going on for a little over a year, according the dates on the earliest messages. Ashton read through half the papers before finding anything that stuck out.

He read carefully and then called Ava as he took the papers and left the lab.

"Take a look here," he said as he handed the papers to her in the bullpen. "I think that's important. Like very important."

"Tell me. It'll take forever to read through all these."

"I don't think Teagan and Connor broke off the affair because she got cold feet. Teagan wanted something in return from Connor. She wanted desperately to be accepted back into the art world. When Connor couldn't, or wouldn't, commit to any promise, she dropped subtle hints that she might let it slip to Margueritte about the affair. When he laughed her off and told her that he knew she wouldn't do that, she got mad. She demanded that he start using his influence to get her back into the New

York City art world or she would tell Margueritte. There was nothing subtle about the last threat. And, by the way, the digital file is sitting in your email. Chandra sent it over earlier. Might want to keep an eye on that because they are the geek squad; cyberspace is their space. That's how they communicate everything."

"Okay." Ava checked the email. "There's another file here, too. It's from Teagan's phone; text messages to Director Leonard about Rusty. She was worried that Rusty's behavior would escalate, and he was starting to scare her. She knew about his violent temper and was asking Ms. Leonard what her best recourse would be."

"Ms. Leonard didn't mention that when we spoke to her," Metford said. "Why wouldn't she mention that to us?"

"I don't know, but you know that means we have to ramp up our efforts to find Rusty Moore," Ava said.

CHAPTER EIGHTEEN

The Stakeout

"I HAVE TO SAY THIS IS THE FIRST TIME I'VE DONE A STAKEOUT AT A library," Metford said.

"It's weird, I give you that," Ava said. "But with the pressure mounting at the office, we need to find someone to give us answers, and preferably that will be Rusty Moore."

"He's been out of the area since Teagan's murder," Metford reminded her. "If he did something, or knows something, he probably won't be back for a while."

"He's a war veteran with a possible mental disorder. He might not even be gone. He might just be laying low because of all the police presence. If he suffers from PTSD, that kind of scene would set it off, I'm sure."

"That's why we're here after hours."

"Was that a lightbulb above your head?"

"Are we seriously going to sit here all night waiting on him?"

"We'll give it a couple of hours, and then I'll check back in with Ashton and see what he's got, if anything that we could follow up on. Dane and Santos could stay here and wait on Rusty."

"And fall asleep in the process. We're all going to have sleep disorders by the time this is over."

"Stop complaining. It's nothing we're not used to already. How many hours a night do you sleep anyway?"

"That's not the point. I enjoy every minute of my nightly naps, and I miss them when they're taken away."

"It's the small things in life, eh?" She grinned, understanding completely how he felt.

"Heads up," he said, pointing to the spot between the church and the strip mall. "Movement."

Ava walkied Dane and Santos. All eyes were on the dark figure making slow progress toward the library property.

"Looks like he's going to the tables at the end of the property," Ava said.

"People eat lunch there; maybe checking for leftovers."

Ava gave the order for everyone to wait for the man to come into plain view under the streetlight and stop. "I don't want to startle him too soon; he'll bolt and we might not catch him."

The man came into view and stopped at the trashcan bolted to the streetlight pole.

"Is that him?" Metford held up the only picture they had of Rusty Moore. "It looks like him, but is it?"

Ava took a look at the black and white picture printed on plain paper. "That's him." She pressed the walkie button. "Wait in the car; we'll approach first." Dane and Santos didn't answer back, but a quick glance in the side mirror showed them giving the 'okay' sign.

Ava opened her door slowly and peered around it to get a better view of the man.

"You sure that's our guy?" Metford asked in a whisper.

Ava nodded and motioned for him to come on. She stepped away from the door and pushed it shut.

The man was bent at the waist and reaching into the trashcan. At the sound of their approach, the man's head swiveled up and toward them. His eyes narrowed as he straightened up. He had a fast-food wrapper clutched in one hand.

"Rusty Moore?" Ava asked, walking briskly with her badge held out. "Mr. Moore, we're FBI, we just need to—"

"Shit, he's running," Metford said, taking off after him. "Rusty, stop. We just need to talk to you."

Two car doors slammed behind Ava, but she was in pursuit and didn't look back. Dane quickly caught up with her, zigged to the right, and peeled off toward the church. Metford ran straight toward Main behind the man.

At Main Street, the man took a sharp right, and Metford lunged at him, missing him by only a few inches. Metford tumbled, rolled back onto his feet, and Ava dodged around him, hugging close to the church's wall. The man turned right again.

"Dane, heads up!" she yelled.

Metford and Ava rounded the corner and burst out into the alley simultaneously just in time to see Rusty dodge Dane and continue down the alley past the burned restaurant. Farther down, he was blocked on his left side by the high fence around the abandoned warehouse site and on his right by the solid back of the strip mall building. He had no choice but keep running straight.

Just as he was about to pass the back of the hardware store, Santos flew into view and tackled him to the ground. She wrestled him onto his stomach, straddled his back, and had the cuffs on him by the time Ava, Metford, and Dane made it to her.

"What's going on?" the man panted as Santos and Dane dragged him to his feet. "Why are you arresting me? I threw the food back in the trash. I've done nothing wrong."

"Then why'd you run?" Santos asked. "Innocent people don't make a habit of running from the FBI like their lives depend on it."

"I'm always getting busted by the cops for going through the trash-cans, but a man's gotta eat."

"Right. Whatever, Mr. Moore. Now you're going in for questioning," Ava said.

"Mr. Moore?" the man asked with a confused tone.

"This could have been so much easier if you had just stood still," she continued. "But you ran, Rusty. Why did you run? Feeling guilty about something?"

"About Teagan, maybe?" Metford said.

The man shook his head, as if he couldn't believe what he was hearing. "Rusty, Mr. Moore, Teagan, I don't know who you're talking about. My name's Bob Gilmore."

"Get him back to the office," Ava told Santos and Dane. "We'll meet you there."

He was put in the back of their car amid a flurry of denials as to his identity.

"You think that's Rusty?" Metford asked as they got out at the office.

"Of course I do. You don't believe him, do you?"

"He seemed pretty genuine."

"I would too if I had killed someone and was trying to save myself."

They went inside and went to the interview room. They stood outside for a minute before announcing their arrival. The man was still saying he wasn't Rusty Moore. Dane exited the room.

"He's still insisting that his name is Bob Gilmore and that we have the wrong man. Says he knows who Rusty is, but not where he is. He's been arrested several times up in North Fairhaven for stealing food out of that same convenience store where Mac Norrie was Monday night."

"If he's been arrested recently, they'll have his fingerprints on file. Check his prints," Ava said.

Dane nodded and walked away briskly.

"This could be bad," Ava said.

"No kidding," Metford agreed as they stared in at the man.

Santos held up the full sheet print of Rusty Moore and looked from it to the man sitting across from her.

"She's even reconsidering it," Metford noted.

"Not helping, Metford." Ava crossed her arms and fretted about the possibility that they had made a huge mistake. "I can't stand here and wait." She opened the door and went in to face the man. "Where were you from Monday night until Tuesday morning, Mr. Moore?"

"I told you, I'm not him!" the man yelled. "Bob Gilmore; that's my damn name! I want a lawyer. There. I don't have to talk to you anymore." He glared at her defiantly.

"I can hold you as a witness, and you don't get a lawyer. How's that? Cooperate with us, and we'll see if we can't work something out. As of right now, you're not being charged with anything, but Teagan Reese is dead. She was murdered. Do you know anything about that?"

"No. I don't even know who she is, so how would I know anything about her death?" His voice had gone shrill and started to crack.

Santos gave Ava a look that said to back down a little. "Okay, Mr. Gilmore. Teagan worked at the library where you were tonight. Were you, by any chance, near that property on Monday night or early Tuesday morning?"

He shook his head. "No, I wasn't. I don't remember exactly where I was, but it was probably up Northside. It's easier to get good food up there, and I only leave when the cops are heavy on my case."

Dane entered again carrying a small electronic fingerprint reader. "Put your right index finger on the screen, please."

The man looked dubious but stuck out his finger toward the light. Dane pressed it, rolled it slowly, and the print appeared on the small screen. She let go of his finger. "Let's get the middle one." The man complied, seemingly intrigued by the gadget. Dane got his thumbprint next and then stood. "I'll run it against North's files. Might take a few minutes." She left the room.

"She's checking to see if I'm lying about my name?"

"She is," Santos said, turning the picture around and sliding it to him. "Because this is a picture of Rusty Moore."

His eyes went wide as he picked up the paper. "Holy canola, that guy looks like he's my twin almost."

"Almost? He looks just like you," Ava said.

"No. His ear's different right here." He tugged at his earlobe. "His nose is bigger than mine, too. I have Mama's nose. Dad always said it was too feminine for a man's face." He turned the photo back to them, still chuckling. "I can see why you thought I was him in the dark like that."

Ava snatched the picture and looked at it. The man who claimed to be Bob Gilmore turned his head to the side, posing so she could get a good look at his nose and earlobe. Ava dropped the paper and walked out feeling like she'd been kicked in the stomach.

"It's not him, is it?" Metford asked.

Ava put a hand over her eyes. "Nope. It really isn't. Dane's confirming it with his fingerprints." She blew out a long breath.

"It's not the end of the world. It will be fine."

"You know the worst part?"

"What, that your powers of perception aren't superhuman?" He put up his hands and feigned fear. "Oh, no, you're only a mortal after all." He grinned.

"I'll have to explain to Sal how in the hell I made this mistake. She's going to think I don't cover all my bases before I act. I've screwed up and missed things already that I shouldn't have; that I wouldn't have if I was on-track up here." She put a finger to the center of her forehead.

"Hey, you'll get back to your old self soon enough. Until then, we're a team. We've all got your back."

Dane came back looking glum. "Bob Gilmore." She held up the confirmation.

"Dammit. Cut him loose, buy him a cheeseburger for his trouble, and meet us in the Reese neighborhood. I have to get something before Sal gets wind of this."

She and Metford left immediately.

Dane and Santos arrived in the neighborhood at midnight, and Ava stationed them on the west side on Alameida Street while she and Metford parked on Sysco Street near the eastern end. For three hours, she fidgeted in the seat. Everything was uncomfortable, and her mind wouldn't let go of the fact that she had screwed up with Bob Gilmore—a man who only resembled their person of interest. Sal was going to have her head on the wall for it, and she had no excuse to even offer.

At four in the morning, two people walked onto Sysco from Barker Street on the east. They strolled by Ava and Metford without noticing them.

"Just teenagers," Metford said.

"Didn't even see us," Ava said. "Probably Jerri Mondale that Dane and Ashton told us about. They said she had sneaked out to meet her boyfriend and was sneaking back in when she saw the man in Brad and Teagan's yard that morning." She looked at her watch. "Same time, too."

"Lets you know this is business as usual for them."

Ava radioed Dane and Santos, told them about the teenagers, and told them to meet them at Mandy's Burgers for breakfast.

"Is Mandy's open this early? It's only four in the morning."

"She opens at five. It's wait here another half-hour or wait there." Ava started the car and pulled onto the road.

"There sounds good. Better than here where no one is going to show up, obviously."

"That's my thinking, too," she said.

As they sat in the parking lot waiting for Mandy's to open, Ava fiddled with her phone.

"Are you planning on calling in the order or what?"

"No, I'm debating whether to call Margueritte Aldridge."

"Why? She's going to be at the office in a few hours. She probably isn't awake yet, and even if she is, she can't get here sooner than her flight."

Groaning, Ava shoved the phone back into her pocket for the third time. "I hate waiting. I feel like I should be doing something more."

"Like what? Ashton is working on the digital side of things; we've run every lead we have into the ground tonight. Literally. We're stuck waiting for the Aldridge interview."

"Or for Brad and the kids to show up, someone to find them, Rusty to be found, and Furlong to return from his damn vacation." She threw her hands up. "Wait, wait, wait. Hurry up and wait some more."

"I think you're hangry and tired."

"Hungry and tired. No, nix that. I'm starved and exhausted."

"You're angry-hungry. Hangry." He grinned. "Get it? I saw that on a commercial."

"Really?" The diner lights came on and a woman unlocked the front door. "Let's go," she said, getting out.

Over breakfast, there was hardly any talking. The entire team looked as exhausted as Ava felt, but they didn't have time to sleep, barely time for breakfast, but she thought a working break wouldn't count against them.

Once everybody started eating, the conversations started. They were mainly about the case except for Santos. She was ill-tempered.

"What's wrong, Santos?" Ava asked directly.

"There's no progress on this case. It feels like we get pushed back three steps every time we take two forward."

"We'll be okay. We always figure it out. Sometimes, it just takes a little more time."

"Yeah, well, you're not the one it's going to look so bad on, either. Me? I'm just getting back after that big ordeal of being mixed up in Miguel Acosta's crap. This is not going to look good on my record."

"You were cleared of all wrongdoing, Jillian. Your record and your name are clean and clear. You started in the middle of this case, so it'll be my head on the platter if it goes sideways, not yours."

"I just hate it when an investigation stalls out. I always feel like I could be doing more and that it's somehow my fault it's stalled out."

"I'm the same way, but there's nothing we can do right now but take a step back, keep assessing the evidence, looking at any new leads, and wait for all the moving parts to align."

Santos chuckled tiredly and rubbed her eyes. "There are a lot of those, aren't there? All our persons of interest are yet to be located."

"By the time we get back to the library, it'll be almost time for the Aldridge interview. While I'm doing that, you and Dane could try finding Bosworth again."

"He splits his time between here, Boston, and New York City. Big rich businessman or something. But we can do that. Better than sitting on our thumbs."

"Indeed, it is," Ava said, glad she could calm Santos.

After a few minutes, she realized that in the process of calming Santos' worries, she had also calmed her own. Was that what Dr. Bran had meant when she said Ava needed something else to care for, to nurture, and focus on? Something besides her own anxiety and worries? She smiled to herself. That's exactly why Dr. Bran had suggested a plant or a pet. That didn't mean she was going to rush to the shelter any time soon, though.

CHAPTER NINETEEN

The Very Important Man

At six-thirty, Santos rushed to Ava. "We found him. George Bosworth the third."

"That's great work, Santos. I told you everything would eventually fall into place."

"He's on his way here now. Do you want to sit in on the interview?"

"I'll watch from outside. You and Dane found him. It should be your interview."

"Come on down in fifteen minutes."

Ava gave her a thumbs-up.

Fifteen minutes later, Metford came from the breakroom with a mug of coffee. "There's a fresh pot in there, if you need a pick-me-up."

"Don't sit. I'm going down to watch the interview with Bosworth. Want to come?"

"They found him. That's awesome. Sure, I'll watch. Has to be better than waiting on the Aldridges to arrive, or watching you look at the clock and your watch every two minutes."

"Clocks can be interesting," she said, making her way down the hall.

"Yeah, sure. So much action and adventure there."

"Lots of action. Do you know how many actions it takes just to get the second hand to move once?"

"I'm going to stop you right there, ma'am. If you want to talk minutiae, you need to find Special Agent Ashton. You two would hit it off famously."

They arrived at the viewing area.

George Bosworth was a big, round man in an expensive gray suit. His face was broad and had rolls at the sides and under his chin, but he was still clean-shaven. He laid his cellphone on the table in front of him.

"Mr. Bosworth, we got your name from the list of top donors to the library in Fairhaven," Santos said cordially.

"I'm aware. You told me that on the phone. And it's the Fairhaven Library and Center for Art Culture; not just *the library*. I wouldn't make such generous donations to a regular public library because they do not offer enough culture, or anything else, to their patrons. Now, could we get down to brass tacks here? Unlike some, I'm a very busy man." He cocked one eyebrow as if indicating Santos was not very busy.

"We're just looking for some information. Teagan Reese, the librarian, was murdered there Monday night or early Tuesday morning. Did you know her?"

He shrugged. "I knew who she was, of course. Newly appointed. Used to be of some significance in the New York art world." His phone rang and he held up a hand as if to silence Santos. "I have to take this." He answered the phone and carried on a five-minute conversation about a business transaction.

Ava started for the door, but Metford stopped her. "Let Santos handle it. We're just observing. She'll put him in his place when she's tired of it."

Not liking that he was right, Ava took a deep breath and crossed her arms as she forced herself to remain outside looking in.

Bosworth put the phone down again. "Okay. Continue."

"I just told you that Teagan Reese was murdered, and you don't even have a reaction?"

He shrugged again. "What can I say? Bad things happen. It doesn't change my loyalty to the center, if that's what you're worried about."

Santos scoffed. "No, sir. That's not it at all. Where were you Monday and Tuesday?"

He laughed. "Now I'm a suspect?"

"Where were you?"

Ava shifted. "She knows that man on the video wasn't Bosworth. Anyone can see that."

"She knows what she's doing," Metford assured her.

"I was on a cruise until Wednesday. I flew out of Boston on Wednesday and returned here to finalize the merging of a smaller broker-age company to one of mine. That's why you were lucky enough to catch me as I was preparing to leave for Boston again." His phone vibrated and he picked it up.

"Is that a normal—"

He flipped up the hand again. "Just a moment."

Santos bit her lip and dropped her head.

Bosworth finished texting and laid the phone down again. "Now, I believe you were going to ask if that's my normal routine, and yes, it is. I split my time between the three places often. If I'm lucky, I get to stay somewhere for more than a week, but that doesn't happen often. The cruise might appear to be a vacation on the surface, but I was conducting business even then." His phone rang again and he picked it up.

Santos stood and walked out. She handed the file to Ava. "I'm going to punch the pompous bastard."

Ava took the folder and went in. "Mr. Bosworth, could you please hold off with the phone calls and texts until we're done here?"

He ignored her until he finished. He put the phone down and looked at her with fire in his eyes. "I'm sorry, I don't think we've had the pleasure."

"Special Agent James," Ava said. "Now, could we get back to the ques-tions? We'll be done much sooner if you leave the phone until afterward."

"Special Agent James," he said in a civil but commanding tone. "I am a very important man. Many people depend on me and the decisions I make. Timely responses are a necessary part of my life. If you can't abide by the interruptions, that is of no concern to me. What you're doing here is a monumental waste of my time and yours. I know nothing about the death of your librarian, and I don't care. I was on a cruise at the time of her murder. You can check. Now, if you don't mind, leave me to my busi-ness and I'll leave you to yours." He took the phone, stood, and went out the door, leaving Ava fuming at the table.

Metford was grinning like an idiot when Ava walked out of the inter-view room.

"I think we should put him on the suspect list. He's too flippant and self-absorbed to be completely innocent in this."

Metford burst out laughing as they walked back to the bullpen. "That's just because the old man got under your skin."

"No, it's not. Did you see him in there? He even said he didn't care about Teagan's murder," she said, her voice rising on the last word.

"And he gave a verifiable alibi. You know he wasn't the man on the footage. You even said so yourself when Santos was in with him."

Ava turned away from the bullpen and into her office. She couldn't think with Metford laughing. More to the point, she couldn't work knowing he was right—the old man had gotten under her skin, and it had taken only a brief interaction for her to lose her cool.

Her phone rang and she snatched it angrily. "James here."

It was Connor Aldridge calling to confirm their meeting time.

"Yes, sir. I'll see you and your wife when you get here."

She met them at her doorway twenty minutes later and led them to the interview room.

"Mrs. Aldridge, if I could ask you to wait out here. I need to speak to each of you alone." She turned Margueritte to a small room across the hall. "There's coffee there and water. Help yourself."

"Thank you." Margueritte sat primly on a chair facing the door and with her back to the window with the best view.

Ava led Connor to the interview room and opened the door. "Thank you for agreeing to speak with me today. Just have a seat, please."

"I'm still not sure what all this has to do with us."

"You're the top donor to the Fairhaven Library." She sat and found the updated list to show him.

He smiled and the cut on his lower lip was prominent. "Yes, I'm a big supporter of art and culture, and we like to support our hometown."

He seemed proud, but something lingered in his eyes. Was it fear, worry, sadness? Ava couldn't tell.

"I see you have a cut on your lower lip just there." She pointed to her own lip to indicate it. "How'd that happen?"

"Oh, that? I got that moving an art piece about a week ago."

"Was that here in Fairhaven?"

"No, it was in Manhattan. I was helping prep the new gallery. Working with a much shorter man; the load tipped and I caught the brunt of it." He smiled nervously. "With my face."

Ava didn't smile. She opened the folder and pulled autopsy photos of Teagan Reese. He looked down at the pale, dead face of the pretty librarian, and he blanched. He quickly looked away.

"Are you sure that's how you got that cut, Mr. Aldridge?"

"Yes, it was an accident. You can call the man I was working with to verify it. There was blood everywhere from it."

She pushed a crime scene photo showing blood on the floor and bookshelves. "No, that's what it looks like when there's blood all over the place, Mr. Aldridge, and I'm just going to go out on a limb here and say that's not what it looked like at all when you *accidentally* cut your lip in New York."

"What? God, I don't want to see these." He pushed the photos back toward her.

"I know you and Teagan were having an affair, Mr. Aldridge. A long affair. Over a year. That's some record, I must say. She was bugging you about using your influence to get her back into the art scene. You wanted her to divorce her husband and bring the kids to live with you. What were you going to do, divorce Margueritte and marry Teagan? Play daddy to her kids? Or were you more of the mind to put her up in a fancy apartment in New York and weave her artwork back into the tapestry of your world up there?"

He stuttered, shut his mouth, and shook his head.

"It's okay, Mr. Aldridge. Things like that happen every day. I'm not shocked. You're a powerful man. A rich man. And Teagan was a beautiful, independent, headstrong woman who was asking too much of you. It was the final push when she threatened to tell Margueritte about the affair if you didn't comply with her demands, wasn't it? You never wanted Margueritte to find out. You'd do anything to keep her from knowing. And you argued with her. The situation got out of control and you hit her."

"No, I didn't. There was no affair. I'd never hit a woman."

"And when she fought back, you pulled a gun and you shot her. First, you shot her in the chest. She fell to her knees, and you knew you had to finish the job. You stepped forward and shot her in the head." She shoved the autopsy photo forward again and jammed her finger on the bullet hole in Teagan's head. "You did that because you didn't want your wife finding out about the affair, didn't you, Mr. Aldridge?"

Tears rolled down his cheeks and he crumpled forward holding his face in his hands. "No, I didn't hurt her. I swear it on my life. I was having an affair, and no, I didn't want Margueritte to find out, but I never hurt her."

Ava showed him the emails between him and Teagan. "Did you ever try to get her what she asked for, Mr. Aldridge?"

"No, but I was planning a meeting with a gallery owner and an agent next week. That's part of what I was setting up in New York, but I had to keep Margueritte in the dark. I didn't want to explain the situation."

"So, your wife doesn't know about the affair?"

He wiped his face and composed himself. "No. And I would very much appreciate if it stays that way."

"Mr. Aldridge, this is a murder investigation. Your affair is the least of my concerns. If you didn't want your wife to find out, maybe you shouldn't have cheated. I'll do what I can, but I won't let this hinder my investigation."

"Thank you." He looked like someone had ripped his heart out when his gaze fell on the autopsy photo.

Ava put it back into the folder. She didn't like seeing it, either. "I need to know where you were from Monday afternoon until Tuesday morning, Mr. Aldridge."

"I had dinner with my wife at Blanchard's on Monday evening. Afterward, we attended a play at Sorenson's Theatre, and then Margueritte and I left for New York City around seven on the morning Teagan was found. We drove up there. I don't care for flying as much as my wife does. Sometimes, a man just needs to be able to unwind and take his time. We heard about Teagan's death on the local news, and after that, I really needed some time to think. It was horrible trying to hold myself together with Margueritte right there beside me." His breath hitched and he put a hand over his mouth. A few tears escaped and ran down his face.

Were those real tears, or just tears of terror that he had been found out and would likely spend the rest of his life in prison? Ava let him cry for a moment as she tried to assess whether the crying spate was genuine or just a good act.

"Why are you crying, Mr. Aldridge?" She scrutinized the emotions on his face even closer.

He wiped his eyes with thumb and forefinger and inhaled deeply. "Teagan's dead, and I haven't had a chance to properly grieve." He motioned toward the door. "Margueritte is always close. It is heartbreaking. Whether you believe me or not, I loved her. And I love my wife. That might seem contradictory, but I assure you, it is not." He sniffed loudly again, clasped his hands tightly in his lap, and pulled his shoulders back. "I don't want to lose my wife, too, Agent James. I've lost enough. If she sees me like this over Teagan's death…" He blew out a breath and seemed to deflate right in front of Ava.

With no evidence to hold him, charge him, or arrest him, Ava decided it was best to move on and question Margueritte before she lost herself in trying to figure out if Connor was a murdering liar. Her gut was giving her nothing. Her mind threw all sorts of doubt on the crying, though.

Her experience with Jason Ellis had tainted her detective's brain with doubt. Would she ever be able to work past it?

"I think I have all I need for now. You can go to the waiting area. I'm going to call your wife in now." Ava stood and opened the door.

With something like terror in his eyes, he stopped before crossing the threshold and looked directly into Ava's eyes. "Please, I know you have a job to do, but don't let it include hurting my wife and ruining our marriage."

She let go of the door and stepped past him into the corridor where she stopped and turned to face him. She wanted to tell him off, tell him he was an idiot for cheating in the first place, but she didn't. Couldn't. Instead, she kept her mouth shut and shook her head as she turned and walked away toward Margueritte's room.

Opening the door, she found Margueritte Aldridge sitting primly on the edge of a chair clutching her purse to her. She looked as if she were afraid of contracting some disease if she relaxed and accidentally touched any surface.

"Mrs. Aldridge, I'm ready for you now." Ava forced a small smile and held the door.

"Where did Connor go?" Mrs. Aldridge walked by Ava and into the corridor with perfectly measured steps to go with her flawless posture.

"He's gone just to the other waiting area, there." Ava pointed to another small room. "This really shouldn't take long. I appreciate you taking the time to come down and speak with me."

"Yes, yes, of course. Terrible business about the librarian."

Mrs. Aldridge went straight to a chair and sat without waiting for Ava to offer it. It was Ava's chair. She was almost sure Mrs. Aldridge knew that. It showed that she was a woman in charge; a woman who took charge, took care of things without being asked, and she made sure she appeared superior to others around her.

"Mrs. Aldridge, I need you to sit in the other chair, please." Ava forced another small smile.

"Why?"

Ava cleared her throat and pointed to the camera. "That's the number one reason right there. We need to be able to clearly see your face during the interview."

"Oh. I don't understand why it matters, but that's fine. We all have our little duties, don't we?" She moved to the other chair. "Did my husband also have to be told to sit facing the camera?"

"No, ma'am. He waited until I showed him where to sit, and it was never even part of the conversation."

Mrs. Aldridge chuffed under her breath. "So good at waiting to be told what to do, but not good at all about taking the reins and making decisions. Just like a man, isn't it?" Her smile was a bit repulsive because it was too wide, too toothy, and out of place on her face.

"I wouldn't know. So, did you know Teagan Reese well?"

While Margueritte was explaining how well she knew the decedent, Ava was taking note of how well she dressed. Mrs. Aldridge dressed to the nines. Her makeup was thick but precise, and her jewelry was large and expensive. Showpieces that bordered on gaudy. The dye in her hair was recent as the roots weren't showing yet. Ava guessed it was a week old. There was no chemical odor, so it couldn't have been applied within the last two or three days.

"I didn't know anything about the murder until you called and asked us here for an interview. I knew Teagan well enough to know she was a lovely woman. Just lovely, and this is abhorrent. Who could do something like that to such a beautiful young mother?"

"I don't know, Mrs. Aldridge, but that's what I'm trying to find out. Do you have an alibi for Monday through Tuesday?"

"Alibi? Am I somehow a suspect?" She laughed.

"Just making sure I perform my little duties to the best of my ability. It's a standard question that I put to everyone in the case."

Anger flashed through her eyes, but she quickly averted her gaze and recovered her tight composure. "You say she was murdered sometime Monday night?"

Ava nodded.

"Well, I had dinner with Connor that evening. We went to Blanchard's in the city, and then we attended a play afterward. We left for New York City the next day between six and six-thirty, I suppose. It was terribly early, so I'm afraid I don't remember exactly. Connor insisted on driving." She flapped a hand in the air as if swatting a pesky fly. "If you have never driven to New York City, you have no idea how horrible it is. I don't know why he doesn't fly there every time, but I can assure you that I will be doing so. It takes three hours to get there, longer when you factor in stops to eat, stretch, and use the restroom. And, God, those awful, repugnant public restrooms…" Her face wrinkled and scrunched in distaste. "Positively the most disgusting places I think I have ever been."

"Which theater did you attend?" She checked her notes from Connor's interview for the name he had given.

"Oh, goodness, the only reputable one on this side of Maryland, dear. Sorenson's Theatre, of course."

"Thank you, Mrs. Aldridge. I think that's all for now. If I need anything else—"

Margueritte was at the door before Ava opened it. "Of course you'll call," she said with just enough snark to get under Ava's skin.

"You bet I will." She opened the door. "Can't forget about those little duties, can we?"

Mrs. Aldridge nodded once, curtly, and pursed her lips together tightly.

Ava put on the interview notes that someone needed to go to Blanchard's and Sorenson's to inquire whether the Aldridges had been at those establishments on Monday evening.

She was glad they were finally gone, but she knew she would be dealing with them again later in the investigation. There was something about Connor's story that led her to believe he was hiding something.

CHAPTER TWENTY

Russell "Rusty" Moore

A VA AND METFORD WALKED INTO THE CONFERENCE ROOM together. The rest of the team was coming in to get and give updates.

"I just interviewed the Aldridges," Ava said, getting everyone's attention. Once they settled, she continued. "Their stories match, but there's not really a big surprise there."

"Yeah, they've had time to make sure they match," Santos said.

"If they needed to," Ava said. "They ate dinner and then went to see a play on Monday evening. We need to verify their story to make sure. They had dinner at Blanchard's and then went to Sorenson's Theatre afterward. I don't want phone calls for this; I want face-to-face questioning. It's hard to interpret someone's tone over the phone, but it's pretty simple to look someone in the eye and know if they're lying."

"Do you really think anyone at Blanchard's would lie for the Aldridges?" Santos asked. "Someone at Sorenson's might, I get that, but Blanchard's?"

"These people have money to throw around, and if I don't miss my guess, they are used to throwing it on top of problems to make them go away," Ava said. She didn't like that she was so jaded, but considering what she had experienced in prior cases, and interactions with rich and powerful people, she felt justified.

"Have you ever eaten at Blanchard's?" Santos directed her question to the team.

Scoffs, dry laughs, and head shakes all around were the answer she received.

"You don't do anything so undignified as *eat* at Blanchard's," Metford said. "You *dine* at Blanchard's."

This was met with a few more very dry laughs. He was right. It was very likely that none of them would ever be able to afford to dine there. Ava didn't mind at all.

Sal came to the door. "Russell Moore has just been located." She handed Ava a piece of paper. "Act quick before he bails again. Duty cop just saw him going into the Salvation Army by the library."

"We're on it," Ava said. "Metford, you're with me. We'll go in the front. The rest of you will come with us and spread out around the place to make sure he doesn't get away again."

They all met up in the parking area between the burned down restaurant and the Grace Food Pantry and Shelter. The Salvation Army was on the next block to the east.

Rusty sat inside on a stool holding a bag when Ava and Metford entered. He looked up at them with wide eyes and his hands clenched tight around the bag's handles.

"Mr. Moore?" Ava asked.

He stood so abruptly that the stool toppled. He gripped the bag to his stomach and took a step backward, away from Ava.

"Mr. Russell Moore?" she asked again, not moving forward. "We're Special Agents James and Metford. We just need to ask you a few questions back at the office." She took one step forward. "If you'll just come with—"

"I did not do anything. You cannot arrest me!" he yelled, pointing a shaky finger at them.

"You're not under arrest," Metford said calmly. "If you'll just come with us, we'll be done and you can go about your business in less than an hour."

Ava side-glanced him. There was no way to determine how long an interview of that nature would go on, but if the sugar-coating made Rusty go with them more calmly, she could overlook it.

Rusty shook his head. "But I did not do anything wrong."

Speaking reassurances to Rusty in her most calming voice, Ava moved until she was within arms' reach of him. Though visibly uncomfortable, Rusty allowed her to escort him to the vehicle without a physical altercation. The ride back to the office was silent.

After putting Rusty in the interview room, Ava and the team stood outside watching him for several minutes.

"Looks like a junkie jonesing for a fix," Santos said. "Doesn't exactly scream innocent to me."

"He's just nervous," Dane said, her arms crossed and her attention directed on the monitor screen.

"Probably scared out of his wits, too," Ashton added. "Especially if he is innocent." He looked at Santos pointedly.

"Well, I'm not ruling him out just because he might be scared and nervous," Metford said. "Who's taking lead on the interview?" He turned to face Ava.

"I will," she answered without looking at the team. "You come in when I motion. Might need some backup when I apply pressure."

She went into the room. Rusty watched her take a seat. His gaze followed the folder and clipboard she carried. She kept quiet as she set up, wanting him to make the first move and break the silence.

"What is that?" He nodded at the folder. "Whatever is in there, I had nothing to do with it."

"Mr. Moore, do you know what happened to Teagan Reese?"

He blushed to his hairline and ran a hand over his hair as if making sure it was presentable. "She is pretty. She sits there with all them books and looks like a painting. She is real nice to me. Most people are not so nice to me." His hand fluttered to his shirt, which he tugged at, and then he sat straighter with a satisfied smile. "Did she do this? Tell you guys to pick me up so she could surprise me with a birthday present? She said she might just surprise me big-time for my birthday."

Confused, Ava stared at him. It was clear that he had a seriously diminished mental capacity. She had expected a different reaction, perhaps even a violent outburst, but not what she was witnessing.

Rusty looked expectantly toward the door, then at the big two-way mirror, and back to the folder. "Did she send me a card or a letter?" He pointed and leaned closer.

"No," Ava said, pulling the love letter from the folder and closing it hastily. "But you sent her a letter, didn't you, Mr. Moore?"

It was Rusty's turn to look confused.

Ava held up the note and raised her eyebrows, checking for any sign of recognition on his face. When there was none, she flipped the paper toward him and slid it across the table. "Did you write this to Teagan Reese?"

His eyes moved back and forth in jerky motions as he read the letter. He mouthed each word as his finger slid along the paper. After finishing, he chuckled nervously, blushed deep red again, and dropped his head.

Pointing toward the letter, but not making eye contact with Ava, Rusty said, "That was supposed to be private. That was for pretty Teagan; not you. You are not s'posed to read other people's private things." He glanced up at her. "Did she give you that or did you steal it?" Anger flashed across his features as he dropped his head again.

"Mr. Moore, do you know what happened to Teagan Reese?" Ava asked again as she replaced the letter into the folder.

He used both hands to clutch the bag to his stomach and chest again. "That was not nice." He cut his eyes toward the folder. "She should not have let you see that."

"But you did write it, correct?"

"Yes, yes, yes," he said, punctuating each nod. He looked more frantic as his gaze darted from the door to the mirror to the window at the other side of the room. "Can I see her now? I do not like this." He began to rock side to side in his seat. It started as a slight movement and became more pronounced after only a few seconds.

He threw Ava's game off. She had expected denials, and then she was going to apply the pressure by showing him the autopsy photo, but she couldn't do that to him. Given his state of mind, it might be more than he could handle.

"Mr. Moore, when did you last see Teagan? I need to know when you put this letter in her office and when you saw her last." She lifted the folder to indicate the letter she had put in there, and a few papers fell from it, fanning onto the table.

She slammed the folder over the picture but it was too late. Rusty had seen it.

"Why do you have a picture of her like that? This is not a good surprise," he said, his voice rising in volume with each word. A scream escaped him and crescendoed as he flung the bag away.

Ava recoiled, dragging the folder and the papers under it to the edge of the table and off it as she stood. "Mr. Moore, please sit—"

He was around the table, knocking Ava backward with his shoulder like a football player, and grabbing the photo from the floor. "Pretty Teagan!" he bellowed. Still clutching the photo, he turned on Ava.

The door burst open. Metford and Santos rushed in, grabbing Rusty by the arms, but he jerked free, keeping the horrible image of Teagan crumpled in his left fist. Ava almost made her feet before Rusty slammed into her, teeth bared in a scream. They hit the wall, Ava taking the brunt of the impact, and Rusty swung wildly, landing punch after punch. Her face, her shoulder, her upper chest, her kidney.

Metford grabbed him again, but Rusty threw his head to the side and busted Metford's lip. Blood flew. Santos wrapped her arms around Rusty from the back. Before she could lock her hands together, he reared his head back, screaming wordlessly, and Santos took the shot at the corner of her right eye. Her head rocked back, and Rusty grabbed her right wrist, twisting as he spun on her. He shoved the picture in her face.

"What did you do to her? What did you do—"

Metford shrugged off the sling he had been wearing since he and Ava had been attacked by the car and he tackled Rusty from the side, getting him in a bear hug.

Rusty thrashed and gnashed his teeth. Metford kept loosening his grip to slide his arms down further and avoid being bitten.

"I can't reach his hands!" Ava yelled. She tried to get the zip ties around his flailing hands but it was impossible.

Santos grabbed one hand and pinned it to the floor with her knee. Her expression seemed to be one of panic as she pushed a palm against the side of his face, pressing his head against the floor. Grimacing with the effort, she lifted one knee from the floor so all her weight was supported on the hand against his face and the knee pinning his hand.

Rusty wailed. He redoubled his struggles, and Metford lost his grip. Santos bounced her weight onto her knee and twisted it. "Calm down!" she yelled. "You'll break it if you don't!"

It was more likely that Santos would break his hand as she twisted her knee into it. Ava straddled Rusty's back but still couldn't get the ties on his one loose hand. Santos snapped a traditional cuff around the wrist of his pinned hand and dragged it to the center of his back. Ava wrestled the other hand to the same position and finally snapped the other cuff into place.

As soon as the cuffs were on, Rusty bucked and turned to his side. Ava flew to the floor, landing on her knee and hand. Before Metford could grab the man and haul him to his feet, Rusty kicked out and caught Ava in the side, sending her sprawling.

Then Rusty was on his feet and pinned to the wall by Santos and Metford. After realizing he could fight no more, tears streamed freely down his face. It was the sound of a heartbroken child wailing and sobbing.

Metford and Santos marched him to a cell without any further incident. Ava went back to the interview room to clean it up while Metford and Santos were checked for injuries.

A few minutes later, Metford stepped into the room, his arm in a fresh sling, and handed her a crumpled and slightly torn photo.

Ava took it from him and sighed as she stuck it back into the folder.

"He didn't want to give it up," Metford said, tilting his head toward the folder. "Still think he's a suspect?"

Ava nodded.

"You do?" The astonishment in his voice was obvious.

"Yeah. His outburst proves just how dangerous his temper is." She motioned toward his arm and face. "Look at you. Busted lip, arm injured worse than before, and I bet you're going to have a few mad bruises to go with them. And Santos, how bad is she hurt?"

"He sprained her wrist pretty good, and she'll have a shiner for a while, but I think she's mostly okay."

"Cara Marks told us how dangerous he could be even without a weapon," Ava reminded him.

"So did Mac Norrie, in a way."

"Mr. Moore was physically violent toward a much smaller female, used a knife in a rage, pointed a gun, whether real or not, at her in anger." She was counting off the offenses on her fingers. "You get the point."

"So, now you're thinking Rusty might be the killer because he was jilted by Teagan the same way he was rebuffed by Cara Marks and he just snapped. That leaves Connor Aldridge, who you thought was hiding something, off the hook. Is that about right?"

She chuckled, but it was an odd sound. It hurt her side where Rusty had landed his last kick. It was likely that the ribs there were badly bruised, and she was grateful his foot had not hit her in the face.

"That's about right. The whole direction of this case is shifting again," she said.

"I think I'm going to get motion sickness before we get this one straightened out."

Ava's phone rang and she answered. After a moment, she hung up. "Gotta get upstairs quick. There's been another shooting, and we drew the lucky straw."

"But we're right in the thick of this case," he complained.

"And Sal wanted an update on it. She also said to make sure you understood that getting your ass kicked twice on one case was not a valid reason to whine about working the new case." Ava punched the elevator button.

"She did?" He looked alarmed for a second and then scoffed. "No, that was all you."

"Ah, getting smarter every day. Soon, I won't be able to get anything by you, will I?" She grinned, not daring enough to try laughing again. That was okay, though. Lately, she had not found much worth laughing about.

"So funny. Where's this new shooting?"

"The burned down restaurant a block over from the library. Homeless man."

"Seriously?"

It was a rhetorical question, and Ava didn't bother answering. She completely understood the shock.

CHAPTER TWENTY-ONE

Another Shooting

Friday

THURSDAY FADED INTO FRIDAY AS AVA AND THE TEAM WENT OVER the crime scene at the husk of a restaurant only a block from the library where Teagan Reese had been killed at the beginning of the week.

Friday, just after midnight, Ava and Metford canvassed the area around the new site for any potential witnesses. The homeless encampment across the road was full of people who saw and heard nothing. Same thing for the camp behind the restaurant. Even Mac Norrie was conveniently absent from the scene.

"This about par for the course," Metford said as another young man denied seeing or hearing anything. "Is everybody around here deaf and blind?"

"You know how this goes. We just have to keep asking until we find someone who isn't afraid to—"

"Tell the truth; admit they saw or heard a man being killed. Yeah, I know the drill. But I get sick of it."

Ava agreed wholeheartedly with him on that aspect of their jobs. It was not only frustrating, but it was also disheartening. Especially when it was obvious that someone, and probably a few people, had no choice but to hear or see what happened.

Instead of feeding into his current mood, she changed tack. She needed to steer him back to the necessary route of finding where the victim had lived and who he knew on the streets. "The victim's name was Arthur Erwin. He was homeless and it's likely that he lived around here somewhere close. He was shot twice, and the site is so close to the library that I can't help wondering if the two incidents are related somehow."

"I don't think they are. What would a homeless man and Teagan Reese have in common that would make them both targets of the same killer?"

"That's exactly what we need to find out. The lab will test the wounds to see if they might be a match for Teagan's; maybe the same weapon was used in both murders."

"Guess that's worth a shot."

"There was one casing at this site. Forensics found it embedded in a piece of wood that had been almost completely burned to a cinder by the fire. No other physical evidence like footprints around the body and no trace evidence on it. At least none that's useable."

Ava searched the shadows of an alley as they passed. Two people lingered just beyond the reach of the streetlight. The silhouettes exchanged something in a small package. Ava motioned toward the alley. "Over there," she said just before directing the beam of her flashlight at the two.

The two whipped to face the bright light, their eyes large and round set into ashen faces. At first, Ava thought it was two juvenile boys.

"Hey, you!" she called. "We need to ask you some questions."

The two figures faced each other for a split second and then bolted like scared rabbits toward the other end of the alley. They knocked over pallets, trash bags, and any debris they could lay hands on as they ran.

Ava and Metford chased after them, jumping and dodging the random items as they closed the distance. At the end of the alley, the two split directions. One went right; the other turned left.

"I got the one to the right," Metford said, veering off in that direction. Without answering, Ava turned left. "Stop! FBI!" she yelled.

The person did not stop, but they did slow at a steady pace. Ava kept her pace, and when she was only a few feet behind, she grabbed the back of the person's shirt. They both tumbled to the ground and rolled a couple of times. As soon as they stopped, Ava scrambled to her feet. The person she had been pursuing flipped over and held up their hands.

"Please, don't shoot," a young woman said, gasping for air. "We weren't doing anything. I swear."

"Then why did you run like that?" Ava patted the woman down as she spoke. There were no weapons, no package, and only three crumpled dollar bills in one jeans pocket.

"Because you're cops, and cops don't ever just wanna ask a few questions."

Ava stood and offered her hand to the woman. "What's your name?"

"Astrid. Astrid Lange. I'm eighteen."

"Where's your ID? Where do you live?" Ava pulled Astrid to her feet. The girl bordered on being too thin.

"My ID's at home." Astrid looked down.

"Which is where?"

"The shelter." She pointed in the general direction of Main Street.

"Grace or The Salvation Army?"

Astrid looked at the ground. "Grace," she whispered.

Only a parking lot separated Grace from the restaurant where Arthur was killed. "Is that where you were earlier tonight?"

She nodded and crossed her arms.

Ava thought the girl would have run again had she not just spent all her energy trying to get away. "Then, you know what happened at the old restaurant site earlier."

Astrid looked stricken. She didn't nod or shake her head, just simply stared at Ava with those wide, round eyes full of fear.

"Astrid, you need to tell me what you saw."

"Arthur got shot." Astrid turned away and put her hands to her face. "Arthur's dead, and I didn't do anything. I just left him there." Tears trickled down her cheeks. "He wouldn't have done me that way, but I was a coward, and I ran. I ran and I hid, and I didn't say or do anything to help him." She crumpled to her knees and cried.

Ava knelt beside the young woman. It twisted her heart to see someone so young going through so much regret and pain. "Astrid, there was nothing you could have done for Arthur. This is not your fault."

"I should have called someone. I could have yelled and scared the guy away. Who would even want to hurt Artie? He was the sweetest man in the world."

"It was a man who shot Arthur?"

"I don't know. He had on a black hoodie and jeans, but yeah, looked like a thin man to me."

"Okay, okay, that's good. What else did you see? Anything at all."

The sobs diminished and the tears slowed. "Gloves. A handgun and gloves."

"The shooter was wearing gloves?"

Astrid nodded, and her breath hitched. "He shot Artie in the head while he was sitting on the block wall that's still there. We used to sit there and watch the stars. Sometimes, he would even build a little fire." Her laugh was watery. "Not like we had to worry about burning the place down." She stood and put her hands against her sides as if trying to hold herself together. "After Artie fell, the man shot him again. I wanted to do something but I was too scared. I ran and didn't look back."

"The shooter didn't see you?"

"I don't think so. His back was to me and he was bent over like he was looking for something. I figured he was robbing Artie." She melted into another spate of tears. "I'm such a shit friend," she said through the sobs.

"No, you're not. There was nothing you could have done after that first shot, Astrid. Your friend was gone by the time you realized what was going on, I'm sure." The tears needed to stop or Ava wouldn't be able to keep up the questioning. Why did people have to cry so much?

"I could've yelled when I first saw the man walking toward him. I could've ran toward them instead of hesitating."

"And you might have been shot, too. You did the right thing." Ava wasn't sure what the right thing was, but she desperately wanted Astrid to turn off the waterworks. "Did your friend see the man approaching?"

"No, he had his back to the guy."

"Arthur wouldn't have heard the footsteps in the debris on the pavement?"

"He would have just thought it was me. I was on my way over there. I had just stepped out of the back door of the shelter. I know you're not supposed to go out or whatever, but they're really lenient with some of us who don't cause any trouble. They know me and Artie just sit there and watch the stars and talk. He's like the big brother that I never had." She coughed. "He *was* like the big brother I never had."

"Did you see which way the shooter went afterward?"

"I told you, I ran."

"I had to ask. Who were you in the alley with, Astrid?"

"She didn't have nothing to do with any of this. I was just… just…" She took a step away from Ava and hugged herself. "I was buying something to help calm my nerves is all. She wasn't around, she didn't see anything."

"It's okay. You're not in trouble for any of that. I didn't find any contraband on you, but I will tell you that if you've been clean long, you should stay that way."

"It was pot, okay? Not like I'm a recovering heroin addict." She rolled her eyes and shook her head. "Are you going to catch the guy who shot Artie?"

"We're certainly going to try. How long have you been homeless?"

"Since the day I turned eighteen."

Ava understood that meant Astrid had been a ward of the state and had aged out of the foster care system. "How many months now?"

"Five." Shrugging, she made a face that said it wasn't so bad.

"You got a job?"

Laughing, Astrid shook out her long brown hair and tied it back. "Yeah, I'm an interior decorator."

Grinning, Ava opened her wallet and took out a card with some phone numbers printed on it. "Take this. Call any of these organizations and you can get help. They'll help you in whatever direction you decide to go with your life. You're young—"

"Oh, please spare me that lecture. I know my age, and I alone know what I've been through. If one more person tells me I'm young enough to turn this shit-pie life of mine around and make something of myself, I swear, I will punch them in the throat." Biting her lip, she shoved the card into her back pocket. "Anyway, thanks for that. Are we done here? I need to find somewhere to sleep tonight."

"Thought you were staying at Grace."

"With the shooting, they've locked the doors tight by now. I lost my bed, and I'll have to go back later to even retrieve my stuff I left."

"Yeah, we're done except one more question. Do you know who Arthur's next of kin is?"

"Didn't have family as far as I knew. Just me and some of the people living in the camps around here."

"My number is on the back of that card, if you need anything."

"Okay, that's not weird at all, but okay."

"Call anytime. If you remember anything else or you just need to talk." Ava nodded and gave her a thumbs-up.

"Right, because cops care so much." She gave Ava a three-finger salute and turned away.

"Some do. And I'm not a cop; I'm FBI. And I need you to come in later to give a formal statement. At the federal building."

Astrid continued away, hugging herself. The only acknowledgment that she heard Ava was a miniscule nod.

Metford had been unable to keep up with Angel, and Ava met him as she walked back toward the alley.

"A girl outran you?" Ava teased.

"A girl? I don't know what you saw, but that was more like a cheetah in a flannel shirt and jean shorts. And hey, you just let the only witness go. She didn't even have to outrun you."

"She'll come in later and give a statement."

"How do you know she will? She might disappear into the ether and leave us with nothing."

"No. Arthur was her friend. The big brother she never had. If she doesn't come in later today, she'll be there the next. Her conscience won't allow her to not do something that might help catch the killer. She's a foster care child who just aged out of the system, and Arthur was good to her. Probably the first person other than the shelter workers who was good to her."

She related what Astrid had told her about the shooting.

"Sounds like the same guy from the Teagan Reese case," he said as they crossed the road and entered the parking lot near the scene of the shooting.

"Maybe. Astrid said she wasn't sure it was a man, though. And, did you just say the two cases might be related after all?"

"Maybe." He grinned. "We weren't sure if the shooter was a man or a woman either. Looked like a slim man."

"If she was there," Ava began, then stopped walking and pointed to the back door of the Grace Food Pantry and Shelter, "and the shooting took place here," she pointed to the ruin of the restaurant where police line fluttered indignantly in the breeze, "that was a straight line of sight. No obstructions, no incline or decline to hinder her view."

Metford turned and pointed at the streetlight across the street. "Don't think that was much help, but at least there was a little light. Maybe enough for her to see something that caused her to think the shooter was a man and not a woman."

"Like the way he walked or handled a gun," Ava suggested.

"Same way we made the assessment."

The shooter could have been a man or could have been a woman. At that point, no one knew for sure, and no one had gotten a clear look at the shooter's face.

CHAPTER TWENTY-TWO

Secrets, Secrets

Back at the office, Ava and the team worked until sunrise on the new case. Just like with the Teagan Reese case, every time they got a lead, it led exactly nowhere. The best witness they had to Arthur Erwin's murder was Astrid Lange.

"Where are Brad, Penny, and Thomas Reese?" Sal asked as she strolled into the conference room. "Does anyone know?"

The team looked haggard; dark circles under eyes seemed to be the order of the day. Ava stood and ran a hand over her hair. "No, ma'am. We haven't found them yet. No signs at all." Her voice dropped on the last sentence.

"Three citizens gone. Just gone. And not a single lead? I know you're all exhausted, but let's pull this together and find this family. The public, the media, and my bosses are eating me alive on this one. Not to mention there is a father with two small children out there somewhere. They might be in danger or worse. It looks like we're sitting around doing nothing; like we don't care."

"You know better," Ava said in an even tone. "You know we're doing all we can, and we do care. There is barely anything to go on."

"If there's no sign of them, no lead, do more." She tapped her watch. "It's Friday morning. They were reported missing Tuesday. We need answers. Find them." She turned and walked out.

"Ouch," Santos said. "She must really be catching hell over this."

"She's right," Ava said. "We need to find that missing family."

"But we have agents looking for them still," Dane said.

"And police officers across the state have been put on alert to watch for them, too," Metford added.

"What about the BOLO on that pickup than ran us off the road?" Ava asked, looking to Ashton, who had been monitoring the system for any hits and the BOLO.

He shook his head. "Nothing yet."

Ava paced to the evidence board and went over everything. Several minutes later, she left the room and went into Sal's office.

"I hope you have good news, Ava. I'm getting ready to go upstairs for another meeting about this Reese case." Sal picked up papers, laid them aside, grabbed an empty portfolio, sat in her chair, and stood back up in the span of time it took her to speak the few words.

"Not exactly, but I do have a different angle on the case that might get us somewhere."

"What angle is that?"

"I was just going over the evidence again, and... what if Brad is a victim instead of the perpetrator?"

Sal put the papers into the portfolio and closed it. "Victim?"

Ava nodded eagerly.

Seeming to consider it, Sal gathered more papers and put them with the portfolio in a briefcase. "I don't think so. I do know that finding Brad is key to finding Penny and Thomas, and right now, they are my biggest concern."

"I agree, but finding the killer is key to locating Brad. That's why we keep hitting dead ends. Brad didn't leave of his own accord; he and the kids were taken by whoever killed Teagan."

"Ava, I don't have time to argue about this. Just find Brad. It's most likely that the husband killed the wife and took off with the kids. That's how these cases go most often, and that's what I think happened here. Double your efforts in finding Brad." She glanced at her watch. "And that's an order. I have to get upstairs before I'm late to the latest ass-chewing." She swung around the desk and past Ava.

"You won't even consider—"

"I can't consider anything else at the moment. I'm sorry. Locate Brad Reese and you'll find those two kids." She glanced back from the hallway. "And the killer. Case closed."

"Right. Because it's always that simple," Ava said to the empty air. She went back to the conference room.

"That look says it wasn't the outcome you'd hoped for," Metford said.

"What's up?" Santos asked.

"I think I'm going to buy a punching bag for home. It was that kind of outcome." Ava moved to the evidence board again.

"Don't let Dr. Bran hear you say that," Santos warned. "She'll say you have anger issues that result in violent outbursts."

"Sounds like you know from experience," Metford said.

"Something like that," she answered.

"We need to double our efforts to find Brad Reese," Ava said, turning to the team. "Is there any new information about him?"

"I can check with the others right now," Dane said.

"Do that."

"I can go to the lab and see if there's anything new from the electronics at the house."

Ava hummed acknowledgement then went to the board and read over the list of electronics taken from the home. A laptop and cellphone were among the items.

"What's going on in your head?" Metford asked, walking up beside her.

She put a finger on the list. "If Brad is the killer, why would he leave his cellphone at home when he took the kids and ran off?"

"Maybe so he couldn't be traced to wherever he was going. Or maybe he just forgot it. How many times have we walked out of the house only to get down the block and have to go back to get the cell?"

"Don't count me in that group. I don't do that."

"Must be sad to never be in the most elite group in the world. How's it feel to be left out?"

Ava glared at him. Was he kidding? Was he serious? She couldn't tell. She was too tired to hash it out, and he was likely too exhausted to know whether he was serious or not. "Don't be a jerk right now."

"Whoa, I was kidding. Somebody needs a nap."

Dane walked back into the room with a carafe of coffee and set it on the coffee station. "I've got news. News and coffee."

Santos and Metford headed for the coffee.

"What news?" Ava asked in an irritated tone.

"Brad purchased a gun two weeks prior to Teagan's death." Dane handed Ava the paper.

After reading over it, Ava sighed inwardly and turned to the evidence board to place it. "Well, that certainly makes him look bad."

"What kind of gun did he buy?" Metford asked, handing a cup of coffee to Ava.

"Nine-millimeter. Ruger LC9," Ava said, hating that it was even the same caliber gun as the detective had first mentioned. "I need to know the caliber in Teagan's shooting for sure. Where's the lab report on that?" She flipped papers on the table looking for the report.

"Still at the lab," Metford said. "I'll call and put a rush on it."

"Thank you. While you're on the phone with them, put a rush on the same report for Arthur Erwin."

Metford stopped with the phone in his hand. "You know, that gives us more information about our killer." He pointed to the copy of the gun sale receipt.

"How so? He prefers nine-millimeter?" Ava asked. "That's a very common caliber. You know that."

"Yeah, but the Ruger LC9 is small. Like small enough that a lot of men, myself included, have trouble handling and shooting it with any accuracy."

"You're saying it's a woman's gun?" Santos asked.

"Kinda, yeah. But men with small hands like it, too."

Ava turned back to the board and noted the information right on the receipt. The killer really could be a smaller-built man or a woman. Ava looked at Brad Reese's photo. He wasn't very small, but he wasn't large either.

"Can someone scan through the evidence and find me a picture of Brad and Teagan holding hands or standing with their hands close to each other?"

Santos and Dane nodded simultaneously.

"Why do you need something so specific?" Santos asked.

"So I can get an idea of Brad's hand size."

Ashton came through the doorway with papers held aloft. "Ava, we found something big. Well, they found it while I was over—"

"What is it?" Ava asked, holding out her hand.

"Brad Reese searched for Connor Aldridge's address on the internet. He put it into his phone's GPS, too. Before you say it, I am already working on getting the tracking information from his phone company to see if Brad was at the library during the time of Teagan's death." He smiled.

"Thank you, Ash."

"Well, don't look so pleased. Curb your enthusiasm for the first break we've had," he said with a teasing tone, though his eyes announced his annoyance.

"I just argued with Sal that Brad was probably a victim in all this, and now I have to go tell her that it looks like he might be the killer. I was dead wrong about him and—" She shut her mouth. Ranting was never a good look, and admitting that she was wrong *again* in the case of Teagan Reese didn't make her feel any better about herself.

She held up a hand. "Thank you, Ash. Seriously, this is great. Let me know as soon as you have that location information."

"Will do."

Sal had returned from the meetings. She was probably in a mood that warranted stepping lightly around, but Ava had to tell her the new information she had learned. Chagrined, she knocked and waited for Sal to answer.

The door opened swiftly, and Sal stood there with a grim expression. "Ava," she said, turning away. "Come on in." She took a seat behind her desk. "Better be good news. I need some right about now."

"It's about Brad Reese."

Sal made a rolling motion with one hand, the irritation on her face becoming more prominent. "I've said it before, this isn't a mystery novel; don't leave me in suspense."

"Right." She related the information about Brad's search and cell-phone GPS history.

"Okay, but that has nothing to do with Teagan being murdered. Not connected."

"He bought a gun two weeks before her death," Ava blurted.

Sal stared at her for an awkward and silent moment. "Is it the same gun that killed Teagan? Are there ballistics reports?"

"Not official reports. Not yet, but they are working on them. And the same caliber gun killed Arthur Erwin. Nine-millimeter."

"What type of gun did Brad Reese buy?"

"Ruger LC9."

"Can it be matched to Teagan's death forensically in any way?"

"We're working on it. Ballistics and lab. I found a witness to Arthur's murder. She's supposed to be in to give an official statement later today."

"A witness, and you didn't bring her in already?"

"She'll be here, and I'm hoping she brings her friend with her just in case they saw something."

"What friend?"

Ava told her about Metford being unable to catch the other girl who ran from the alley. "Astrid says the other girl saw nothing, but I don't know if that's true. If she did see anything, I believe Astrid will talk her into coming here as well. Arthur was like her big brother, and she is ashamed that she didn't do more to stop his murder."

Sal shook her head and exhaled deeply. "It's your case; handle it how you see fit, but don't get my ass chewed any more than it just was. You screw up, I catch it from everyone above me."

"I understand."

"Thank you for updating me on the Brad Reese situation. Now, if he bought that gun to shoot his wife, why was he searching Connor Aldridge's address?"

"Connor and Teagan were having an affair. At first, we thought it was only a rumor started by a jealous coworker, but turns out, it's true. We found email correspondence and Connor admitted to the affair."

"Ruger LC9…" Sal tapped the desk with one finger. "Did Mrs. Aldridge know about the affair?"

"Connor said she never found out and he wants to keep it that way. He asked for discretion on our part while we investigate."

"Good work, but go find those kids and their father. If he shot his wife, the kids might be in more danger than we first thought."

Ava left the room and immediately called Brad's parents.

"Mr. Reese, can you put me on speaker?" she asked, stepping into her office and closing the door.

"Yes, what's happened now?" he asked.

The sound on the other end of the phone opened up and Ava could hear the yapping Yorkie doing what it did best.

"Did you find my son and my grandchildren?" Mrs. Reese asked.

"If they're doing their job, they have, but you know they're not," Millie stated.

"Please, Mr. and Mrs. Reese," Ava said. "Did Brad know how to shoot a handgun? Had he ever taken classes, gone to ranges, showed an interest in firearms, anything like that?"

"No," all three voices said at the same time.

"No, Agent James," Mr. Reese said. "Our Brad didn't like guns. He said they were for violent people—"

"Criminals, is what he said," Mrs. Reese corrected. "He thought all guns should be outlawed and dumped into the deepest part of the ocean. Guns kill people."

"Mom, guns aren't autonomous," Millie said in a condescending tone. "People use guns to kill each other. Same as baseball bats and kitchen knives. Should all the knives and bats be dumped in the ocean, too?"

"Excuse me," Ava said. "Why would Brad suddenly, just two weeks ago, purchase a handgun?"

The other end of the line fell oddly silent. Even the dog shut up for the span of a breath.

"Brad wouldn't have bought a gun," Mr. Reese said in a disbelieving voice.

"If you found one at his house, maybe whoever took him and the kids left it there," Mrs. Reese suggested.

"They're right," Millie said without the inflammatory condescending tone for once. "Brad wouldn't buy a gun. He hates them, and besides, he isn't afraid. Not like he's in fear for his life, but maybe he should have been, considering. If he'd had a gun, whoever took him and my niece and nephew wouldn't have been able to kidnap them. He would have protected them at any cost."

"He did purchase it. He bought it with his bank card. His ID is on file at the store."

"He said nothing to us about it," Mr. Reese said in a low voice that made him sound like a defeated man.

"I don't believe it," Mrs. Reese said. "I don't… think he… would…" Her voice broke and Mr. Reese comforted her.

"No one here knew about the gun purchase, Agent. It's a shock to us given his lifelong stance about guns—handguns in particular."

Ava thanked them and hung up.

Buying a firearm and telling no one about it just before his wife ends up dead did not put Brad Reese in a good light. Ava had hoped that perhaps he bought the gun as a gift for someone in the family, but she hadn't really expected that. Hope was still free.

CHAPTER TWENTY-THREE

And More Secrets

B ACK IN THE CONFERENCE ROOM, AVA CALLED EVERYONE'S ATTEN-
tion. "Dane, Santos, I want you two to go back to the Reese's beach
house and check for any sign of a firearm, and of course, any sign of our
three missing people. The gun was a shock to Brad's family. Apparently,
he was a lifelong advocate of eradicating guns. Especially handguns."

"We're on it," Santos said, standing.

"And on your way back, canvass around the Arthur Erwin site, as
well. We need to know if any of the homeless saw anything. I know they
denied it at first, but I believe they were just scared to talk. Find out why."

"What do you want me to do?" Metford asked.

"You're with me. We're going to deep dive into Connor and
Margueritte Aldridge's lives. If they owned a cat ten years ago, I want to

know about it. They're public figures; it shouldn't be very difficult to get information on them."

"Sounds like loads of fun," he complained.

"You've got a busted wing, what else is there right now?" she snipped.

"I hate riding the desk. You know that."

"You're no good to me out there where you could get hurt worse or cause someone else to get hurt. Suck it up. You'll live." She patted his shoulder as she headed to the other end of the room where the laptop sat. "I could let you help Ashton over in the geek lab."

Metford stood quickly. "I'll flap over to my desk with my one good wing and work all day, thank you. No more complaints."

"That's what I thought." She laughed and stood. Following behind Metford, she took the desk across the aisle from him. "I'll take Connor; you take Margueritte."

They worked for an hour. The only sound was the whir of the shared printer at the back of the room.

"This Connor Aldridge has a lot going on," Ava said. "Those sponsorship programs for struggling artists seem to have great effect on artist popularity." She stood and retrieved more printouts. "Like here. The artists who come out of this program seem to shoot straight to fame and fortune within months, but participation in one of these two programs seems to lead to low-levels of recognition and sometimes even obscurity."

Metford reached for the papers. "Some of the enrolled have disappeared?"

"From what I'm finding, yeah. Like, missing person reports filed and everything. Some of the cases are still open, too." She showed him another stack of printouts. "I've got them right here. Three cases that were filed within the last year and all three of them were enrolled in the last program just a month or so before going missing. All three cases are still ongoing."

"What about that gallery opening that Connor and Margueritte were supposedly at in New York City right after Teagan was found dead?"

"What about it?" Ava asked.

"Has anyone questioned any of the artists in attendance there?"

"We haven't. I don't know if the detectives on the missing person cases have spoken to anyone involved with the programs or not. It might be worth checking out, though. Good idea, Metford. See? Clip a wing, expand the mind."

"So funny."

"We need to make a list of all the artists that were at the gallery opening. Some of them will undoubtedly be in one of Aldridge's programs, and some might have noticed something off about him or his wife."

"You're working with the idea that Connor might have shot and killed Teagan because of their affair."

"I am. All the angles are worth looking into, but Teagan was an artist at one time. She lived in New York City. She was acquainted with Connor back then. When she already had a new life started here, she struck up an affair with Connor and threatened him if he didn't help get her back into that particular art world."

Metford *hrm*ed. "I thought that, too, but what about Brad and the gun purchase? Maybe he found out about the affair, went by the Aldridge house but they weren't there, and so he went to the library and confronted Teagan. Things got heated and out of hand; he shot her in the heat of the moment. That would explain why he placed her back in the chair and draped that sweater over her head."

"Makes sense."

"And what if it was just a murder of opportunity? Those aren't as uncommon as people think."

Ava groaned and rubbed the center of her forehead. "This case is going to make me crazy."

"That implies that you aren't already."

"Very funny, now get back to work before I clip your other wing. Get some artist names from that gallery opening. What was the name of the gallery, even?" She realized she had failed to ask either of the Aldridges during their interviews.

"Vibrant Vault."

"Vibrant Vault? What a name. Vault makes me think of a locked vault in a bank, not art."

"I don't pretend to understand anything about art or the people who produce or procure it. Just doing my job here."

After another half-hour, Ava stood and stretched. "I got about ten names, and I can't read through anymore articles right now. A lot of the names repeat, and I would bet your list looks a lot like mine."

"I have five names and they all repeat through the various media and articles, but all five of them were at the Vibrant Vault grand opening or christening, or whatever they call it." He handed her a piece of paper with handwritten names.

"Ciro Trapani, Sharelle Kim, and Neely Parker. Let's take those three and research where they are now. They seem to be the ones who are involved with recent events."

"I have Ciro Trapani pulled up here. New York driver license, twenty-four years old, lives in the Chelsea Art District. Looks like he has an apartment in his name over in Greenwich Village, too."

"Whoa, someone has some serious money. Is he married, have kids, live with roommates?"

"Not married, no kids on record, and you'll have to give me a few minutes to find out about the roommates. I'm not Ashton. I'm just learning how to navigate through the records systems."

Ava pulled up everything she could find on Sharelle Kim. Another artist who lived in Bushwick. A twenty-eight-year-old female living alone, unmarried, no kids, no car, and was in one of Connor Aldridge's sponsorship programs.

"If Ciro Trapani shares living costs with roommates, I can't find them listed anywhere in any of his records," Metford said.

"Sometimes roomies don't get listed on leases or any other official paperwork, but we will say he lives alone and assume he does not when we go to speak with him."

Metford's eyes flew wide. "Wait, what? When we *go speak with him*? As in, we're going to New York City? To all these artsy-fartsy neighborhoods?" A look of dread crossed his face.

"If I can get clearance, yes, we are. Might as well wipe that look off your face. Neely Parker lives in East Harlem. She's twenty-three and she's in a sponsorship program funded and run by the Aldridges. Single, no car."

"What about Sharelle Kim?"

"Same story. They each have a driver's license but no car, both in an Aldridge sponsor program, both at the grand opening of the Vibrant Vault."

"Which is also in the Chelsea Art District on West 24th Street. If it was any closer to 11th Avenue, it would have been the corner building. Prime location for visibility."

Ava chuckled. "Now you're a real estate guru to the elite gallery owners of New York City?"

"No. It's common sense that if you own a business that relies on the public seeing the work or services or whatever you are offering, you want it in a building that gives you the highest possible visibility. That would be a corner property in this case."

Ava's phone rang and she answered. After a few seconds, she hung up. "Well, the lab results came back on what kind of gun killed Arthur Erwin. I'll give you three guesses and the first two don't count."

"Ruger LC9."

"How did you get so smart?"

"It's the crystal ball I keep in my desk. What about prints on the spent round?"

Ava shook her head. "There were none."

"Without a round from the library shooting, there's no sure way to know if it's the same gun in both crimes."

"Or if it's the same Ruger that Brad bought recently." Ava stood. "I told you this case was going to make me crazy." She clapped his shoulder. "And if I'm going crazy, you get to tag along for free." She headed toward Sal's office.

After twenty minutes of explaining why it was important to go talk to the artists in New York City, Ava sat back and clasped her hands in her lap. Sal had not been impressed with the idea of Ava and Metford running off to the city in the middle of looking for the missing Reese kids.

"You know what?"

Ava's heart tripped a couple of beats and straightened out. "What?"

"Sometimes I really don't understand your take on things, the way you process evidence, or hell, even the world, but I do understand that you always get results. Normally, I would say no, you can't go, and you certainly can't drag Metford away from this search, but I just realized how much time you two have spent compiling all this information about these artists and the Aldridges." She looked down at the papers Ava had given her. "You might as well follow-up at this point, but I want it wrapped up in twenty-four hours and your butts back here with a report. Understood?"

"Yes, ma'am. Thank you. You won't—"

"Uh-uh. Stop right there. Just go. Just you and Metford. Everybody else stays here and keeps digging for leads on Brad and the kids. And I want someone ready to interview Solomon Furlong, who, as I understand it, still isn't answering his phone, and we still don't know for sure where in Mexico he went."

"Yes. We have been unable to locate him. He is due back from vacation sometime between this evening and Sunday evening, though."

"Make sure the others know what's going on, and get out of here before I change my mind."

Ava hurried to the bullpen. "Thank you."

"How did she take the news about the gun?" Metford said, standing slowly.

"Not great, as you'd expect. It's just another twist we didn't need adding another complicated layer to an already-convoluted case." She grabbed her files. "My go-bag is in the car already. Where's yours?"

"My car."

"Let's go. We only have twenty-four hours, and I have to call the others so that someone is ready in case Solomon Furlong shows up. They're staying here to continue investigating leads in the Reese case."

"Are we flying or driving?"

"No way to get a flight this spur-of-the-moment. You know that." Ava hit the unlock on the key fob while she was still forty feet from the car. "Hurry it up and get your bag."

"It's a minimum of a four-hour drive, what is five minutes going to hurt?"

Five hours later, Ava stepped out of the car in Chelsea. She eyed the building in front of them and pointed. "Fifth floor," she said and looked back to the paper in her hand.

"That's what it says." Metford headed for the front door of the apartment building.

CHAPTER TWENTY-FOUR

NYC, First Trip

Ciro Trapani

A
VA KNOCKED ON THE DOOR TO ROOM 508. MUSIC PLAYED INSIDE
the apartment, but no one came to the door.

"Maybe he has a dog or a cat that he leaves the music on for," Metford said.

She knocked again, louder.

After a few seconds, Metford turned to leave. "I vote that we head to his place in Greenwich Village and see if he's there."

Ava knocked once more, and Metford gave an exasperated sigh as he turned back to face the door again.

"Hello? Who are you?" a man's voice asked in a heavy Spanish accent from the other side of the door.

"Mr. Trapani?" Ava asked.

There was a long pause before he spoke in an irritated tone. "You have me at a disadvantage. State your business or leave."

Something tapped against the door on the other side, and the fine hairs over Ava's body stood straight out. She pushed Metford past the door on one side, and she moved to the other, her hand going to her gun.

"Mr. Trapani, we're FBI. We just need to ask you some questions about Connor and Margueritte Aldridge," Ava said.

The chain lock rattled, two deadbolts slid back into the door, and the door opened revealing the visage of a man walking away.

"Come in and have your questions, but you must follow me to my work. Someone always disturbs me when I'm working. If it's a good work, I get more interruptions."

Ava followed him, scanning the place for anyone else. In his hand, she saw a large paintbrush and realized that could have been what she heard tap lightly against the door. Ciro Trapani stepped from the dimly lit living room through an open set of French doors onto a small balcony.

"Ask, ask, ask, and then show yourselves out." He turned to a giant canvas, flourishing the paintbrush with more drama than necessary. Ava couldn't make heads or tails of the abstract shapes already on the canvas. "What did Connor do now to get the FBI on his ass?"

Ava stepped forward. "Were you at the grand opening of the Vibrant Vault Gallery a few days ago, Mr. Trapani?"

Without hesitation, he said that he was. "Anyone who is anyone was there. If they were good according to Connor and Margueritte, they attended. It's not really optional if you're in his sponsorship programs." He grinned but still didn't look at Ava or Metford. The painting was more important than his unwanted guests. "Is that all?"

"No, actually, it's not. Were Mr. and Mrs. Aldridge at that opening as well?"

He sneered at her before returning his gaze to the painting. "Is that a tricky question? It's their gallery; their newest baby. Why would they not be there at its birth?"

"Standard question. Were they there the whole night?"

"I don't know when they left. It's a funny thing... I don't care when they left either. I am not their keeper."

"I take it you don't care for the Aldridges?" Metford asked.

Trapani stood back and admired the painting for a moment, spared Metford a disgruntled look, and dropped his brush into a five-gallon bucket. Water splashed as he chose from an array of fan brushes.

"I work for them. How much does anyone like their boss?"

"So, you don't like them. Why?"

"I never said I don't like them. I just don't keep close tabs on them. It was a grand opening. I had more things on my mind than where they were all evening."

The painting was comprised of broad strokes of dirty-white overlaying clashing colors that had been put together like a child's attempt at reconstructing a Monet. How he ever became famous for such horrid work was beyond Ava's comprehension or explanation.

"Why are you here breaking up my concentration? If you are done, you can show yourselves out now. I need to work and I can't do it with you here. Besides, why do you care where the Aldridges were that night?"

"Did Connor ever talk to you about his life in Fairhaven?" Metford asked.

Trapani shrugged with one shoulder and dropped the fan brush into the bucket of water. He wiped his hands on a towel. "I know some about it, why?"

"Did he ever mention Teagan Reese?"

Trapani's hand tightened around the end of the towel, and his gaze shifted between Metford and Ava rapidly. He dropped his gaze to the painting. The muscles in his jaws bunched as he tossed the towel toward a patio chair where there were a few clean hand towels. "No."

Ava and Metford exchanged a look. She was sure Trapani recognized the name, and she saw in Metford's eyes that he caught the recognition, too.

"You never heard her name before?" Ava asked.

"I told you, I don't know her. Never heard her name." He chose another brush, seemingly at random, and picked up the palette to turn his full attention back to the easel.

"Mr. Trapani, if you know Teagan Reese, or if you ever heard Mr. Aldridge speak about her, we need to know. This is a federal investigation. We'd hate to find out later that you knew something and withheld it. Withholding information is a—"

"I don't know her and I don't give a damn about your *federal* investigation," he said forcefully, turning to glare at her.

"She's dead. Murdered at work," Ava said.

"Okay. What does that have to do with me?" He turned to the painting once more.

"She used to be an artist here in the city. Painting. Just like you. I heard she was pretty good."

Trapani let the paintbrush drop to his sides momentarily. "So? Lots of people are artists."

"She wanted to come back. That might have upset a lot of people, huh?"

"Why would that upset anyone? Listen, I really need to get this piece finished. I have a showing—"

"It might upset artists who don't want the competition. Take you, for instance. If Mrs. Reese came back on the scene, she might oust you from your position in the art world."

"She might take the art world by storm," Metford added. "Be the new golden child, so to speak."

He sneered and scoffed, raising his palette and brush again.

"Connor Aldridge was going to use his influence to get her back on the scene here. Maybe he thought it was time to shine the spotlight on some actual artwork that was worthy of the spotlight instead of…" Ava motioned toward Trapani's work in progress and wrinkled her nose, "… whatever that is."

Trapani spun on them, anger flaring. "That's it. I want you to leave." He tossed down the palette and brush. Paint splattered onto the floor of the balcony. He raised a hand and pointed to the door they had entered. "Now. Get out and don't come back without a warrant. I can't be bothered with your nonsense while I'm trying to work." His voice grew louder, and his expression stormier with each word.

When Ava and Metford didn't move fast enough to suit him, Trapani shoved between them and yanked the door open.

After they stepped out the door, Ava turned and smiled at Trapani. "You know, this isn't a good look, Mr. Trapani."

"You want information about Connor, you go speak to him. Eh?" He slammed the door.

Ava and Metford went back to the car.

"Did you see that painting?" he asked, buckling his seatbelt.

"How could I not?" Ava looked to the list of names and addresses.

"That's what passes for top tier artwork in the Aldridge world. Maybe I should become a painter."

"Artist," Ava said. "Painter makes me think of someone who paints the outside of houses or something."

"I wouldn't hire him to even do that. I think he knew Teagan Reese by the way he acted."

"He had at least heard her name before, but it might be because she used to be an artist."

"Or because Connor had bragged about the affair to his top, pet artist. Aldridge and Trapani seem to be joined at the hip when it comes to this art stuff. If an article mentions one of them, the other is mentioned in the same article."

"For some reason beyond my comprehension, Trapani is Aldridge's cash cow right now. His paintings sell for thousands. Of course they're joined at the hip. The minute Trapani's work drops in popularity, Aldridge will just choose another artist to take his place."

"Where to now?"

Ava pointed to the list. "Sharelle Kim is next."

Sharelle Kim

In Brooklyn, Ava and Metford stopped at the HQ for one of Connor Aldridge's artist programs. It wasn't the glamorous high-rise building Ava had pictured in her head. Instead, it was at the end of a building that also housed Loco Taco Spot, Mary's Dry Cleaning, and Mad Money Check Cashing.

"You think it's a coincidence that the Aldridge Rising Star headquarters is right next to a dry cleaner and check cashing service?" Metford asked.

Grinning, Ava shrugged. "Probably not." She pointed to Loco Taco Spot. "Tacos are only a buck each. No starving artists here, huh?"

He laughed. "Good one." He leaned to see the taco storefront. "Are they seriously only a dollar, though?"

"We don't have time for you to eat a bunch of gut grenades and have to stop for bathroom breaks every few minutes." She opened the door and stepped out.

"Yeah, well, you might be able to function on air and caffeine, but I need actual food."

"And that isn't real food. Can't be if they're only a dollar each." She opened the door and walked in.

Aldridge Rising Star was small. The low-pile carpet was stained, and the furniture sported a fine coat of dust. The top of a computer monitor peeked over the counter, and a woman stood from the seat. She adjusted her glasses and smiled pleasantly.

"Welcome to…" she gave her scripted welcome.

Ava and Metford held their badges out, and Ava introduced them.

"Oh, I see," the woman who had introduced herself as Babette, Babe for short, said. She adjusted her glasses again and pursed her lips.

"We're here looking for one of the artists in this program. The way we understand it, the sponsored artist will have a residence paid for by the program. Is that correct?" Ava asked.

"Yes. That is correct. Some will live in a large house with other artists who share a similar level of talent. Others will have a small apartment to themselves."

"That sounds…" Ava glanced at Metford. It sounded creepy to her, but she knew, to a young artist just starting out, it would be a hook.

"Sharelle Kim, ma'am," Metford said. "We're looking for Sharelle Kim."

"Oh, I'm not supposed to give out information to anyone like that. It's a safety precaution. You understand."

"We're not just anyone," Ava said. "We are federal agents investigating a federal case."

Babette's eyes widened and her lips all but disappeared as she pressed them together harder. She nodded and sat at the computer again. When she stood again, she looked worried.

"I'm sorry, but it looks as if Miss Kim dropped out of the program some months ago. Once the artist is out of the program, they cannot remain in the program housing."

"Where did she move to?" Ava asked.

Babette shook her head. "I have no way of knowing, I'm afraid. We don't keep tabs on artists who are no longer interested in our services. I'm sorry."

"What was the address she gave when she was in the program?"

Babette got the information and gave it to Ava. "She was a waitress?"

"That's what she put on her intake forms."

Ava thanked her and left.

In the car, Metford took the piece of paper. "That's in Brooklyn."

"The Bushwick neighborhood," Ava added. "Artists go there because of the culture and art everywhere."

They drove to the Bushwick address. It wasn't in one of the nicest apartment buildings, but it could have been worse. The hallway to her unit was dim. The fluorescents that still worked were yellowed. Some flickered, some burned steady and buzzed loudly. Two of the doors had been tagged with spray paint, and the carpet had a large hole in the middle of the corridor. The concrete had a scorch mark.

"Someone tried to set fire to the whole place," Metford said.

"Might have been an accident," Ava said, pausing in front of Sharelle Kim's door. "This is it." She knocked and waited a while but there was no answer, not a sound coming from within.

They left and walked two blocks to The Spice Rack restaurant listed as Miss Kim's job before she was in Aldridge's program but she was not there either.

"Why would Sharelle Kim drop from a program that was paying her rent and utilities to come live here?" Metford asked.

"Maybe Aldridge's group-home for wayward artists wasn't for her."

"Group-home for wayward artists? Where did that come from?"

Ava blew out a long and exasperated breath. "I'm just tired."

"I'll drive, then. I can still drive, you know."

"Not that kind of tired, Metford." She pulled into traffic and a driver laid on the horn. She paid no mind to it even though Metford flinched and swore. "Put Neely Parker's address into the GPS, would you?"

Metford did. "Says we're forty-one minutes out."

"Where was that address?"

"East Harlem."

Neely Parker

The twenty-three-year-old blonde answered the door and smiled at Ava and Metford. "May I help you?"

They showed their badges and introduced themselves.

"Could we come in and ask you a few questions, Miss Parker?" Ava asked.

Neely shifted her weight, looked nervously at them, and then nodded. "Sure, but I don't know what the FBI would want to talk to me about." She snickered and closed the door behind them. "I'm just an artist."

"That's what we wanted to ask you about, Miss Parker. You're in Aldridge's Rising Star Artist sponsorship program, correct?" Ava asked.

"Well, yeah." She laughed again and waved a hand around. "You didn't think I could afford something like this on my own, did you?"

"It is a big place," Metford noted. "Live here alone?"

"God, no. Five others live here with me. Well, most of the time, anyway."

"Does the program supply all this for the artists staying here?" Ava asked, indicating the sixty-five-inch TV mounted high on the wall of the living room, and the furniture.

"Every bit of it."

"Do you know Connor and Margueritte very well?"

"Kinda. I guess. It's not like I go to dinner at their place or anything, but I know them pretty well." She shoved her hands into the pockets of her jean shorts and cleared her throat lightly.

Ava asked her about Teagan Reese and received the same answer she had gotten from Ciro Trapani.

"Do you know Ciro Trapani?"

"Duh. Every artist knows Ciro. His tagline is *From a zero to a Ciro… that's what the program did for me.*"

"What does that mean?" Metford asked.

"He went from a nobody to being the top artist in Connor's circle."

Ava couldn't hide her shock. "That's a surprise." She quickly pointed to a canvas propped on an easel near the window. It was still strange and abstract, but something about it made it a lot more pleasant to look at than Trapani's piece. "Is that yours?"

Neely beamed and then looked embarrassed. "Yeah. I just finished it. That's why I'm still here while the others are at the gallery meeting. I'm falling behind a little."

"Do the Aldridges force you to produce art on a schedule?" Metford asked.

"No, but they prefer it if we make ourselves work through the blocks and slumps that come along with any creative lifestyle."

"Prefer it or demand it?" Ava asked.

Neely glanced above Ava's head toward a corner and then shook her head. "They don't force us to do anything if we don't want to." She looked to the painting.

"Neely," Ava said, stepping a little closer and choosing to use the woman's first name. "You can tell us if anything is going on that's not on-the-level in this program. You won't get into trouble."

Neely shook her head and gave them a big smile. "I don't know what you're talking about, Agent. This program is the bomb. Without it, most of us would be starving in the street. Or, at least, living in a hovel and trying to scratch out an existence." She laughed and the sound was full of tension. She glanced above and behind them again.

Metford turned to face the large kitchen and then stepped to Ava's side. He whispered, "There's a camera up in the corner behind us."

"Okay, Miss Parker. Thank you for speaking with us. Could you, uh, show us out and point us in the direction of a restaurant? Agent Metford just reminded me of the time, and we haven't eaten yet."

"Sure thing," Neely said, nodding dramatically. "Come on." She walked with them to the inner door. She opened it and stepped into the vestibule then opened the door that let out onto the sidewalk.

Ava and Metford stepped out, and Neely rushed to Ava's side. "You need to speak to Lucia Garcia Martinez. She works two blocks that way in Muy Caliente. She's a waitress." Neely ducked back inside and trotted toward the inner door.

"That wasn't suspicious at all," Metford said.

"No. I'd say everything is just peachy-keen here at the Artist Abode ala Aldridge." She pointed in the direction Neely had pointed. "I say we go speak to Miss Lucia Garcia Martinez and see what she has to say about the Aldridges."

"Her name was listed as a recipient of an Aldridge sponsorship," Metford said. "I remember the name because she has two last names. And she ain't hard on the eyes either."

"I'm glad your memory is so good. Maybe you can pick her out when we get there."

"Gladly," Metford said, speeding his pace a bit. "But only if we can get something to eat while we're there."

"Get it to go."

CHAPTER TWENTY-FIVE

Lucia Garcia Martinez

Lucia took Ava and Metford's order. She was diminutive, her eyes were bright, and her wit was quick. She was the total package, and Ava remembered they called smart, pretty, and talented girls a triple-threat back in high school. That's just what Lucia seemed to be. Ava pointed to a period painting of Mexican aristocrats.

"Look at the artist's name," she said.

"Gorgeous and talented," Metford said. "That's art, not whatever it was Ciro Trapani was doing."

"Vandalizing the canvas is what I'd call it."

Lucia returned. "I just rung up your order. It should be about ten minutes or so." She stepped out from behind the register and began wiping down the counter with a cloth.

"Lucia," Ava said.

The young woman looked up, the smile dropping as she saw the badge in Ava's hand. "Okay. You're FBI." She flipped a hand up. "Doesn't get you a discount."

"We would like to speak with you about Connor Aldridge and his wife. We know you were in one of the artist programs they sponsor."

Lucia let loose a string of words in Spanish that were too fast for Ava to decipher, but she was sure the woman had cursed multiple times before she took a breath, and gave them their total.

Metford handed his card around Ava's arm. "Lucia, Neely Parker told us to come speak with you."

"Neely?"

Ava nodded. "We just came from her place."

"Follow me." She briskly took them into a part of the dining area that wasn't in use. There were pocket doors to separate it from the main dining area. "It's okay. We can talk freely in here."

"Neely had only good things to say about the Rising Star program, but she also told us where to find you," Ava said.

"There was a camera at her place, and she wouldn't open up to us about the program or Connor," Metford added.

"Oh, it's not just him. It's her, too. Margueritte. I was accepted into the six-month program they run in Fairhaven, Maryland. It's close to the beach where I live."

"Wait, the Aldridges run a sponsor program in Fairhaven?" Ava asked, looking to Metford, who shrugged.

"Yes. That's where I live, so that's the one I signed up for."

"If you live in Fairhaven, what are you doing here?" Ava asked.

"I only come here when I want to show pieces to galleries. That's why I'm here now. I'll be here for two months, maybe three, and then I'll go back home and work until I have more ready. Wash, rinse, repeat. There's a convention I'm here for right now, too. I have paintings, sketches, sculptures, everything set up. That's where I go after work."

"Did the Aldridge program help you?"

"Oh, yeah. Paid for a place to live, food, utilities; we even had access to two little cars, but we were highly discouraged from leaving the house and property. They tried to make it so we didn't need to." She sighed. "Then I quit the program. Connor's type of fame and fortune came at too high a price."

"What do you mean?" Metford asked.

"That means that halfway through the program, he starts paying special attention to me, telling me how famous I could be if only my work was a little better. Then one day, he says he can give me more fame, promise me fame and all the money I would ever need, if I would just do something for him."

"Sexual favors," Metford blurted, his eyes flaming.

"He wanted me to pose nude in front of a CCTV camera for an audience of men who appreciate the beauty of the female body. That and nothing more, he assured me. He flashed a stack of cash at me and said that was just for one ten-minute session and that there was much, much more where that came from. At first, I thought it was like nude modeling for artists learning how to draw the female form." She rolled her eyes and scoffed. "I was wrong. It was just for a bunch of old perverts who wanted to watch me... *do things.*"

"What did you do when you learned that?"

"What do you think I did? I broke ties with the Aldridges and their nasty program. I stay away from anyone associated with Connor and Margueritte. I don't doubt that they would retaliate."

"Why would they retaliate if you only refused to pose for them?"

"Maybe I didn't just refuse. Maybe I threatened to tell the police," she said, pulling her long black ponytail over one shoulder and trailing her fingers through it.

"Am I understanding that Margueritte was in on the posing nude for men situation?" Ava asked.

"I don't know for sure that she knew, but I have enough reasons to think the old bitch went right along with it. If there was money to be made, Margueritte surely had a hand in it."

They talked a few more minutes and then Ava asked about Teagan and Connor.

"Sure. He talked about her sometimes. Said he thought she'd be a good fit in our program in Fairhaven, even. I thought it was a little weird because she was married with a couple of kids from what I knew. Why would she want to come live with a bunch of younger, single, childless women who were just starting out? I wouldn't. Anyway, she was with Connor on a couple of occasions. I saw them with my own eyes."

"Was he trying to bring her back on the scene as the next superstar?"

Lucia shrugged. "I guess. Teagan used to be an artist. A good one, but to be real, she's a has-been in the art world. Connor would talk her up and feed her ego to her face, but he laughed behind her back and told his friend that if anyone found out he was screwing that washed-up has-been that his rep would be down the toilet. He'd lose his power and influence and he'd be ruined."

"His friend saw them together, too?"

"I guess. I mean, I don't know for sure, but the guy agreed with Connor."

"Did the friend have a name? Do you remember what he looked like?"

"His name was Karl, but I can't remember the last name. But he was rich just like Connor and Margueritte."

"And he was at functions here or in Fairhaven?" Metford asked.

"I saw him in Fairhaven and here. He warned Connor to keep the affair under the radar, to keep it quiet at any cost because they couldn't afford for Connor's programs to fall apart."

"Why do you think that was?" Ava asked.

"I don't know what it meant then, but after Connor got all hands-on with me, I got an idea. I wanted to tell Teagan, but I didn't want to get that close to anything concerning Connor. I held off for the last three months since I've been back living in Fairhaven, and now I'm here again. I wanted to tell her when I returned. I planned on it. I kept rehearsing how I would approach her with my suspicions and what I'd heard, and I didn't. I regret it now." She put her hands in her lap and looked down. She swiped a tear but didn't look up. "Maybe if I had said something to her, it might have saved her life."

"What do you think was going on that was so bad she was killed for it?" Ava asked.

Lucia looked up at her as if she had made a sick joke. "He offered me money to do nasty things in front of a camera for *an audience*. A dedicated audience of men. That's a form of trafficking, isn't it? How many others did he propose the same thing to? How many of them took him up on the offer? Besides, when that Karl guy said to keep the affair quiet at any cost ... after Teagan's death, I figured that must've been a threat or a directive or something."

The pocket door slid open a few inches and a tall woman with dark hair smiled apologetically and informed them their food was ready.

Lucia smiled to them both. "I have to get back to work now." She stood.

"Wait, Lucia," Metford said. "Would you be willing to testify if we find that—"

"Yes. Yes, I am willing to testify to everything I've told you. If it means making other women safer, yes."

"Would you mind coming to the office when you're back in Fairhaven and giving an official statement?" Ava asked.

Lucia glanced at Metford as she took Ava's card. "I will help you, but only if you can promise that I'll be safe. You have to promise me that you will keep me safe."

The woman appeared at the door again. "Rush incoming. Just got two ten-tops and a couple."

"I'll see you when I get back home. You can pick up your food from the front counter." Lucia rushed away, leaving Ava and Metford to grab their eats and show themselves out.

"Well, that was an info dump," Metford said.

"I think there's more to it. She didn't have time to tell us everything. Like how she heard Connor and Karl's conversation."

"Eavesdropping while the men were at the beach property," Metford suggested.

"Why would they talk about the affair there if they didn't want anyone to know about it?"

"Right. Maybe at a gallery showing or something like that. Where's the beach house, anyway?"

"That's something else we didn't get," Ava said. "We'll search for it when we get back home. Let's go see if Sharelle Kim is home yet."

He held up the bag of food as he got into the car. "What about this? We just going to let it get cold?"

"No, I'm going to drive while you eat."

Sharelle Kim

Sharelle was not at home but she was at work.

"What do you want to know? I'm trying to work here." Sharelle crossed her legs and looked around at the few customers scattered throughout the dining area.

"The Rising Star Artist program you were in," Ava said. "We need to ask a few questions about that and Connor Aldridge."

"Margueritte, too. His wife," Metford added. "You know them, I assume?"

"Yes, I know them."

"Did the program help you?" Ava asked.

"Of course it did. Gave me a place to live, food to eat, and the utilities were paid. Almost anything we wanted, we got. Are we done now?"

"Just a minute more," Ava said. "If the program was so good to you and for you, why did you drop out?"

"I said it was good to me, not for me." She gestured to the restaurant with its cheap lighting and cheap seating. "Otherwise, I wouldn't be starving in the land of plenty, would I?" She stood. "That it?"

"Why did you drop out, Sharelle?" Ava continued.

Sharelle cocked a hip, crossed her arms, and gave Ava a defiant look.

"Okay, what about Teagan Reese? Ever heard of her?"

Sharelle shook her head, but the flicker of surprise that ran over her face told a different story. "Listen, my job is as far away from Connor and his program as I could manage. I don't know anything, I don't hear nothing out here. I just want to be left alone to live my insignificant little life in my own way. Now, I gotta get back to work before I get fired. That happens and I lose my apartment. Goodbye." She turned on her heel and flipped her long braids over her shoulders, revealing her ear.

Above the lobe, the ear was badly disfigured. Sharelle quickly tilted her head forward and the braids covered it once again.

"What happened to her ear?" Metford whispered.

"I don't know, but maybe it's the reason she doesn't want to talk to us about the Aldridges."

As they walked from the side toward the front, Sharelle came from the kitchen carrying a tray full of drinks. Ava stepped in her path and slid her card into one of Sharelle's wide apron pockets.

"What's that?"

"My card. In case you change your mind about talking to us."

Ava left with Metford.

"We need to stop somewhere and go over what we have now," Metford said.

"We will. Then we're going to hit the Chelsea gallery."

"Fine, but we need to regroup first. We've got a lot more information now, and you're not even slowing down long enough to breathe, let alone process it all and see how and if it fits with our case—which is finding out who killed Teagan and where her family is."

"I know what our case is, Metford. I don't have to come to a full stop to process the information and see if it fits. You might, but I don't. If you can't keep up, at least don't slow me down."

He got into the car, chagrined. After a few miles, he turned to her. "You're hangry. Probably low blood sugar levels are making you this way."

"No, I'm this way because it's how I am. Stop trying to analyze me." She gripped the wheel tighter. It was Jason Ellis, still. He preyed on her mind and her heart even after all the months that had passed, but she didn't want to talk about it. Least of all with Metford.

"You weren't always like this. You're going at this thing like your life depends on it."

"Somebody's life might. Two somebodies, actually. Penny and Thomas Reese; maybe their father's life, too. They lost their mother already. Don't you think that's enough for a four- and six-year-old to lose?"

"How are you going to be any help to them if you drop from exhaustion? Or a damn heart attack?"

"I'm not old enough to worry about a heart attack. Exhaustion either. I've been through worse." She snapped a look at him. "Recently. So, drop it."

After a short break to put together their information and get coffee, Ava and Metford headed to Vibrant Vault only to find that the gallery was closed until further notice.

CHAPTER TWENTY-SIX

Back in Fairhaven

ETFORD PARKED THE CAR AT THE FAIRHAVEN FIELD OFFICE AND turned off the ignition. "Rise and shine," he said loudly.

Ava groaned from the passenger seat and lifted her head. "Well, I feel rested," she said sarcastically. She rubbed the right side of her face and head where it had been pressed against the window and door.

"Could be worse," he said, cheerily.

"How?" She worked her jaw and reached for the cold coffee she had bought two hours earlier.

"I don't know. You could have had no sleep at all." He opened the door and stepped out. "Thanks, Metford. I'm glad you insisted on driving back home," he said to himself.

She drudged out of the car. "Fine. Thanks, Metford. I'm not saying I feel better because I'm sore all over, my head hurts, and my face aches now."

"You should go home and get a few hours of sleep and take a shower. Then you'll feel better."

She raked her fingers through her hair and put the elastic band around it again as they walked toward the entrance. "I'm fine."

"Suit yourself." They entered.

"Usually do." She headed straight for Sal's door. "I'll give her updates; you give them to the rest of the team. We'll meet in the conference room."

She knocked at Sal's door twice before realizing that the lights were off inside. The door was locked as well. Muttering a swear, she stepped to her own office and went inside. The door was unlocked. She swore again. Losing sleep was affecting her worse than she had previously thought.

Dropping the file on the desk, she picked up her phone and called Sal. Fifteen minutes later, she finished giving the updates from New York City.

"And you think the Aldridges are trafficking young, gullible artists? The Aldridges who support the art center and library? Those Aldridges?"

"I think something is going on. We found that several of the artists who were accepted to the Rising Star program disappeared afterward. There are two other programs, but none of those artists have disappeared. The opposite happened to them. They're famous, and some are rich."

"Perhaps the Rising Star program caters to a higher-risk group than the other programs. The ones who are on drugs, who have no families, few ties; you know the group I'm referencing."

"Yeah," she said through a yawn. "I do, but that's not what's going on here. At least, I don't think so. The people who disappeared were from different backgrounds and cultures, and most of them, although not well-to-do, weren't street urchins or junkies. They didn't have rap sheets. Maybe Teagan stumbled onto some information she shouldn't have, and Connor got rid of her to keep it from getting out."

"You said Lucia agreed to give a statement and that she would testify against him if it came to it."

"That's what she said. And that he did try to traffic her; not to mention he had his hands all over her and it was unwanted physical contact."

"But how long ago was that incident?"

"Only a few months."

"Shit. Bring Connor in. Rattle his cage and see what falls out."

Ava hung up and went to the conference room.

"No, it's my cup," Dane stated loudly with an angry expression. "I don't want to drink after any of you. Hand it back." She pointed to Metford's coffee cup.

He pulled it back and shook his head. "I just got this from the break-room. Yours is over there by the board."

"Why don't you both take a cup, go wash it, make another coffee, and just shut up for a minute?" Santos said, walking rudely between them to get to her spot at the table. "The rest of us would appreciate being able to work in peace."

Ashton held up a paper. "The blood spatter analysis from the library came back."

Ava took it from him. The paper had no case or file number on it. She turned it toward him. "What's this, Ashton? There are no numbers to match this to anything. It could be a report from any case."

He took the paper back and stood. The dark circles under his blood-shot eyes had darkened to a concerning bruise-brown color.

"I adjusted the printing parameters and forgot to change them back. The numbers are there, just got cut off during printing."

"We can't afford that kind of mistake, Ashton. Fix it, and don't let it happen again."

"Sorry." He stepped out of the room.

Dane and Metford continued to bicker about the coffee cups. Santos pressed her fingers to her temples. "Ava, could you do something about this elementary school arguing? Please?"

The overhead fluorescents made the dark rings under everyone's eyes show. Ava couldn't imagine how bad she looked and didn't want to.

She held her hand out to Metford and made the give-it-to-me gesture, and with the other hand, she did the same to Dane.

"What?" came their twin questions.

"Give me the cups, please." Seeing their hesitation and suspicion, she said, "Now. Let me have them."

They did. She walked to the trashcan and dropped them in. "Problem solved. Metford, we need to pick up Connor Aldridge and bring him in as per Sal's orders."

"Whatever gets me out of here." He eyed Dane as he stepped past her. "I'll be in the car."

"What are we doing?" Santos asked.

"Keep working on narrowing down the leads to Brad and the kids. Sal's catching hell over this one again and she wants answers."

"You know those kids can't be in good shape," Dane said. "Even if they are still alive, which I very much doubt."

"Get another coffee and go take a walk, or go to the gym and do a little workout, Dane. You too, Santos. If you need it. Get your blood flowing, get all the negative crap out of your head, and then get back to work. Think we could do that?" She waited for a reply. When one wasn't forthcoming, she turned to leave. "Good. Let's get to it, please."

As she went out of the room, she heard Santos say, "And that's why we say crap rolls downhill."

Dane laughed. "And lucky us; we're at the bottom."

Ava walked on, glad they weren't arguing for the time.

Metford was behind the wheel when she reached the car. "Nope. Move it. I'm driving," she said, dangling the keys. "Remember, you gave them back as soon as we were inside."

"You sure?"

"Positive. Don't want you driving when you're mad. It'll keep me alert anyway." She swung in and shut the door as soon as he was out.

"Mad? I'm not mad. That was my cup. Dane's just so tired and stressed that she forgot where she left hers. She's not thinking clearly either. Why would I switch out cups with her? And you tossed both of them in the trash." He laughed. "Can't believe you just chucked them out like that."

She pulled onto the road. "Solved the issue, didn't it?"

"For sure."

As Ava pulled the car into the Aldridge driveway, her eyes followed the line of the paved drive all the way to the house. The line continued to draw her eyes to the front porch with its four white columns. The columns drew her attention higher to the third-floor balcony and three dormer windows. For the first time, she recognized the artistry of the estate. Its layout was like that of a painting, and she was driving on the center line of that painting.

"There!" Metford shouted, pointing out the passenger window. "Stop, turn around! There goes Connor in his car."

Ava turned the steering wheel hard and drove off the paved path into the grass, around a tree, and back onto the paved driveway.

"Come on, give it the gas, Ava. We're going to lose him. He's running."

"He's got something to hide, then," she said, punching the gas.

"Left, he turned left. Go, go, go."

Pushing the accelerator even more, Ava gripped the wheel and shifted slightly in her seat, preparing for the sharp turn at the stop sign. The tires screamed against the pavement, and then the car jerked straight. Connor's black Mercedes weaved in and out of traffic smoothly. Ava did her best to follow suit, but her movements were jerky, unsure, and dangerous. She let off the gas a little and their speed dropped. Nearly swiping a car in the left lane, she braked, letting the car move to the lane in front of her.

"Idiots," she exclaimed. "Can't they see the lights?"

"He's gone," Metford announced. "We've lost him. You think somebody tipped him off that we were coming?"

"No. We're the only ones who knew besides Sal, and she gave the order."

"Maybe one of the artists in New York told him we were there asking questions and he got spooked."

"He was told to make himself available for questioning," Ava said.

"Doesn't mean he will. If he goes back to the city, he could disappear for a long time."

"We're heading back to the house. Have to make sure he's not there." She turned and went back to the estate.

She rang the doorbell and knocked on one of the massive double doors. The chiming doorbell echoed through the interior of the house.

"Sounds like a cavern in there," Metford said, leaning to peer through a long window by the door.

"The ceiling must be twenty feet high. Bet you can hear everything in a place like this."

"Apparently Margueritte didn't hear him sneaking in and out for his affair."

Ava rang the bell and knocked again.

After a moment, she turned away. "Let's get back to the office. There's nothing more to do here."

CHAPTER TWENTY-SEVEN

Adjusting the Profile

SAL HAD ARRIVED AT THE OFFICE AND SHE MOTIONED TO AVA AS she and Metford entered.

"Uh-oh," Metford said, gesturing in Sal's direction. "Doesn't look happy."

"Would you be if the suits were on you about this case?" Ava veered off and went to Sal's office. "We lost him. I know, it's probably my fault. Metford saw Connor making a break for it and I didn't react quick enough—"

"Ava, stop and take a seat for a minute."

She did so.

"The Behavioral Analysis Unit has offered to help on the Teagan Reese case because there are two kids at risk."

"Okay, so what do they need? Or, are you going to let them help?"

"Of course, I said yes. The whole team is tired. I'm not blind, Ava. I see what this case is doing to everyone involved. Ashton is practically asleep at the wheel, making careless mistakes he has never made. Santos looks like a pressure cooker ready to explode, and I don't even need to state the obvious with the other two. And you. You're manic, and you look busy and productive, but you're starting to chase your tail. You need a fresh set of eyes or two looking over this with you. Leni Wagner and Dr. Vikram Sur will arrive within the hour. After their assessments, see where you are. If you need more help, the rest of the BAU team can be here later."

"Thank you." Part of Ava wanted to be angry that Sal had called her out, but she knew the observation was right. "I'll go tell the others. I know they'll be glad, too."

"See that the others cooperate with the BAU. I know tempers are on weak leashes right now, but we need this."

Ava agreed and went to the conference room to prepare for the meeting.

"Why do we need outside help?" Santos asked. "That just makes it look like we don't know what we're doing."

"No, it doesn't reflect badly on any of us," Ava said. "If anything, it shows interdepartmental cooperation. People coming together to help solve the murder of a loved and respected figure in Fairhaven, and to find her remaining family. Those kids are on everyone's minds from the state governor all the way down to Penny and Thomas' playmates."

"What if they change what we've already established?" Metford asked.

"If they have a different take on the crime scene, maybe we should take it into consideration. It's their area of expertise."

"Looking at pictures and telling a story is considered an expertise now?" Metford scoffed. "We go out in the field every day and put our lives in danger to save people, but the BAU can sit in their nice, air-conditioned offices and look over images on a screen, and they never have to draw their weapons." He drained coffee from a paper cup.

"But we do, Agent," a woman's voice sounded from the doorway.

Metford jerked in that direction with a guilty expression.

"See, it's right here." The woman patted her side. "And we do go out in the field. Just not as often as you do." She set her briefcase on the table and smiled levelly at each team member.

"And often not for the same reasons," a man said in a thick Indian accent. He removed his hat and put it on top of his briefcase. "Dr. Vikram Sur." He motioned to the woman. "Leni Wagner. We are here to help, not step on any toes."

"We only want to help get Penny and Thomas Reese home safe. Their father, too."

Ava introduced the team and made a blanket apology for anything that was said, or might be said that could be taken as offensive.

"No worries," Dr. Sur said. "We know tempers flare under stress and lack of sleep."

"Sleep deprivation is serious," Leni said. "That's the other reason we volunteered to help." She motioned to the board. "Now, if you don't mind, we just want the crime scene photos without notes or opinions or input to start with."

Santos made a disgruntled sound and Dr. Sur turned to her. "It isn't that your opinions and observations aren't valid, Special Agent Santos. We are supposed to be a fresh set of eyes for you, and we can't form our own analysis if yours is already in here." He tapped his temple and nodded before taking a seat.

Leni followed suit. "You can stay, leave, or tell us to use another room, if you like. We just ask for no input until we've finished our assessment."

"We'll stay, if it doesn't distract," Ava said.

Leni laughed. "Oh, this is a tame crowd compared to what we are becoming accustomed to. We work under very stressful situations sometimes."

"What, the AC goes out and you have to turn on a fan?" Metford quipped.

Leni pinned him for an instant with her glare. She blinked and it was gone. "No, Special Agent Metford." She folded her arms on the table and stared directly into his eyes. "Have you ever stared into the eyes of a serial killer? A true serial killer with no one around to help you even if you screamed? Have you ever felt the blush of blood where his knife's edge kissed your throat?" She tilted her head to the left and showed a thin scar on her neck.

Metford shook his head and glanced at Ava. Ava turned away and pretended to be interested in the coffee station that had been stocked with paper cups, plastic lids, and cardboard heat sleeves.

"Well, I have. I was his pet monkey performing a parlor trick for his entertainment. I knew as soon as I failed to entertain, he would kill me."

"I didn't mean to—"

"It's fine. But I wouldn't be so eager to judge others without knowing them at least a little."

Ava handed Dr. Sur the stack of crime scene photos and pointed to the screen at the other side of the table. "The tablet there controls the images on the screen. Just don't open the associated file for the images and you won't see the notes."

"Thank you," the doctor and Leni said in unison.

Suddenly, it was as if Ava and the team didn't exist. Leni and Dr. Sur were good at shutting out distractions. Leni hadn't been wrong about that. Which serial killer had she survived? Probably wasn't her boyfriend or love interest, but still there was a common thread. A tenuous, fragile fiber that ran between her and Ava. Was there a bond there or was it just Ava's mind wanting to feel a connection?

Desperation. That had to be it. She wanted so badly for there to be someone out there who had gone through something similar and survived, thrived, and even excelled afterward that she was imagining there might be some connection.

Leni looked well-rounded and level-headed. She was probably in her mid-forties, dressed professionally in a pantsuit, her emotions were definitely in-check, even with Metford's friction. But there was that one crack in her façade when she pinned him with the blackest look … It had lasted a second; maybe only a fraction, but Ava had seen it.

She smiled inwardly. Leni Wagner wore a mask, and that mask had at least one crack where the real Leni could peek out and be seen. It made her human. And it gave Ava hope that, one day, she could also be in control of herself so well and seem so comfortable at her job and around people again.

"Okay, we are ready." Dr. Sur readied their notes while everyone moved into place around the table.

"We went by the library on the way over here," Leni began, "but the crime scene and any evidence of a murder have been cleaned. Obviously. We wanted to get an idea of the layout, foot traffic around the area, and visibility from outside and inside."

"Then we looked at all these shots—kudos to the photographer, excellent job—and we have a profile. The killer is very methodical." He pointed to the wide shot of the crime scene. "Possibly even a hitman because of the 'double-tap' kill shots. You would be wise to look at suspects who are meticulous in nature, don't have a wide social group, few friends, and maybe exhibit some sociopathic behaviors that would have been noticed over the years."

"And would likely have caused him trouble in school," Leni added.

"Maybe ex-military?" Santos asked.

"Not likely," Leni answered. "With his meticulous nature, you would think that, but he has no problem going from stone-cold and reserved to outright brutal and deadly. A man like that wouldn't last in the military or law enforcement."

"It is obvious that he does not care to get his hands dirty." Dr. Sur pointed out the scene manipulation. "He must have gotten blood on him from moving the body." He pulled another photo up on the screen. "And from what we saw earlier at the library, he must not have worried too much that he would be seen even though it's a straight shot from these two windows to where the murder took place."

"It was dark outside and the lights in that area inside were on," Leni said, pulling off her glasses. "Well, it's almost like he was begging to be seen."

"He wanted someone to see him commit murder and then move the body, stage the scene?" Dane asked.

"No. Not really. More like, it was a brazen bold act of defiance. More like he didn't care if he was seen. He had that much faith in his ability to still get out of the situation."

"He might have exhibitionist qualities that would have resulted in trouble at school and, or, trouble with police," Dr. Sur added.

"We are looking for an exhibitionist, sociopathic hitman who has feelings?" Metford asked. He turned the tablet and pulled up the picture of the sweater draped over Teagan's head. "That's a sign of what? Remorse, right? I didn't think sociopaths felt remorse, or much of anything, actually."

"We didn't say he was a sociopath," Dr. Sur corrected. "Only that he likely exhibited some sociopathic tendencies that would have been noticed by others and would likely have caused him significant trouble throughout his life."

"That's right," Leni chimed in.

"Okay, he's not a psychopath who suffered a bout of the feelings, so what is he?" Santos asked.

"He might be psychopathic," Leni said. "Not sociopathic. Psychopaths are generally more complicated, more predictable, and sometimes, much smarter than sociopaths who are given to outbursts of rage when things don't go as planned. Most psychopaths can control their emotions, and they exert that control onto everything in their lives from their own personal, daily routines to their partners, kids, coworkers, and even their kills."

"I would say you are looking for a white male between twenty-five and forty-five. He's not a large man but has an average build. Probably can't keep steady employment because of his overbearing and controlling nature. If he does have a steady job, it's probably in a factory where he repeats the same processes every day," Dr. Sur said.

"And he can blend in with a crowd but he prefers to not be in a crowd," Leni added.

"Why do you think he's not a big guy?" Dane asked.

"Because it's obvious that, at some point, the victim got away and procured a weapon. It's also obvious from the wounds on her palm that she used that weapon repeatedly on her assailant. If his plan was always to leave her to be found in her chair at her desk, he would have bound her or overpowered her and shot her in the chair. That would have made the murder and his escape much simpler."

"Why did he move her?" Ava asked.

"That chair was where he wanted her to be found. That's what he wanted everyone to see. The scene in his mind had to be forced onto the scene of the crime."

"Then why cover her head like that?" Ava asked.

Leni lifted one shoulder. "A number of reasons. Regret and remorse come to mind first but that's not it. Not quite. He could've covered her head while she was on the floor if it was regret or remorse. Maybe he knew her personally and it was a sign of respect," Leni offered.

"Or, maybe he was told to do this and he didn't want to," Dr. Sur said. "If it was a hired hit, which I still think. Two kill shots. It's like a signature. Heart and head. Both to make sure the target is dead."

"We had another murder just a block from there," Ava said. "Homeless man but he was shot in the heart and the head."

Leni and the doctor exchanged a look. Leni turned to Ava. "Have you explored the idea of a serial killer?"

"It crossed our minds. How certain are you of the profile you just gave us?"

"Very," Dr. Sur said. "It is our area of expertise to look at photos and tell a compelling story." He grinned at Metford, who shook his head and chuckled good-naturedly.

Ava took the suspect list from the board. "That would put Russell Moore right at the bottom of the list, I would think." She explained a little about each suspect for Leni and Vikram.

"Brad should be at the bottom, too," the doctor said.

"No," Santos said. "Recently, he bought a gun that's the same caliber as the one used in the murders."

"What about Connor?" Dane asked. "Where should he be on the list?" She looked to Ava and Metford. "You guys just came back from New York. What did you find out about him?"

"That he could be methodical, cold, misogynistic, and manipulative," Metford said.

Ava nodded agreement, thinking about Lucia's story. "I say Connor stays at a solid number two on the list. Solomon Furlong is at the top for me right now simply because we haven't been able to speak with him. He dropped off the face of the earth right after Teagan was killed. Seems like something a killer would do to save his own skin."

"He hasn't arrived back on any flights or ships yet," Dane said. "Ashton is monitoring those. If he's your number one suspect for Teagan, what about Arthur Erwin?"

"Maybe coincidence," Ava said. As soon as it was out of her mouth, she wished she had not responded.

"What are the chances of two murders so close together that used the same caliber gun?" Santos asked.

"I know," Ava said, thumping into a seat. She read over evidence while the others talked more. "Hey, what about the prints we got?"

"What prints?" Metford asked.

"From the table at the library and Penny's dresser at the Reese house? Where's that report? They were a match to each other, but did they match anyone in the database?"

Everyone shrugged in turn. Ava groaned. "Who was in charge of getting the lab results on those prints?"

No one seemed to know for sure.

"Want me to go ask Ashton if he got the reports?" Dane asked.

"Yes, thank you," Ava said. "Metford, call the Aldridges' phones and see if you can get anyone to pick up."

He stood and walked to the far corner where he took a seat by the window with his phone in his hand.

"Solomon Furlong," Dr. Sur said. "Does he fit the profile?"

"He's a thirty-seven-year-old white male with a temper. He's five-ten and thin. He's a meticulous man who planned this vacation for months. He wanted the librarian position that Teagan got and he was angry about it. He openly disliked her but was usually able to be professional, if cold, toward her at work. They had the one heated argument, though, and there were witnesses."

"I don't know if he fits," Leni said. "But he sounds like a good candidate. If he's been on vacation out of the country, which I assume it's out of the country since you have a man watching flights and ships coming in."

"Yes, Mexico, but we don't know where exactly he is staying. He's due back between now and time for his shift Monday at the library."

"He left after Teagan's death?"

"Yes." Ava sighed. "But so did Connor and Margueritte Aldridge."

CHAPTER TWENTY-EIGHT

The Flip

WITH THE ALDRIDGES IN THE WIND, AND SOLOMON FURLONG playing off-grid in Mexico, Ava was stuck. She should have known her next move, but she had painted herself into a corner.

Metford stood. "Not surprisingly, the Aldridges aren't answering any of their phones, and their assistants, managers, and gallery workers don't know where they are either. They haven't been seen or heard from since they returned to Fairhaven."

"What about Furlong? Any word at all?"

"Ashton's monitoring that. He hasn't said anything to me. No texts, no emails, no calls from him."

"Okay, we can do this."

Metford sat at the table. "Do what, exactly?"

"Solve this case, Metford," she replied. "If the Aldridges are running, that means they have something to hide. Innocent people don't run like that. If Furlong doesn't return over the weekend, I'm going to assume he is also hiding something. Maybe he was in on it with the Aldridges."

"You think both Aldridges had something to do with Teagan's death?"

Ava scrubbed at her cheeks with her palms to get the blood flowing. Standing, she shrugged. "It's a theory."

Metford looked at Dr. Sur. "Would a woman fit your profile?"

"No. I don't believe a woman could have done this. I still believe it was a white male. Twenty-five—"

"To forty-five, yeah, we got that part," Ava snapped. "Could the murder have been perpetrated by more than one attacker?"

"We saw nothing to indicate a second attacker," Leni said. "It's not completely outside the realm of possibility that a woman did this, but the chances are astronomically low."

Ashton barged into the room and moved straight to Ava. "I found something. Connor Aldridge owns a gun." He held the report out to her and then swiveled his head toward the new people in the room. "Oh, hello. Sorry to interrupt." He turned back to Ava. "Who are they?"

Dane walked in and shut the door. Ava nodded to her. "She didn't tell you the BAU sent over a couple of people to help on the case?"

He shook his head and turned to Dane in confusion.

"I did tell him. He was brain-deep in the computer and didn't hear me, or he just didn't pay attention. I'm learning that's a thing with techies."

"Do you have any idea how many distractions I deal with every hour while I'm trying to do my job? More to the point, do you know how many are actually worth listening to?" He made a zero with his thumb and forefinger. "That's how many. But I found this, so it was worth not hearing you."

"Did you hear her ask about the fingerprints?" Ava asked, hoping his temper would calm. Ashton had always been the level one, and she didn't like what she was seeing and hearing from him.

"Really?" He spun to face Dane. "What fingerprints, and what about them? Can't anyone pick up the phone and call the lab besides me?"

Ava put a hand on his shoulder and he turned to face her again. "Sorry, Ava. I know; I'm over-reacting." He took a deep breath and asked his question again.

"The ones found in the library and the ones found in the Reese house. Did we get any hits on any of them yet?"

"I've heard nothing, but I can rush the lab."

"Thank you." She read over the paper he had given her. "Connor Aldridge bought a Ruger a little over five years ago."

"Same kind of gun that killed Teagan Reese," Santos said.

"And Arthur Erwin," Dane added.

"I think I can get a warrant with this," Ava said. "I'll talk to Sal."

The Aldridges were not home when Ava arrived. Wherever they had absconded to, they were not in a hurry to get back or answer their phones.

"Where do we even start searching in a house this size?" Metford asked, looking up at the grand staircase and the balcony that extended in front of the many rooms on the second floor.

"That's why we brought extra agents," Ava said.

"I think we could have used a few more, to be honest," Dane said.

"We have three floors and outbuildings, people," Ava announced loudly. "Let's split off into pairs and work our way through this monstrosity. And remember people, make this search count."

Metford followed her up the stairs. "We're taking the second floor, aren't we?"

"Yes. That's the most likely place to find a handgun."

"Is that some statistic you got from Ashton?"

"No, it's just logical that if Connor bought a handgun for personal protection, it would be handy when he felt most vulnerable."

"Which would be when he's in bed for the night," Metford said, finishing her thought.

"Exactly."

They reached the landing and assessed the layout. Ava pointed to the right. "Master will be one of those two. They look to be the largest."

The first room they went into was enormous and grandly decorated with expensive furniture and even more expensive art pieces, but the room had not been used in a while. A fine layer of dust had settled on the dresser and bedside tables. They searched it anyway but came up with nothing concerning a gun.

The next room looked as if someone had tossed it.

"Looks like a robbery scene," Metford said.

The bedclothes were tumbled to the center and hung to the floor on one side. A drawer on one bedside table was open and a costume necklace with big gaudy fake pearls dangled from the corner. A garishly bright blouse lay on the foot of the bed. Ava supposed it was fashioned after a Picasso painting. The closets stood open. Clothes hung half-off hangers, strewn across the floor, and several hat boxes had been tumbled into a pile in the corner of the walk-in.

"Somebody left in a hurry," Ava said. "Check the closets for any sign a gun is or was there. I'll take this one." She stepped into the far left walk-in and flipped on the overhead light.

Margueritte had some questionable fashion choices but they hadn't always been so bright and bold and garish. Looking at her dresses, Ava could follow the decline of Mrs. Aldridge's fashion sense. Some of the clothes looked as if they hadn't been worn in years. It was a fault with the very rich that they could hang on to frivolous, useless things instead of donating them so someone else might benefit from them.

Metford came to the door. "Nothing in his closet. Need help in here?"

"No. There's nothing in here either." She exited the closet and headed to the bedside table.

Metford did the same on the other side. There was nothing in either table except that fake necklace.

Kneeling, Ava lifted the corner of the covers off the floor and looked underneath the bed. "There," she said, popping her head up over the mattress to point. "On your side up next to the wall."

Metford bent and carefully retrieved a gun box. He set it on the bedside table under a lamp. "If he was going for easy to reach, he failed."

Ava came around and Metford opened the small gun box. "It's dusty and there are prints," she said. "Be careful of them."

The box was empty.

"I knew it wouldn't be that simple," he said. "Of course they took it with them."

"Let's get these prints through the system and see who they belong to." She lifted the prints and scanned them into the system remotely.

"That's one gadget I'm glad we have," Metford said.

"Me, too. I just wish it gave results faster."

"Too bad we didn't use it at the library. Maybe we'd have those results back."

She messaged Ashton about the library and Reese home prints. When he didn't reply immediately, she sent a message to the lab requesting a rush on all evidence for the Reese case.

Santos met them in the foyer. She held a portfolio out to Ava. "Found this in a box in one of the pantries off the kitchen," she said. "Thought it might be important."

"What's in it?" Metford asked as Ava took it and flipped it open.

"Information on the sponsor programs the Aldridges run. Did you see anything in here about the one they run in Fairhaven?" she asked Santos.

"No, but I didn't read everything in there either. All the ones I saw were listed in New York City and looked like a couple out in Los Angeles."

Ava and Metford exchanged a look. Los Angeles had never been mentioned either.

Ava's phone dinged with a notification. "Hit on the prints already," she said, opening the message. "Margueritte's prints are the only ones on that gun box."

"And you were just wishing for faster results upstairs," Metford said. "Guess it was granted even though it wasn't helpful."

"Yes, it was."

"How? The prints all belonged to Mrs. Aldridge. Of course, she handled the box. It's in her house. She lives here."

"But the gun was registered to her husband, and he's the one who bought it."

"And? How does that help us prove that he is the killer?"

"It doesn't. It gives us a new suspect, in my opinion. Those prints were fresh. No dust had settled over them yet. She handled that box very recently."

"So, we have a shiny new suspect to check out," he said half-heartedly. "Fantastic."

CHAPTER TWENTY-NINE

Margueritte Aldridge

A VA LEFT MESSAGES ON EVERY ALDRIDGE NUMBER SHE HAD WHILE she was still in their home. "I say we find out all we can about Margueritte while we're waiting for a return call. Maybe we can find out where they went."

Metford snorted. "Like we're expecting a return call."

"They can take their sweet time. We're here, let's see if we can find something to point us in the right direction. I know the laptops and cellphones are gone, but let's see if we can find—oh, I don't know—pictures, saved newspaper clippings. Something about their community around town. Who are their friends?"

Unfortunately, they weren't able to glean much from the frames on the walls—very few had actual photographs in them, and most of those were not of the Aldridges.

"They're so involved with this artist program, they don't keep any info about it at home?" Metford griped.

Ava stood up from a sideboard she'd been sifting through. "Where's the office?"

"The nook off the other side of the living room," Dane said, pointing to the right.

They hurried to the room and rifled through desk drawers and file cabinets. Since their warrant couldn't cover them fishing for digital information through the computer, they had to directly search by hand without overstepping bounds.

"Bingo." Ava help up a small rolodex labeled CONTACTS.

"She had it on paper?" Santos asked incredulously. "What is this, the nineties?"

"I had a hunch. Margueritte seems pretty old-fashioned. Not the type to have it on the computer," Ava said, flipping through it. The list was short. No more than ten names with contact information and only one of them was a Fairhaven number.

"Margueritte doesn't have many friends, and only one of them here in Fairhaven, it seems. A Ms. Jean Maxwell." She flipped the paper so he could see the address. "And we're going over there to speak with her."

Ava and Metford took the short drive to Jean Maxwell's house. It was a large white house styled similarly to the Aldridge estate but not nearly as large.

A woman with straight, silver hair cut into a stylish bob answered the door. She smiled with confusion. Ava explained the situation quickly, and Ms. Maxwell invited them inside.

"Are you sure she's missing? Maybe she just didn't answer the phone," Jean said. Worry etched deep lines across her forehead and at the sides of her mouth.

"That's the same thing in this business, Ms. Maxwell. Are you sure you haven't heard from her or Mr. Aldridge?"

"No, I've not. God, I hope she's all right."

"That's what we need to find out," Ava said. "Do you have any idea where she might have gone?"

"No. I don't know. She goes anywhere and everywhere. They travel, you see. They have money enough to do that, and I'm glad for her. She deserves to wake up in the morning and just decide she wants to take the weekend in Hawaii and be able to do it." Jean smiled wistfully.

"If she was upset about something, where do you think she would go?" Metford asked. "Are there any special places she liked to just get away to? Her and Mr. Aldridge together, or just her alone?"

Jean put a finger to her lips and the lines above the bridge of her nose deepened and drew downward. "The only place I can think of is New York. They have several properties there. If she's not there, I don't know where to even begin looking."

"Could you call her from your phone and see if she answers?" Ava asked. "I've left messages on all their phones and neither of them has called back."

"I will. Anything if it will help." Jean handled the cellphone like an old pro. She left a voicemail asking Margueritte to call back as soon as she got the message. Jean tried three other numbers for Margueritte and then called two for Connor. She got the voicemail each time. "I'm sorry. I'm at a loss. I just hope they're okay. Her no-good brother hasn't been around, has he?"

"Well, I didn't know anything about a brother. I don't know if he's around or not," Ava said. "Maybe we should contact him. If something is wrong, she might have called him for help." Ava did not think anything was wrong with Margueritte or Connor; not the way Jean was thinking, but it didn't hurt to let her believe that.

"No, no. If there was anything wrong, he's the last person Margueritte would call for help. Nothing but trouble, that one. Always was as a kid, and as an adult, he's even worse. I just hope he had nothing to do with her disappearance."

"I thought he was the last person she would—"

"He was jealous of Margueritte's success; of her money. All I know is that Margueritte told me Grady was in cahoots with some really bad people. Dangerous people. I think it was drugs, but she would never tell me the specifics. She thought Grady would end up right back in prison because of whatever mess he was involved with."

"And you said his name is Grady?"

"Grady Arrowood." Jean put a hand to her mouth and her eyes widened. "You don't think those drug people nabbed Margueritte and Connor, do you?"

"Why would they do that, Ms. Maxwell?" Metford asked.

"Maybe to get Grady to do something they want him to do. A what do you call it? A ... persuasion tactic?" Her eyes went wider. "Oh, no. Maybe Grady took them. He couldn't find work after being in prison, and he was always desperate for money. Maybe he is trying to get them to give him money. Wouldn't surprise me. He never was worth a tinker's damn."

Ava stood. "Thank you for talking with us, Ms. Maxwell. If you hear from either of them ..."

"Of course. I'll call you immediately."

"Thank you." Ava said as she and Metford left.

"This Grady doesn't sound like a good guy at all," Metford said as they got into the car.

"And we're going to find out for sure." Ava drove them back to the office where she immediately went to Ashton for help.

They worked together, pulling up any information about Grady they could find online and in the system. After an hour, Ava smiled at Ashton. "This is good. Thank you for helping me. I know you're stretched as thin as it gets, but you came through again. Mr. Grady Arrowood is going on the suspect list."

She went to the conference room and pinned Grady's name and information to the board. "We have a new suspect. Grady Arrowood."

"What did you find out about him?" Metford asked.

"Only that he was in prison for attempted murder with a gun. He was sentenced to twenty years, got out in less than seven. His rap sheet reads like a resume for *America's Most Wanted*, and they're all violent offences. He keeps getting out of them completely, or with just a slap on the wrist. The address he gives when he's arrested is in New York City, and it is listed in Margueritte Aldridge's name. Her name is on the lease. The building is owned by George Bosworth the Third."

"What? Are you serious?" Dane asked.

"Dead serious."

"Why would she rent a place for her brother in someone else's building?" Santos asked. "Don't the Aldridges own a bunch of properties in the city? Why not put him up in one of them if they're going to help him like that?"

"Maybe she did it because she didn't want anyone to know she was helping," Dane said.

"Yeah, like her husband," Metford said.

"You want to know the weirdest part of all this for me?" Ava asked, directing the question to Metford.

"Yeah."

"Guess who he attempted to kill that got him sent to prison with that attempted murder conviction?"

"I don't know... Margueritte, his super-wealthy and successful sister?"

"Sharelle Kim," Ava said. She watched his face as all the pieces came together in his mind.

"That's why her ear was deformed," he said.

"I bet that's why she refused to talk to you, too," Santos said.

"Yeah, she was scared to death," Dane added.

"With good reason," Ava said.

CHAPTER THIRTY

Scrutiny from Above

S AL WALKED INTO THE CONFERENCE ROOM. "TEAM, I'VE GOT SOME bad news."

Everyone turned their attention to her.

"What's going on?" Ava asked, stepping closer to look at the paper she held.

"The whole team is going to be investigated because of Russell Moore's injuries during his interview."

The room exploded in a cacophony of disbelieving, shocked, and outraged comments.

"Okay!" Sal yelled, holding her hand up to silence the team. "I understand your outrage at this; I'm not happy about it either. Unfortunately, there's nothing I can do about it. This is happening." She held out the paper to Ava.

"He had to be restrained," Ava said. "Metford and Santos were both injured by him. So was I, for that matter. We could file counter-charges for assaulting federal agents."

"Save it, Ava. Everyone, just save it for the interviews. Tell the truth. Tell exactly what happened because this is happening right now. Internal Affairs is here. They've set up in the interview room and are requesting our complete cooperation. They're aware of the pressure we're under and that we are in the middle of this investigation. They've promised to do this as quickly as possible. Metford, you're up. They asked for you to come in first." She handed him a paper. "They'll instruct you where to go afterward."

"I could instruct them where to go," he said blackly.

"Keep your temper in check, big guy."

"I always do," he said, glancing at Ava as he left the room.

The only thing that gave Ava hope about the situation was the swiftness of each interview. She was the last one called in. The other interviews had taken a little more than an hour to complete in total, and averaged about fifteen to twenty minutes for each.

Ava went in and gave all her pertinent information, what she called the vitals. She was answering to two women and two men who were expressionless. Their eyes were cold and calculating as they watched her every move even between questions. She hated the scrutiny, but what choice did she have but to go along with it?

"Special Agent James, do you agree that Special Agent Santos reacted with too much force because of her own recent situation involving—"

"No. No, I absolutely do *not* think that had any bearing on Special Agent Santos' reaction to Russell Moore attacking me and then Special Agent Metford."

The woman waited for Ava to finish and then continued in that cold monotone. "Maybe because of Special Agent Santos' recent altercation and injury, she is not fit for duty just yet. Perhaps she needs some more time to completely recuperate from the trauma."

"Santos was in the right," Ava stated coldly. "Any one of us would have done the same in her situation. There was no way around it, no other way to handle it. Special Agent Metford and I were being attacked and injured by Russell Moore. He had to be restrained. Special Agent Santos is fine for duty."

One of the men cleared his throat. "Russell Moore has serious mental impairments. His lawyer will push that he didn't know what was going on, and that you and your team took advantage of that. The lawyer will say that you and your team pressured Mr. Moore until he felt threatened and snapped. Mr. Moore is also a veteran. US Marine Corps. He has a diagnosis of PTSD from serving his country. When your fellow agents rushed into the room, Mr. Moore feared for his life and acted accordingly."

"But it wasn't acting accordingly. He attacked me, and my people ran in simply to restrain him. Mr. Moore was a murder suspect, and we had good reason to think that at the time. He's also been accused of stalking women, including Teagan Reese whose murder we were investigating at the time."

"Special Agent James, we're done for now. Just so you know, there will be severe consequences if it is found that you and your fellow agents abused a mentally impaired US veteran. The public shame will be even harder to deal with. And as for your career… I hope you have told the whole truth here today. For your sake and the sake of your team," the other man warned.

"And we will be going over all the evidence with a fine-toothed comb," the woman said.

"We will not allow such abuses of power or authority go unchecked or unpunished," the second woman added.

Biting her tongue, Ava nodded once and left the room. One of the hardest things she had done in a while was not slamming the door when she exited the interview room.

Worry knotted Ava's gut as she walked the hallway. What if IA agreed that Santos was too forceful? What if Ava seemed to be too hard on Russell Moore? It hadn't taken long to ascertain that he was mentally impaired in some fundamental way, but she had not known that in the beginning. Was she too hard on him? Was her career in jeopardy? Her freedom?

She was sure the others were asking themselves the same questions, and it would do nothing to dwell on it. The IA investigation was out of their hands.

The Teagan Reese case, however, was not.

CHAPTER THIRTY-ONE

Personal Demons

S ANTOS PACED THE LENGTH OF THE WOMEN'S RESTROOM WITH furious, quick strides. Her heart raced almost as fast as her thoughts. Stopping in front of the bank of mirrors, she stared at her own reflection.

"Stop it," she ordered herself. "You look like a scared rabbit. Are you scared? Are you gonna cry?" She sneered and turned away, disgusted with herself.

Without looking at the mirrors, she turned and ran cold water into her hands to splash on her face. She couldn't let the rest of the team see her falling apart. They already looked at her sideways sometimes. A lot, actually.

"Yeah, they look at you like you're a dried flower that might turn to dust under a little pressure," she said as she glanced up at her reflection again.

Grabbing a paper towel, she scrubbed at her face and walked back and forth again.

How could she fix it? How could she fix the problem that she had caused? Her own recent trouble had come back to haunt the entire team. It was her responsibility to do something about it.

"They'll really look at me sideways now," she muttered. "Maybe I was too rough with Russell. Maybe they're right and I'm not ready to be back on duty yet." She ran her fingers into the front of her hair and curled them, pulling the hair tight. "It was an accident. I didn't mean to hurt him. I was just trying…" She let the thought trail silent as the voice of doubt spoke up in her mind. *To hurt him? Or were you just angry because you were almost killed by a bad guy and you didn't want it happening again? Maybe you just wanted to prove to everyone that you could handle the situation, that you were fit for duty, but…*

"They'll kick me out of the Bureau, and the team won't even care because of all this trouble. What can I do? How can I make them see that I'm fine? That I can do my job? Excel at it, even?"

Suddenly, she stopped as a thought occurred to her. *Solve the Reese case, find the killer, and they'll have no choice but to see that I'm fine. Do something that even they can't do right now.*

She raised her eyes and stared at her reflection again. She didn't look like a scared rabbit anymore. She looked like a woman on a mission.

"So, why are you still in the john pacing like a teenager having a meltdown?" She grinned and left the bathroom.

Connor Aldridge killed Teagan Reese and he had gone back to New York City. Of that much, Santos was certain. Certain enough that she walked out of the building, got into her car, and set her GPS for New York City.

If the team couldn't or wouldn't make up their minds about who the killer was and go bring him to justice, she would do it. That might make up for all the hell she had brought down on them with Internal Affairs.

Before she was out of town, Ava called.

"Where are you, Santos?"

"I… I just thought I would go to Solomon Furlong's house and wait for him to arrive. I can talk to him while you and the others are following your other leads."

"Solomon Furlong's house? He might not be back until Sunday night or Monday morning."

"Or he might be home right now and we just don't know it."

"No, Ashton is monitoring inbound flights from Mexico."

"You gotta let me do this, Ava. I know all the trouble this IA thing is causing, and I know everyone blames me. Let me do this to help; to prove I'm useful and that I'm fit for duty."

"No one blames you for anything."

"Well, I do," she said. "Maybe I just need some time alone, you know?"

Ava sighed. "Okay, fine. But if you see Furlong, you call me immediately. Understood?"

"Yes. Thank you." She hung up and tossed the phone to the passenger seat.

All the way into New York, Santos planned what she would do when she found Connor Aldridge. She mentally prepared for every scenario she could think of. What she didn't plan on was finding him so quickly.

The second place she checked for him, another gallery where a party was in full swing, there he was. She parked the car and watched him. He laughed and clapped men on the back, threw back a shot, walked outside with a wide smile to welcome another small group of peers into the party. His voice was loud, his actions were exaggerated, and he wasn't even trying to blend in. Bastard wanted to stand out. Thrived on it.

Santos' heart thudded hard as anger welled in her chest. She got out of the car, crossed the street, and stood at the side of the gallery just inside the mouth of the alley. Eventually, Connor came out to the edge of the building just where he was still in the multi-colored light washing the sidewalk to greet a couple with that big, stupid smile again.

Santos stepped out between Connor and the couple. Her gun was at her side. "Connor Aldridge, you are under arrest for murder." She took a step forward, and Connor turned to run.

"Don't do it, Connor," she warned, raising the gun. "You run and I'll shoot you just like you shot Teagan. Hands up, get on your knees."

By the time he was on his knees, a crowd of artists, hopefuls, and patrons had crowded around the scene. Santos put cuffs on him, got him to his feet, and guided him to the car.

"Where are you taking me?" he asked loudly as she shoved him into the backseat.

She slammed the door and got in hers.

"I said, where are you taking me?" he demanded.

"Back to Fairhaven to answer for killing Teagan Reese. Now, shut up, if you know what's good for you."

Connor screamed, pleaded, threatened, and offered bribes all the way back to Fairhaven.

"I can't believe this miscarriage of justice has been allowed to happen," he said.

Santos had stopped responding to him a hundred miles back. Ava called her phone, and she warned Connor to keep it down.

"Hello?"

"Hey, any updates about Furlong? Hadn't heard from you in a while."

"Hello!?" Connor screamed. "I said I'm going to sue you, your boss, the entire Federal Bureau of Investigation for this."

"Santos, who's that screaming?"

Santos gave Ava the highlights and was summarily surprised when Ava's response was shock and then outrage.

"You went rogue, Santos!" she yelled. "Do you have any idea what you've done?! Dammit, get him back here. Now!" Ava hung up.

As Santos led Connor inside, he shouted about how and who he was going to sue, what charges he would lay against them, and that no one on the team would have a snowball's chance of ever working in law enforcement again. Not even as meter maids.

Ava met them in the hallway and tried to quiet Connor. She pulled Santos to the side. "Did you at least Mirandize him?"

Santos floundered. "I don't know. I can't remember."

Connor leaned over with a gleam in his eye. "She absolutely did not, and there are dozens of witnesses to that fact."

Ava Mirandized him quickly. "Connor Aldridge, you are a suspect in the murder of Teagan Reese and the disappearances of Brad, Penny, and Thomas Reese. We are going to hold you for questioning."

She motioned for Santos to take him to holding. "And then get back here."

Just as Santos led Connor out of sight, Sal came from the elevator. "Who was that yelling? What's going on now?" she asked Ava.

Exhaling deeply, Ava stepped into Sal's office and motioned for her to follow.

"You're inviting me into my own office? How very cordial of you."

Ava shut the door. "You might need to sit down for this one, Sal."

"Ah, shit." She thumped into her chair. "Hit me with it. What's happened?"

"Santos happened."

Ava explained what had happened as best as she could with her limited information. The silence that followed was more stressful than any showdown with a crazed gunman. When it was broken, it was only a little better.

Sal held up a hand toward Ava. "I don't want to hear whatever excuse you're going to make, or try to make, on her behalf. You're in enough hot water because you're lead on this case. You're the agent in charge of the team, Ava. How could you let her go to New York?"

"I didn't. I didn't know she was going to New York."

"So, what, a team member just goes off without reporting to you, me, anyone, and does whatever the hell she feels like?"

Ava looked down and shook her head. "No. She was gone for a long time after the IA interviews were over. Dane said she had gone to the restroom, and we all figured she was just trying to get herself together. I finally called after I saw she wasn't in there. She said she wanted to go to Solomon Furlong's to await his arrival and speak with him. She said she needed to do that to feel better about what had just happened here."

"No, no. Just stop. Where is your head?" She shot from her seat. "You know what? Never mind. I don't care where it is. Do you know what has possibly just happened to this case? She didn't even Mirandize him, Ava. She went rogue. You will be written up, but she..." Sal took a deep breath, closed her eyes for a moment, and then walked toward the door. "She's done. I can't risk any more trouble for this unit. I won't stand for this kind of behavior."

"I read him his rights, Sal. I did it already. I told him he's a suspect in the murder of Teagan Reese. We found enough at his house to make him a suspect." She bit her lip. That wasn't the truth. Not exactly.

"What you found at his house was a big bunch of nothing to hold him for!" Sal yelled.

"We didn't find anything to clear him either. The gun is missing."

"Stop. I want to talk to Santos immediately." She opened the door and Ava stepped in front of her.

"Please, Sal. The team needs her. She made a mistake. We all make mistakes. We were looking for Connor Aldridge, but she went and got him, brought him back here. Now, thanks to her, we have him in the holding cell waiting to be interrogated. And, just maybe, we can put this case to bed and bring those kids and their father home."

Sal shifted from one foot to the other while myriad emotions played out on her face. "I want to talk to her. I have to. You know I can't let this go."

"Just like the rest of us, she'll learn from her mistake. She won't do it again, and if she does, you can take my badge, too." Ava's chest tightened. Had she really just offered to put her own career on the chopping block to save Santos when she had been so worried only a little while before?

"Doesn't work that way."

"I'll go get her." Ava ducked out of the room and hurried to find Santos before Sal did. Having been in her own bad headspace for months, she thought she could understand why Santos did what she did. Before Sal got hold of her, though, Ava wanted to warn her.

Santos was pacing in an interview room and biting her lower lip so hard it looked close to bleeding.

"Sal wants to talk to you," Ava said.

"God, she's canning me, isn't she?"

"She's mad, Santos. Very mad. Can you blame her?"

Santos shook her head. "I'm sorry, Ava. I forgot. I shouldn't have forgotten to read him his rights. Such a rookie move."

"That's what you think this is about? You forgetting to Mirandize Connor?"

Santos stopped and looked at her as if she'd been slapped. Ava witnessed the realization bloom on her face.

"That's right. The whole thing is a problem because you went rogue; you just did what you thought and didn't bother running it by anyone. You jeopardized this whole case, the safety of the kids and Brad, Connor Aldridge's rights have been infringed upon, and why? We don't even know for sure if he's the killer. You best brace for impact because Sal is demanding to talk to you now. I told her you'd never do anything like this again. Ever." She motioned for Santos to get a move on. "I said if you did, she could take my badge, too, so remember that, and don't do anything like this again."

Santos hesitated. "You said that?"

"I did. Not my brightest moment, I know. You're a good agent who's been through some shit. Me, too, you know." She stopped at Sal's closed door and put a hand on Santos' shoulder. "I think we just need to remember to wash it off after we get through it."

Santos knocked on the door and went in after Sal called out.

Ava headed to get her file together so she could interrogate Connor.

CHAPTER THIRTY-TWO

Interrogation of Connor Aldridge

AVA STARTED THE INTERVIEW BY APOLOGIZING FOR THE WAY HE was brought in even though she didn't really care. It's not like he had been pistol-whipped and hog-tied. And he had run from them, regardless of what he might say, and he and his wife had actively been ignoring phone calls.

"I've got nothing to hide. You already know about the affair and that I was going to help Teagan ... uh ... Miss Reese get back into the art scene. What else do you need from me? I would like to get this cleared up and get out of here without alerting the press."

"Yes, it does tend to tarnish one's reputation a bit when they're a suspect in a murder case, doesn't it?" Ava opened the file. "Tell me again about your affair with the deceased, Mr. Aldridge."

He did, and his story had not changed.

"Refresh my memory, why did you kill her?" Ava asked in a conversational tone.

"I didn't kill her. I had no reason to kill her."

She put the autopsy photo on the table that showed both bullet holes. "One in the head, one in the heart. Ever see what the exit wound looks like, Mr. Aldridge?"

Tears shimmered in his eyes, and when Ava put down the next photo showing the exit wound, he closed his eyes and sobbed.

"I didn't do that to her. Stop showing me those. Put them away."

"Of course. I didn't mean to upset you. I just wanted you to know what happened to a woman you were having an affair with."

He opened his eyes, anger flaring in them. "I screwed her, I didn't shoot her!" he bellowed.

"If you didn't do it, why is your gun missing?"

The anger fizzled and puzzlement replaced it. "My gun? What gun?"

"The Ruger LC9 that was supposed to be in the gun box under your bed at your Fairhaven house, Mr. Aldridge."

"That gun? I don't know. The last time I held that thing was right after I bought it five years ago. I took it to the practice range. After that, I put it in the box and put that under the bed. I'd honestly forgotten about it until now."

"It was purchased a little over five years ago." She showed him a copy of the sale from the store. "And now it's missing. You conveniently forgot you owned a gun, huh? I just can't believe that, Mr. Aldridge."

"It's the truth. I bought it back when I thought I might need it, and then I forgot about it. Jesus, it was under the bed all this time?"

"I don't know, but that's certainly where we found the empty box. Now, why don't you tell me where the gun is?"

He spread his hands, palm-up. "I don't know where it is."

"It's the same kind of gun that killed Teagan Reese and Arthur Erwin. It's got fresh fingerprints on the box, and the gun is missing. Doesn't look good for you."

"Arthur Erwin. Who the hell is that?"

"The second victim. Homeless man who was shot dead only a block from the library after Teagan was killed."

"I think it's time for me to have a lawyer, Agent James. I'm done talking."

There was a knock at the door, and Ava took her folder as she walked out. Dane stood outside. "What's up?" Ava asked.

"It's Mrs. Aldridge. She's here and she's kicking up hell demanding to see him."

"I'll handle it. Thanks. He lawyered up, by the way."

"Got it."

Ava followed the sound of Mrs. Aldridge to the front where she was demanding that someone take her to her husband. She was so mad that she was almost screeching.

"Mrs. Aldridge," Ava said, motioning for her to step into an alcove that offered little privacy.

"Where's my husband, Agent?"

"He's asked for a lawyer, and you can't see him right now. I'm sorry."

"You're not, but you will be. I took a flight down as soon as I heard what happened to him. I want to speak to your supervisor, superintendent, or whoever your boss is."

Ava stood and walked out without a word to get Sal. She returned moments later with Sal.

"Mrs. Aldridge," Sal said, extending a hand, which Margueritte didn't take. "I'm sorry, but Special Agent James is right. You can't speak with your husband just yet, but we're working on it. He's requested his lawyer, and we're just playing the waiting game right now."

"I already spoke to our lawyer on my way here. You best believe he is on his way. He is going to have a field day with this charade. You can't mar a good man's name and reputation like this and get away with it. Murder? Are you all insane?"

"I understand how upsetting this must be, Mrs. Aldridge, but rest assured that we are doing things by the book. We're just trying to find out who killed an innocent woman. If it wasn't your husband, there's nothing to worry about." She looked at her watch. "I have a meeting, so I'll leave you in capable hands."

Margueritte scoffed at Sal's retreating form, and then at Ava. "None of you know what you're doing."

CHAPTER THIRTY-THREE

Another Flip

"**M**RS. ALDRIDGE, WOULD YOU LIKE TO GO TO A ROOM THAT'S A little more comfortable? And private?" Ava asked

"I thought you were going to let me stand out here for-ever with nowhere to even sit. That's the first decent thing you've done, Agent." She whipped past Ava into the hallway and then stopped, realizing she didn't know where to go.

"It's just this way." Ava led her to a small room with a little table, four chairs, and a small sofa set. It was the room where they usually delivered bad news to families of victims that didn't survive. "Please, have a seat and make yourself comfortable. Can I offer you something to drink? Water, coffee, a soda?"

"No, I'm fine." Margueritte placed her purse on the table and sat rigidly on the edge of the seat. "Connor would never hurt anyone. Never.

I don't even know how you could think such a thing about a man who does so much good for this community."

Ava pulled out a report and laid it on the table. "Maybe we're wrong." She slid the paper to Margueritte.

The woman looked at it as if it might be poisonous, and then her gaze fell on her own name at the top of the paper. "What's this?" She dragged the paper to her and read it. "My fingerprints were found in my own house? How did you even get in without permission? You have falsely imprisoned a man for a murder he didn't commit, hauled him across state lines illegally, and you've been in our house lifting my fingerprints as if to accuse me of something? Insane, I tell you. Now, how did you gain entry because if you broke anything—"

"I'm pretty sure the broken lock on your front doors is covered under the warrant to search the premises for a murder weapon."

"What?" She blanched. "Murder weapon. I told you, Connor did not kill that woman."

"Can you tell me where the gun is, then?"

Stammering, Margueritte asked, "What gun? We don't own a gun. I don't believe in them."

"Ah, I've heard that so many times. You wouldn't believe me if I told you the number. Now, where's the gun, Margueritte? If we have it, we can test it, rule it out, and your husband is free to go home. If not, we have to hold him."

"I told you, I don't know anything about a gun."

"Funny because the gun box under your bed is where these prints were lifted from. Did you take that gun, Margueritte?"

She scowled. "I won't say anything else until our lawyer gets here."

"Oh, you're not being questioned as a suspect, but if you clam up, we have enough evidence right here to put you on the list, if you prefer."

Margueritte clamped her mouth shut and looked to the door.

"You don't have to say anything, but there are other lives at stake here. Remember Brad, Penny, and Thomas? We still haven't located them. If you don't talk to me now, and it's later discovered that you did know something, you can be charged with several crimes. Everything from impeding a federal investigation to murder charges if those three are not found alive. If anything happens to any of them, or if it already has, and you lie to me, I'll make it my life's mission to send you away forever."

Margueritte fidgeted, floundered, and started to speak several times but ultimately closed her mouth before she could. Fetching around for something to say that might save her ass was not a good look on the powerful, tightly-wound Mrs. Aldridge.

"Go ahead, Mrs. Aldridge. I'm all ears," Ava said, sliding the paper back and forth under her finger.

"I don't know anything. I didn't even know we had a gun. That's all I'm saying."

"I know you're lying, though. And so do you. You definitely knew about the gun." She tapped the fingerprint analysis. "This proves it. If you're lying to protect your husband or yourself or someone else, I don't know, but you aren't doing yourself any favors."

"I want to be left alone until our lawyer gets here."

Ava went to the door. "If you need anything, I'll be around."

CHAPTER THIRTY-FOUR

New Evidence

ASHTON FOUND AVA IN THE CONFERENCE ROOM PORING OVER EVI-dence. She looked up when he said her name.

"Please tell me you have something solid," she said, holding out her hand for the report he had.

"I hope it's solid enough. It's the forensics report on that bone fragment we found at the library."

Ava took the paper but didn't read it. Instead, she waited for him to supply the information. "Yeah, what about it?"

"They said it's a deer bone fragment that most likely came from the handle of a hunting knife. You've seen that type of knife, right?"

"Are you implying I have a bone-handled hunting knife?" She tried to grin but the humor of it fell flat for her.

"You might. You go fishing and hiking. Outdoorsy woman like that might have one or two hunting knives."

"No, I don't, but I have seen them before. I've also seen pocketknives with bone handles."

"Not the same thing, and apparently not the same type and grade of bone according to the report." He pointed to the report. "It's all in there, so I won't bore you with the details."

"I appreciate that."

"Anyway, they said the piece of bone probably broke off when the handle impacted something hard and sharp."

Ava whipped her head toward the board. "Like the corner of a librarian's desk." She went to the board and flipped the pictures up until she found the one she was looking for.

"Yes, that would qualify as hard and sharp." Ashton took the photo and squinted at it. "I'll pull the images up on the screen so we can see them more clearly."

Ava took the picture back and squinted at it. If the knife had been in play during the murder, where had it gone? And why wasn't it used?

The pictures came up and Ashton scrolled to the relevant set. Ava stood a few feet from the large screen and pointed to the desk.

"Right there. Can you zoom in?"

"Of course, silly mortal." He grinned and zoomed in on the desk.

"Now, come help me search for any marks."

He walked closer and leaned toward the screen. "I think it might be this one to her left." He put a finger on the screen just below the corner.

"I see it. Can you zoom more or will it decrease the quality?"

"Pfft." He went back to the computer, and within seconds, the corner had doubled in size and was rendering.

Layers of crisp, sharp color dropped over the image of the blurry desk until it was so clear that it seemed almost as if it were in the room with them.

"That corner has definitely sustained damage on the apex," Ashton said, nodding. "Want me to print that?"

"Yes. Add it to the board, save the image as a new file." Ava looked over the crime scene notes. "Right under that corner is where the bone fragment was found."

"It begs the question, where is the knife now?" Ashton said.

"And if it was there during the attack, why wasn't it used?" She stood in front of the screen again. "Zoom out so we can see the whole scene again."

"What are we looking for? There was no knife at the scene."

"I know. I'm just trying to figure out why it was there and not used. If a killer bothered to pull a knife, why would he ultimately shoot the victim instead?"

"Maybe the victim fought back, knocked the knife from his hand. That's when it struck the corner and broke off that fragment we found."

"Why not just pick it back up and finish the job as intended?"

"Because …" He squinted at the screen and rubbed his chin. "Because it slid somewhere he couldn't reach it. Under a shelf, or under the desk."

"Or some of the other furniture. Right." She sat in a chair and swung her hands at the air in a downward arc several times, trying differing angles of descent.

"Uh, what are we doing?"

"I'm trying to put myself in the attack. If someone came at me from the side or back with a knife, and I had no professional training, how would I engage?"

"First off, you wouldn't 'engage.' You would react."

"Right. Like if a bee flies toward your face, you just instinctually swat it, not thinking about what happens after or where it will land."

"Exactly."

"Get a pencil and come at me from behind like it's a knife and you're going to stab me."

He hesitated.

"Now, Ashton. Come on, we don't have all day."

He did as asked.

The first strike sent the pencil-knife flying wildly to her left. The second strike sent it straight up and it fell on her lap. Several attempts later, Ashton called a halt.

"Maybe she wasn't sitting when he approached, and how do we know he came from the side? Maybe he came from behind and put the knife to her throat. Like such." He stepped behind Ava and reached around to place the pencil at her throat with his left hand.

Ava grabbed his wrist and pushed it downward as she stepped back. The pencil hit the edge of the table.

"That's it. She didn't completely panic and react wildly," Ava said. "She was standing, or she stood when she realized he was behind her, and this is the result."

"Once the knife was out of his hand, she turned to the other side and grabbed that salt lamp to use as a weapon," Ashton said, chuckling as they moved around the end of the table.

Ava made a break for the door and Ashton swiftly cut her off.

"She hit him with the lamp," Ava said, mock-swinging at his face.

Ashton stumbled backward and reached as if for his gun. "Seeing he was about to lose the victim who had now seen his face and disarmed him once, the attacker pulled a gun and shot her in the head. She fell. He shot her in the heart."

"And the rest is in the reports," Ava said. "That was good, Ash. I didn't realize you could pretend so well. Never thought you techies had much in the imagination department."

"Are you kidding? We have to have great imaginations."

"Why?"

"We get through our days by pretending we're saving the world from the infinite threat of annihilation. We are superheroes in our own minds."

"Seriously?"

"No, Ava. I was making a joke."

She laughed. "I knew that." She noted the new scenario on a sheet of paper and put it on the board. "What about the prints? Did anyone ever get a report on them?"

"You mean the hundreds of sets from the library?"

"Yeah, that would be the ones."

"I will check, but don't hold your breath. That was a lot of prints to run." He worked at the computer for a few minutes. "One set returned a hit. There's a note that says you told them to flag the report if any turned up to be Grady Arrowood's prints."

"Only one set came back as his?"

"Yes. Lifted from a book on Mrs. Reese's desk."

Ava went to the computer and read the report. She smiled and clapped Ashton on the shoulder. "This is good news. No, this is great news."

"Why is that great? I feel like I've missed some fundamental things in this case."

"You did, but it's been moving fast. Grady is a convict. He's a repeat offender on violent crimes, and the system just keeps spitting him back out onto the streets. And, he just happens to be Margueritte Aldridge's brother."

Going to the board again, Ava wrote Margueritte's name on a piece of paper and added it to the suspect list. On another, she put Grady's name. "Time to get all our little duckies in one pond."

She left Ashton standing by the computer looking confused.

Sal agreed that they should send someone to arrest Grady at his New York City address. After making several phone calls and following all protocols, Sal nodded.

"It's done. Local PD will pick him up. I'm sending Agents Stinson and Cash up to bring him back. Chief approved use of the plane, so, it shouldn't be more than two hours before Mr. Grady Arrowood is here."

"Thanks."

"Glad to help," Sal said. "I want to find those kids and their father; bring them home safe. The sooner, the better."

Ava agreed fully. "They'll let us know if they find the gun, right? They will search the place for it, won't they?"

"Stop worrying, Ava. You're giving me ulcers. You can't do it all; you can't micro-manage every aspect of the case. Sometimes, you have to trust others to do their jobs and do them well."

"Without that gun, though…"

"Grady might not be the killer, so the gun might do you no good."

"At least if I have it, I can use it as leverage to get one of them to talk. I'll take a good old-fashioned confession or finger-pointing session that leads me to the truth."

CHAPTER THIRTY-FIVE

Brother Grady

THE ALDRIDGES' LAWYER SHOWED UP AND WENT IMMEDIATELY TO his top priority client—Mr. Aldridge.

Ava went to see Margueritte.

"I told you, I'm not talking until the lawyer is finished with Connor and he can sit in on our conversation, Agent. You're wasting your time."

"I thought you'd want to know that you've been upgraded to a suspect on our list."

"That's preposterous. I've never heard such a ridiculous thing in my life." She cackled and motioned to herself. "Do I really look like someone capable of murder?"

"It's not about looks, Mrs. Aldridge. It's about evidence, and we have enough to make you an official suspect. We need to interview you, so we're going to put you in an official interview room. Come with me, please."

"I most certainly will not. I'm staying right where I am." She crossed her hands in her lap and turned her head to the side.

"Mrs. Aldridge, this can go one of two ways, and it's your choice, but if I were you, I'd take the easy way." She motioned for her to move.

"What's wrong with this room? I don't need to be in an interrogation room if I am not going to speak with you."

Ava dangled her cuffs. "I can put these on you and march you through the place for everyone to see, but in my opinion, silver clashes with your outfit."

Margueritte made a displeased sound in her throat and stood. After snatching her purse from the table, she hoisted her head high, pulled her shoulders back, and walked out past Ava.

Around the corner and down the corridor, there were several doors on either side marked as interview rooms. Connor was in the fourth on the left side. Ava put Margueritte in the first room on the right. She wanted to be able to walk Grady past Margueritte's room so she could see that he was in custody.

"Right here, Mrs. Aldridge." Ava made sure the vertical blinds were open and pushed aside. "There you go. Now you won't feel like you're in prison. You can see what's going on out there in the corridor. I'll be back in a while; just make yourself comfortable." She smiled, and it was not returned.

Ninety minutes later, Grady Arrowood arrived. Cash and Stinson escorted him toward the interview rooms, and Ava jogged to catch up with them. "I need him in there. Interview D."

"Got it," Cash said.

"I got a D for you, Sweetheart," Grady said, blowing her a kiss.

Stinson yanked up on the cuffs and Grady went up on his toes. "Okay, okay, I get it. Ease up."

Ava let them take Grady past Margueritte's window and then she walked by. She glanced in at Margueritte as she passed. The stoic mask completely crumbled, and Ava saw the horror on the woman's face. That was a good sign.

"Need one of us to stay?" Cash asked.

Ava looked at Grady. His cuffs were anchored to the bar on the table. "No, but thanks for the offer. I think I can handle him."

"Woo-hoo, I wish you would handle me." Grady laughed and bucked in his chair, making lewd gestures.

Stinson stepped back into the room, but Ava put her hand on his chest to stop him. "Not worth it, Stinson. He's trying to get a reaction. Just go; I've got this."

Stinson and Cash left, and Ava shut the door behind them. She flipped the blinds closed and turned on the In-Use sign so no one would walk in unannounced.

"Ooh, goody. A little privacy, huh?"

Ava dropped the file on the table. "Get over it, Arrowood. You know why you're here, and you know how serious it is."

"Nah, why don't you get me up to speed on all this, sweetheart."

Ava ignored his attempt to get a rise from her and gave him the rundown on everything.

"And what does any of that have to do with me?" he asked.

"Well, your prints were found at the crime scene, Grady. I'd say that's pretty damning."

"Not at all. I grew to love books and reading when I was in the pen last time. I was just there looking for a book to borrow."

"From the librarian's desk?"

"She was going to check it out for me." He smiled and remained smug. "Good luck trying to make that stick."

"Why were you in the library in Fairhaven when you live in New York City?"

"Now, that is a good question." He pretended to study on it for a second. "Oh, I was visiting friends, and just saw the library and thought I'd stop in and see what all the fuss was about."

Ava queued the video footage from the hardware store. She hit play and pointed to the screen. "Is that you, Grady? Didn't know about that camera, did you?"

He narrowed his eyes at the screen and shrugged. "That could be one of about a million men. But it's not me. Why would I go to the library after hours?"

"How do you know it's after hours?"

"Well, look. The place is dead empty. No cars, only a few lights burning. You know, the city should really invest in some good lighting and cameras for that place. Make it a hell of a lot safer."

Ava clicked off the video and stared at him. He was so cool and calm about it. Had he been let off so many times that he thought this time would be the same? Minor punishment for a major crime.

"You're just a real tough case, aren't you, Grady?"

"You've got me chained like one, don't you?"

"Yeah, I guess we do. Hey, guess who you walked by out there in the hallway on your way to this room?"

"The Pope."

"Margueritte Aldridge. Oh, what's that look about? She's your sister, isn't she?"

"Okay, all right, so maybe I know a little something about this librarian's death, but that don't make me guilty of murder."

Ava sat back in her seat. "Now you know something about it? That much of a change just because you learned your sister is here. That's interesting. She's a suspect, too. So is her husband."

Sweat glistened at his hairline, and the smug expression was gone. His eyes darted ceaselessly, and he shifted in his seat.

Ava fanned her face with the file. "Getting a little warm in here to you? I think I'm going to go talk to your sister for a while now. Not getting anything but smartass comments from you." She stood.

"No, wait. I'll tell you what I know. Just..." He motioned crudely for her to take her seat.

She sat. "Better talk fast, Grady. I don't have much patience left."

"Margueritte found out her old man was boning the librarian. She probably flew into a jealous rage." He jabbed an accusatory finger at the air. "That's what happened. I would bet everything I own on that. Margie probably killed the librarian."

"Everything you own? What would that be, Grady? The clothes you're wearing? Way I understand it, you've had a little trouble finding and holding a job since you got out of prison." She leaned in and lowered her voice. "You don't own anything, do you? It all belongs to your rich, successful sister. The same sister who is ashamed of having you for a brother. The sister who hides you away from her peers, friends, and even her husband. Tell me, does Connor even know you exist?"

A tic started up in his cheek, and he gave her a death glare. "I told you what I know. She found out Connor was cheating with that librarian chick and she probably killed the woman."

"That *librarian chick* has a name. Teagan Reese. Now, why would you think Margueritte would be capable of killing Teagan? Your sister just doesn't strike me as the type to lose control and do something like that."

"You don't know her. She can go into blind rages. She told me about the affair, and she threatened to kill that—Teagan—then. I talked her out of it."

"She threatened to kill Teagan, and you talked her out of it."

"Yeah."

"If she told you all that, she would have come to you if she had gone through with it."

He shook his head.

"Yes, because you are the only criminal element in her life. She has been very careful to make sure everyone and everything around her, in her life, is the opposite of you and your lifestyle. It's like she was trying to forget about you, the no-good, troublemaking brother that had plagued her all her life."

"That's not true." A vein pulsed in his forehead. "She threatened that woman, and she was serious about it. I'm telling you that she is probably the one who committed the murder."

"And if I go ask her about all this?" Ava motioned to him. "Is she going to break down and admit it?"

"I don't know. I doubt it. Would you?"

"I am not a killer, Grady, but you are. Or, you tried to be. Remember Sharelle Kim several years ago?"

His face flushed deep red and he broke eye contact.

"You tried to kill her. With a gun. Margueritte, on the other hand, has a sparkling reputation and nothing but one speeding ticket on her record."

He dropped his head. "I paid for that mistake. I did my time."

"Part of it. A very small part, but we won't get into that. What about Brad and the kids, Grady? Where are they?"

"Who?"

"Don't play games. We're way past that. Where are they?"

"I don't know. You'll have to go ask Sister Margie; she's the killer."

"Do you have proof of that?"

He shrugged and concentrated on his hands.

Ava asked more questions, but he remained quiet.

CHAPTER THIRTY-SIX

Sister Margie

"MRS. ALDRIDGE, JUST SO YOU KNOW, YOU DON'T HAVE TO SAY anything until your lawyer decides you are a high enough priority to come in here. Also, just so you know, it might be in your best interest to reconsider."

"Why would I do that?"

"Did you see who walked by your window a few minutes ago?"

Margueritte swallowed hard and averted her gaze, but her shoulders and back remained ramrod straight.

"It was your long-lost brother, Grady Arrowood. He's just in the next interview room."

After clearing her throat, Margueritte made eye contact with Ava, and though it was a tenuous thing, she held it long enough to seem unflustered. "What do you want, a gold star for your efforts at digging up my dirty secret? Can't choose your family, Agent. God knows if I could, I would have chosen almost anyone else for a brother. He's been the bane of my existence since I drew my first breath."

"Wow, the love. I mean, it's thick between you two, isn't it? The way you talk about each other amazes me. And yet, you give him everything he has. And even though you do, he accuses you of cold-blooded murder. That was with no prompting from me, mind you."

"He did not. That's ridiculous."

"He did. I assure you, he most certainly did. And all I did was tell him that you were here and that you were a suspect. It was like punching a hole in a dam. Just, whoosh. Spilled it all in one go."

Margueritte's face turned ashen, and she pulled her clasped hands to her stomach.

"Where are Brad and Penny and Thomas? I'm only asking because Grady said for me to go ask Sister Margie; she's the killer."

Margueritte's head snapped up and she sneered. "I hate it when he calls me that. Little bastard always called me Sister Margie when he had thrown me under the bus for something I didn't do and he knew he would get away with it."

"He seemed adamant that you knew where the remaining Reeses were. Just tell me, and we can sort all this out after they're safe at home again."

"I don't know where they are. I don't know because I didn't have a part in any of this. I didn't have a part in it because I'm not a killer," she said in a loud, stern voice.

"With the evidence we have, you'll both go to jail unless we find out what we need to know and unless you tell me something I can use." She tapped the folder. "Your prints all over that box."

"They could've gotten on that box years ago. It's my house. I touch things. That's what we do in our own homes; we touch things."

"The prints were fresh." She opened the folder and took out the report. "It's all in there, if you want to read over it again. The box is in the lab now. They're checking the interior for prints as well."

"They can't get prints from fake velvet."

"Really?"

"I'm not stupid, Agent. They can't get prints from that sort of material."

"You're not stupid, but you're not real smart either."

Margueritte looked confused.

"How did you know the interior of the box was lined with fake velvet unless you knew about the box? That means you did know about the gun, and you lied to a federal agent. We have Grady's prints at the library; your prints on the gun box; a missing Ruger LC9, which is the weapon used to kill two people here in Fairhaven over the last week. I think you better start talking."

Margueritte's mouth moved but nothing came out. She stood, one hand on her hip, the other across her midsection as if she might hurl.

"Mrs. Aldridge, you found out about Connor's affair with Teagan, and that's why she was executed, wasn't it?"

Margueritte's eyes bulged and she settled back onto the chair. "He was what?"

"You knew about the affair."

"No, I... Connor would never cheat on me. I'd know if he did something like that."

"The game is over. Grady told me how you went to him when you found out. He also said you threatened to kill Teagan even then, but he talked you out of it."

"That's—"

"Ridiculous. Right. You've said that a lot, but it's not ridiculous. You found out about the affair, you killed Teagan, and your brother helped you stage the scene, right?"

After several minutes of back and forth, Ava pulled out the crime scene photos. "That's what he helped you do, isn't it?"

"I don't have to respond to that. I won't. I refuse."

Ava's phone rang. It was Sal.

"You'll want to see this report from Grady's place in New York," Sal said.

"On my way." Ava hung up and went to the door. "Think about it. You want to spend time in prison because you won't roll on your brother, that's up to you. I'm happy to see both of you in jail for this." She left the room and headed to Sal's office.

CHAPTER THIRTY-SEVEN

The Final Round

M ETFORD STOOD OUTSIDE SAL'S DOOR TO HEAR WHAT WAS GOING
on.

"We've got him," Ava said. She held the papers out to Metford. "We really got him."

"I want to be in the room with you. You went in alone with Russell Moore and it went south in a hurry."

"I've got him restrained. Cuffed to the table."

Metford shook his head. "No, I want to be in there, too. This involves me."

"All right. Fine by me."

They went to Grady's room.

"Oh, bring in backup, did you? I was talking; there was no need to bring him." Grady yanked against the cuffs, rattling them loudly against the bar. "Not like I'm going to attack you."

"Mr. Arrowood, the team at your apartment building found something very interesting," Metford said. "It's an old two-tone pickup registered in your name."

"It was in the parking garage," Ava said.

"The report said it looked like the driver hit something with the front of it," Metford said. "Know anything about that?"

Grady smiled. "Nope."

"It also had a bullet hole on the passenger side of the windshield. That bullet came from Special Agent Metford's gun, Mr. Arrowood," Ava said.

"Well, somebody call the cops. I wanna make a report, file a complaint, file charges," Grady said with a twisted grin.

"Your prints were all over the truck—inside and out—and your prints and DNA were on the coffee cup in the seat," Ava said.

"Oh, and just so there's no way you can get out of this one," Metford said, "my bullet was fished out of the seat."

Grady rolled his eyes theatrically. "When did you go shooting up my truck, young buck?"

"When you ran us off the road. Do you know how much trouble you're in for that?" Metford asked. "That could be considered attempted murder of two federal agents. That's just the start of a long, detailed list of charges being written against you right now."

Grady dropped his head, scooted to slouch in his seat, and laughed.

"Something funny about this?" Ava asked.

"If you coulda seen the looks on your faces when I pushed you into that ditch." He bellowed laughter.

"How did you know we were on the case so soon?" Ava asked. "I assume that's why you ditched us that way."

"A little media birdy told me. It was splashed all over the news when the FBI stepped in and took over the case. How could I not know?"

"Why did you kill Teagan Reese, Mr. Arrowood?" Metford asked.

"Was it because she laughed and turned down your juvenile, perverted advances like the ones you pulled on me earlier?" Ava asked. "She hurt your pride, so you got revenge and killed her for it."

Grady laughed and acted as if he wiped a tear from his eye as he shook his head. "Is that what dear Sister Margie told you? *She* is the killer. I don't even know Teagan, let alone Brad, Penny, or asthmatic little Thomas."

"Mrs. Aldridge says you're the killer," Ava said. "Quite frankly, I believe it was both of you."

"And we're all entitled to our little opinions, aren't we, Agent?"

"We have your fingerprints at the scene of the murder. We have your truck, which was used to commit a felony. All the evidence points toward you." She stood. Metford followed suit. "If you want Margie to walk free, keep silent." She walked to the door and waited for Metford to step out before adding. "With your record, who do you think the jury will believe?" She stepped out and closed the door.

"Let him ponder that for a while, eh?" Metford said.

"I just wanted to punch his smug, laughing face. Can you believe the nerve? I need to talk to Sal." She left without waiting for a reply.

CHAPTER THIRTY-EIGHT

Realization

"WHAT'S GOING ON, AVA?" SAL ASKED, HANDING HER A CUP OF coffee. "You okay?"

"It's this case. These suspects. It's driving me up a wall." She sipped the coffee. "Thank you for the coffee. I feel like I need to borrow the heart paddles from the ambulance, though."

"I bet. We're all feeling the pressure and lack of sleep, but we knew what we signed up for with the career choice."

"Grady is pointing the finger at Margueritte and vice versa. It's like the world's worst case of sibling rivalry. He knows he's busted for running us off the road, but still denies killing Teagan Reese. Margueritte is sticking to her story of innocence. She even tried to get me to believe that she didn't know about the affair or the gun."

"She says she didn't know the gun was missing?"

"No, she denies knowing there was even a gun in the house. Says she doesn't believe in guns."

"Maybe she didn't know about it."

"She lied and then stuck her foot in it." Ava related the whole back-and-forth she'd had about the gun and the box, the velvet and the prints.

"And neither of them admits to knowing where Brad and the kids are. Mr. Arrowood said he didn't know Teagan, Brad, Penny, or asthmatic little Thomas," Ava said, imitating his tone and body language. "Or asthmatic little Thomas," she repeated.

Sal tilted her head questioningly. "His exact words?"

"Yes, they are. That lying bastard." Ava set the coffee on Sal's desk and stood. "We never released that detail to the press. He wouldn't know Thomas has asthma unless—"

"He had been around them." Sal pointed to the door. "Go, but tread carefully. You don't want him to clam up or lawyer up before we find out where Brad and those babies are."

"I'll be careful."

Ava opened Margueritte's door and stepped inside. "Mrs. Aldridge, I understand that you had nothing to do with Teagan's death, and you've expressed how horrible you feel over the tragedy, but I need to know what really happened. Those kids are out there somewhere. So is their father. We need to bring them home. His wife, their mother, is gone. Nothing can change that, but if there's even the tiniest hope that they are alive, I need to know."

"I do feel horrible for those kids. And their father. I wish I could help, but I don't know anything about this. I didn't know about the affair." Tears twinkled at the corners of her eyes. "I didn't know my husband owned a gun. And I don't know how my fingerprints got on that box."

"But you do know, Margueritte. You do. You knew what fabric was inside that box. The interior padding is cut out so the gun fits snugly into the depression. If you opened the box and it was empty, you would still know it was a gun case. Is that what happened? Did you open it and the gun was already gone?"

"I wish I could be of more help, Agent."

Ava stopped at the door. "Think about those children, Mrs. Aldridge. They must be terrified, hungry, thirsty, and they don't even know what's going on or why. They don't deserve this."

The crocodile tears dripped but no more followed. "I don't deserve this, Agent." Her voice didn't crack, and all the strength had returned.

Ava thought it had never left. Margueritte had only pretended to be broken up about the case. She was as cold-hearted and self-centered as her brother.

Grady sighed when Ava entered his room again.

"Let me guess, you've found something else to pin on me. Something that will seal the deal and put me away for life unless I tell you what you want to know."

"You watch too much TV, Mr. Arrowood. I can't make you that offer, but you're right about the other thing."

"What other thing?"

"The thing that will seal the deal. Do you own a hunting knife?"

"Nope. I live in the city. Why would I need a hunting knife?"

"One with a deer bone handle."

"Nope."

"We found a piece of the deer bone handle in the library and matched it to a knife found at your place, so you can see why I'm a little confused. The piece we found at the library was broken off when the knife's handle impacted the corner of Teagan Reese's desk."

"I thought you said she was shot to death. That's what's all over the news, too. Nothing about a knife."

"Yeah, funny how the media doesn't get all the little details, isn't it? The knife wasn't used to commit the murder, but we think Teagan fought back and knocked the knife out of your hand. It hit the corner of the desk, skittered out of your reach, and that's when you used the gun."

"You have one good imagination, Agent. Maybe you should give up on this career and go work writing movie scripts for Hollywood. You'd make a much better screenwriter than a federal agent."

"That missing gun has turned up, too, you know."

"Where?" He cleared his throat and glanced around nervously.

"Why don't you tell me, Mr. Arrowood?"

"She had—" He put a hand to his mouth and remained silent.

"She had what? The gun? Good reason? Good enough reason to just throw you under the bus?" Ava leaned toward him. "She told us where to find it, Grady."

A knock came at the door. Ava walked over and opened it. A tall man in his fifties stood there in a suit. "Margueritte Aldridge. I'm her lawyer, Mr. Bell."

Ava stepped out and took him to Margueritte's door. "Your client is in here."

Mr. Bell opened the door, and Ava headed for the conference room, fuming.

CHAPTER THIRTY-NINE

Sprung

LESS THAN AN HOUR AFTER AVA SAW MR. BELL, THE ALDRIDGES were released.

"That can't be right," Metford said.

"Money greases many wheels," Dane said. "Saw it a lot in New York."

Sal entered the conference room. "The Aldridges are out for now. They won't leave Fairhaven, but they're out of here."

"Not even one night in jail after killing Teagan and doing God knows what with her husband and kids?" Santos asked furiously. "But I was at risk of being fired and jailed for what I did. Broken isn't the word for the justice system."

"Santos," Metford said. "Take a breath. We're all upset about this."

"It's not the end of it," Ava assured her. "Grady Arrowood still hasn't asked for a lawyer, and I'm not done with him."

She made her way back to his room but he had been removed back to his holding cell. She went there but didn't rush too much. It gave her time to think out her strategy.

"Well, you might make it as a detective yet," Grady said. "At least you found me."

"You know you're alone in this now, don't you? I mean, your sister at least came to see you before she left, right?"

"What do you mean? Where'd she go?"

"Margueritte's fancy, expensive lawyer, and her husband's power, influence, and money have freed both of them while you're left here to take the fall and rot away in prison, or worse, but you don't have to talk. I understand."

He huffed. "I can't believe that bitch would do this to me. How could she just walk out and not even try to help me?"

"Maybe the same way you tried to sell her up the river and cover your own butt."

"What's going to happen now? I want to know what's going to happen now."

"Your lawyer will let you know, I'm sure. Oh, wait a minute. You don't have one, do you? Can't afford one either. Not since Sister Margie ran off with all her money and her fancy attorney. Or, did you just think you really wouldn't need one?"

He scowled at her through the bars.

"You can have one appointed. That was in your rights, remember?"

"Piss off and leave me alone." He gripped the bars tighter and continued to glare.

"Sure thing, but just know that when this goes down, you're taking the fall for all of it. Money works miracles, as you just saw, and apparently you don't have any." She made it to the door.

"It was her idea," Grady said in a defeated voice.

Ava turned and took a few steps toward his cell. "I'm sorry, what was that?"

"You heard me. It was her idea. I'll tell you everything. Even where to find the recorded conversation we had about it. It's time that high-flying bitch paid her dues like the rest of us have to."

"Well, by all means, start talking. This conversation is being recorded, too, by the way." She pointed to the cameras.

He sneered. "I hope so, because I don't want to repeat this a hundred times. Margie found out about Connor and Teagan having an affair. She said it had been going on for at least a year. That was over a month ago that she came to me with it. She wouldn't divorce Connor because of his money and power, and even though she wanted to confront Teagan, she didn't want anyone to know she had found out their secret. That was supposed to keep her dainty little hands clean.

"She, my sister Margueritte Aldridge," he said, clearly addressing the camera in the corner, "said she wanted Teagan dead. It was the only way Connor would ever stop messing around with her." He looked back to Ava. "She came to me three different times over the last month with updates to her plan. She wanted to hire me to kill Teagan. Said she would supply the weapon even."

"How much did she offer you to kill Teagan? How much was Teagan Reese's life worth?"

"Five hundred thousand at the beginning, but that changed. She wanted me to kill Brad, too. She said if Brad was taken away from here and killed, his body hidden, it would look like he had killed his cheating wife and went into hiding with his kids."

"But then what about the kids?"

"She came back the third time with a final plan. She wanted them all dead. The whole family. Couldn't risk just kidnapping the kids and leaving them alive. They'd talk; and kids are smarter than we give them credit for. So, she wanted Teagan killed at work, Brad and the kids taken away and killed. I was to dispose of the bodies and any evidence, then she would pay me and I could disappear."

"And you accepted that offer?"

"Do I strike you as a saint? Do I look like I'm even a nice guy?"

"You have a point. Continue."

"Brad's body is at Warehouse Seventy-Two, building G, all the way at the farthest end from the loading docks. I wrapped his body in plastic and put it in a wooden crate that had been used to deliver kitchen equipment. Vulcan was the name brand on the crate."

Disgusted at the ease with which he related the details, Ava tensed. "What about the kids, Mr. Arrowood? Where are Penny and Thomas?"

"They're in the same warehouse, but locked inside the little house in there. It's the office, but it looks like a tiny house. Both kids were alive when I left them." He raked his hand through his hair. "That's been almost four days ago now, but I swear they were alive. Scared, but okay. They didn't know I killed their dad." His eyes widened as they met Ava's.

"You admit to killing Brad."

He exhaled slowly. "Why lie when I'm going to tell you where the recorded conversations are?"

Ava got on her phone and called Sal to tell her about the warehouse. "Where is the recording?" Sal was still on the other end of the line.

"There's a loose floorboard in the closet of my apartment. There's a thumb drive under that board. But you'd know that if you really already found the gun."

"Did you get that, Sal?"

"Putting units on it right now."

Ava hung up.

"You lied to me, didn't you, Agent?"

She wobbled her hand back and forth in a 'kind of' gesture. "I wouldn't say lied. Wound you up and let you think what you wanted, though, yeah. Did Connor know about any of this?"

"She would never have told him. He would've stopped her, and then he would've divorced her. She's a bitch, not an idiot."

"Well, the jury's still out on that one. For your sake, you better hope those kids are still alive, Mr. Arrowood."

He blew air up into his face. "Why? Because if they're not, they'll tack on two more life sentences to the two I'm already going to get?"

CHAPTER FORTY

Arrested

I T WAS SATISFYING WHEN MARGUERITTE ALDRIDGE WAS BROUGHT by Ava's office in cuffs. It was even more satisfying when Ava got to interrogate her.

"I heard the conversations you had with Grady about how you wanted Teagan killed and her family disposed of. We've all heard the recordings. Bet you never thought your brother was smart enough to have an insurance policy like that."

She chuckled. "Not much of an insurance policy. He's going to prison, too. In my opinion, it defeated the purpose."

"Well, I can't express how glad I am that you two trust each other so much. Do you have anything you want to say, any last-minute plea deal offers, anything?"

"I'll tell you where Brad and the kids are."

"We already know. The team has already located Brad's body, and the kids are at the hospital."

"They were supposed to be unharmed."

"I have the recorded conversation, Mrs. Aldridge, remember? I heard you tell Grady to kill Brad, stash the kids. Then I heard you later change your mind and tell him to kill them all, that it was too risky to let the kids live."

Real tears spilled down Margueritte's face. "I didn't think he would really kill any of them. They were innocent, really. All three of them."

"Mrs. Aldridge, you offered him five hundred thousand dollars to kill Teagan, and then you told him you'd pay him double that if he would get rid of all of them and then disappear himself. Why would you ever think he wouldn't go through with it?"

"Because we were kids once, too. And our father is all we had. I thought … It doesn't matter what I thought."

"No, Mrs. Aldridge, it does not."

"At least he didn't hurt the kids. That's something."

"Yeah, but they were starving and dehydrated, and there might be permanent damage. The doctors aren't sure yet. As for you, Mrs. Aldridge, you are going to lose everything. Your home, your reputation, your husband, and your freedom. You deserve a worse fate, in my opinion, but I'll settle for that."

In the conference room, the team gathered for the final debriefing in the Teagan Reese case.

"Penny and Thomas are stable," Santos said. "I just spoke with their doctors. Penny is asking for her mom, and they haven't told her anything. They think the shock might be more than her system can handle right now."

"What about Thomas?" Metford asked.

"He's in worse shape. He is in and out of consciousness, and he hasn't spoken yet. The doctors say it could be shock, but maybe a trauma response. It's likely that he will have some amnesia because of the hit on the head. That, by the way, was caused by a fall. Penny told the doctors he fell when they were trying to climb into the ceiling vent to get out. She stood on a desk and he was on her shoulders when they lost balance."

"What about the gun?" Ava said. "Was it a match in Arthur Erwin's death?"

"It was," Dane said.

"So, we're charging Grady with three murders," Sal said. "I talked to him an hour ago, and he admitted that he got worried when the FBI got on the case. He shot Arthur to throw us off his trail. If it looked like someone was killing at random, maybe it wouldn't lead back to him."

"And Connor was really clueless about all this?" Ava asked.

"Looks that way," Sal said. "The recordings of Grady and Margueritte's conversations cleared him."

"The only thing he's guilty of is the affair," Ashton said. "And being a misogynistic, clueless jerk."

"That's a strong opinion," Santos said.

"Yeah, well, I had to go through all his electronic communications. I saw much more of him than I ever wanted to. Got a good look inside his head, too. Some men are messed up."

"What about the hunting knife?" Metford asked.

"It was Grady's. It was in the truck. He tossed it behind the seat and just left it," Ashton said. "Guess he didn't realize part of the handle was chipped out at the crime scene."

"Okay, team. That was good work. Go home and get some much-needed, much-deserved rest. Keep your notes and files handy because you'll be called to court to testify soon."

CHAPTER FORTY-ONE

A Little Recognition

THE FOLLOWING WEEK, THE TEAM WAS BACK TO NORMAL AND TAK-
ing on cases as if what happened on the Reese case was just business
as usual. Ava was amazed at the resilience of her team. Even though
they had been pushed to the edge, they had come out the other side with
a strengthened bond and smiles. It made her proud of them; of herself.

Although she had been doubting whether she really wanted to continue with her chosen career, she stood at the bullpen door and smiled
at her team. Metford, Ashton, Dane, and Santos worked together as dil-
igently as ever.

They had grown as individuals and as a team. That was the mark
of greatness.

"Hey, what's going on?" Sal asked.

"Just thinking."

"Looked like maybe it was happy thinking. If I'm not mistaken, I saw the impression of a smile."

"Nah, it's just the way the light was hitting my face," Ava joked.

"Got a nice surprise for all of you. Want to get everyone into the conference room?" Sal walked away.

"Sure," Ava called after her. She opened the door to the bullpen. "Hey, Sal said to come to the conference room."

"Oh, no," Santos said.

"What'd we do now?" Metford asked.

"Probably another messy case," Dane said.

"No, she said it was a nice surprise for all of us," Ava interjected.

"She's giving us a day off," Ashton teased. "I knew if we just waited long enough and worked hard enough."

"Keep wishing," Metford said.

They made their way to the conference room as a group. It was impossible not to notice how everyone was getting along and interacting without the usual friction. Going through days and nights of no sleep as a group could have made things worse but it had done the opposite. Was it because of the intimacy of being out of their heads with stress and being sleep-deprived? It had to be. That was the most pronounced difference between the Teagan Reese case and the others they had worked together.

In the conference room, Sal stood at the side of Deputy Director Marks. Everyone on the team, including Ava, stood straighter and dropped their grins and the joking.

"Team," Sal said proudly. "Deputy Director Marks has come over here today to speak to you about the Teagan Reese case." She stepped away and smiled at him.

The tension that ran through everyone was palpable. Sal was smiling, but the Deputy Director didn't just drop in to say howdy and have coffee. Ava wasn't sure about everyone else, but she was sure they were about to get lambasted for something they had done wrong.

But he cleared his throat and smiled.

"Congratulations, team. You really made the Bureau look good out there."

The collective sigh of relief was so audible that everyone glanced at each other and giggled.

"This case wasn't easy, and I know you were dealing with lots of moving parts and pressure from up-top. But you saved those kids, which is a win any day in my book. And as far as the Internal Affairs investigations..."

The tension didn't even have time to return before he waved it away. "Consider everything settled. Far as I'm concerned, you took some calculated risks that paid off, and we're grateful."

The whole meeting took less than fifteen minutes. Marks again congratulated them on solving the case so swiftly, and as a token of the Bureau's appreciation, he invited them to a dinner that was going to be held in their honor. It was being held by the Arts Council of Maryland.

And then, he had a flight to catch back to DC. After shaking hands with each of them, he was gone.

"You made quite the impact," Sal said to them. "It's unusual for a team to get recognition like that."

"Do we have to wear a suit to the dinner?" Metford asked.

"Yes, Agent. It's a black-tie dinner," Sal said with a disapproving downturn to her mouth.

"They'll be taking pictures, won't they?" Santos groaned.

"Yes, there will be plenty of pictures of the golden team," Sal said. "Seriously, guys? I thought you'd be more excited for the recognition. This is big."

"We are," Ava said. "It's just so weird."

"Take it," Sal said. "Trust me, take the recognition where you get it in this line of work. It's a thankless job, so let the Bureau and the Arts Council of Maryland thank you in grand fashion."

Later that evening, as she drove home, Ava couldn't help but contemplate how little and how late the well-deserved recognition was for her team. They had accomplished nearly impossible feats to solve other cases, save countless lives, clean up tons of drugs and guns from the streets, and they were just now getting a nod of approval from the Bureau.

Even though it was little and late, she felt a sense of contentment growing in her that she had feared was gone, and her purpose for pursuing the career had been renewed. She could think of nothing she wanted to do more than continue helping others, keeping people safe, and making sure justice was served.

For the time, that was enough.

CHAPTER FORTY-TWO

Residue

"THAT DINNER WASN'T AS BAD AS I THOUGHT IT WAS GOING TO be," Metford said.

"It was nice. Different, but nice," Ava agreed. "I think Santos would have been more comfortable in a dress made of sandpaper, though. Did you see how she kept adjusting it and pulling at it?"

"She grumbled the entire time," he chuckled. "But she looked good. We all did."

Ava thought about it for a minute as she opened the box containing the files for the Teagan Reese case. "Yeah, we did. And we got some great pictures."

"Can you believe they gave us pictures as mementos of the special night?" He laughed. "I thought we'd get a watch, a commemorative badge, or something like that; not five-by-seven glossy group shots."

Ava opened a file and read over it. She closed it and put it aside, remembering how tough the case had been on all of them, but especially how it had twisted her. Had it been the case or that she had still been dragging around the guilt and shame about Jason Ellis?

She decided it had been the latter.

After the case was finished, she had been able to get a grip on her feelings about Ellis. It had come with the sometimes-harsh help of Dr. Bran, but that was okay. If she hadn't been harsh, Ava knew she would not have taken her advice seriously. Why take advice from a push-over?

And strange as it had seemed to her, the whole buying a plant and taking care of it had helped. She wasn't sure what about it had helped, but there had been a noticeable and sizeable improvement in her mindset, emotion-control, and contentment after she bought the thing. And she had to admit, it looked nice in her window, too.

"Weird that Grady had been in prison for trying to kill that scared girl in New York that wouldn't talk to us, isn't it?" Metford asked.

"Yeah, weird because of her connections to the Aldridges," Ava said.

"Guess it really is a small world after all."

"Maybe." She opened her note file and read over some of the things she had jotted down on the fly when she and Metford had been there.

"What's that?" Metford tapped the open folder she held.

"Just some notes from when we were in the city. You remember Lucia?"

"Yeah, she talked enough to make up for Sharelle Kim's silence. Why?"

"I don't know. I just can't stop thinking about all that stuff she said about the Aldridges and their sponsor programs. Something feels unfinished."

"It's odd, but what can we do? We don't have anything to go on but what she said. If there's no case, there's no case."

"What if there is and nobody's looked into it yet? What if all that money and influence has greased the right wheels, and the right people don't know what's going on in Connor's circle?"

"What's going on there, Ava? A bunch of artists living together, probably partying and maybe taking drugs? Producing ugly art that will make them a bunch of money and earn them some fame?"

"What about the ones who disappear and aren't found?"

"They're adults. They can disappear if they choose to. And we know that the lower rung programs took in troubled young artists, artists who had predispositions to addiction especially. We both know what happens to those people when they spiral and there's no family or friends there to anchor them."

Ava nodded and flipped the folder closed. "Yeah, I know. They end up chasing the next fix until they end up dead. Then we get to investigate their deaths or the crimes they committed while they were trying to get that next fix. I know." She took out another folder and opened it. "It's just not right. Something about it stinks. Those sponsorships, the case with Teagan, the Aldridges."

"If this is going to eat at you, why don't you figure out what we can do and let's do it?"

They locked eyes. "You're serious?" she asked.

"As a heart attack."

"Which you are going to have if you don't stop eating that fast-food junk all the time." She pointed to the Wendy's bag on his side of the table.

"I still say your eating habits are just as bad as mine. I've seen you scarf down cheeseburgers like a Viking going at a whole ham."

"Yes."

"Yes, your eating habits are bad?"

"No. Yes to the offer."

He blinked at her in silence. The confusion was all over his face.

She held up the folder. "About the case. You said if I would figure out what we could legally do, we'd do it."

"We will. As soon as you have a plan, count me in."

"We can find out more about Connor's sponsorship programs and see where it leads."

"Might be a waste of time."

"Might not, though."

EPILOGUE

THE WOMAN SAT IN THE DARK SILENCE. SHE COULDN'T REMEMBER how long she had been gone from her home, but it felt like years. The beatings and rapes made the days an endless river of brutality that ebbed and bled into one another. There were no borders, no boundaries anymore. She was Art Exhibit One-Nine-Three: The Abused Female.

"My name is Gloria," she whispered. "My name is Gloria. I'm from Franklin, Tennessee. I went to New York City and met a man." She pushed her memory but couldn't recall the man's name or what he looked like. There had been too many since him. Or, had it been a woman? She didn't think so.

Someone screamed in the distance and Gloria slammed her hands over her ears. "One, two, three…" She counted to a hundred before removing her hands. The screaming had stopped.

Someone knocked on the glass wall at the front of her room. She tried to shrink into the corner. It wasn't time for another exhibit. She'd just been put in the dark, and that meant she had a while to heal at least a little.

The knock came again and tears welled in her eyes.

"Hey, what's going on? I heard you counting; I know you're in there," a man's voice said.

He was on the other side of the glass, but that wasn't right. That was the viewing pit. No one was supposed to be in there unless an exhibition was happening.

"Hey, girl," the voice called. "What's this place? Where are we?"

Gloria risked moving a bit closer to the glass. The dark canvas curtain that covered the outside of the wall prevented her from seeing the viewing pit, but there was a gap at the bottom and up the right side. If she pressed her eye close enough…

The next knock made her yelp and fall backward. She scrambled to get up. "Stop it," she hissed.

"God, it's great to hear you. I'm Danny. What is this place? Where are we? What do they want from us? How long have you been here?"

"Shut up," she said, fear rippling through her. If they heard her talking, even to herself, they would beat her with the stick again.

"How do we get out? Do you know?" The man's voice was much lower. Maybe someone had escaped their room. "No way out," she whispered.

"How old are you?"

"I don't know. Can't remember." Her throat pained with each word.

"How old were you on your last birthday?"

"Twenty," she said without hesitation. That day, she remembered in great and vivid detail. It stuck out in her mind as a reminder to how bright and happy and free her life was before she left for New York. It was just a memory stuck there to torment her, tease her cruelly, and leave her wishing for the death that never seemed to come.

"I'm twenty-three."

Bully for him. If he lived long enough, he wouldn't know his true age, remember his real name, or who took him either.

"Gloria," she whispered. "My name is Gloria." Or was that one of the many names she had been given by the man who beat her, fed her, prepared her for exhibitions, and cleaned her up afterward? Did he have a name? Everyone had a name, but she didn't think she had ever heard his.

"Hey, girl, what's that you're saying? Speak up."

"Shh," she said.

"Why?"

"They'll beat us if they hear us," she said, pushing back to her corner. If Danny wanted to get into trouble, that was his deal. She didn't want any more beatings.

Danny tried talking to her more, but she refused to answer. After a few minutes, he hit the glass hard with his fist. The black curtain was yanked back, and bright, stinging light flooded her concrete room.

Screeching in shock and fear, she shielded her eyes with her arm. Applause boomed and echoed, and she peered out. Her heart thundered and raced. The viewing pit was full. Men, women, all ages and ethnicities stared in at her with expectant glee.

The man's voice came from above, as it always did. "Danny, claim your prize. Claim it for all to witness. This is what you paid for, the moment you've dreamed about. Seize it." The last word faded and the audience took up the chant: *"Seize it! Seize it! Seize it!"*

She'd been tricked. Danny wasn't nice. Danny wasn't a scared victim. He was one of them.

The metal door at the side of the room opened and a man stepped in dressed in black. He wore goggles and gloves. He held his hand out in the light. A small, silver knife glistened in his palm.

"My name is Gloria. I'm from Franklin, Tennessee. I went to New York."

The trailer door rumbled up into the track. "Welcome home, Gloria," the man said.

"That's not my name." She struggled against the zip tie on her wrists and the collar around her neck.

"It's whatever I tell you it is, and I happen to like Gloria. We just lost our last Gloria, and you're taking her place." He stepped into the trailer. "Albeit in a different way. You paint, no?"

"My name is Jennifer."

He slapped her hard. When her head rocked back forward, she spat at him. It was bloody and hit him in the face. He hit her again. That time it was hard enough that she heard her neck pop.

"Now, you'll behave like you've got some manners, Gloria, or it would please me to beat you into submission. Do you understand?"

She didn't, but she nodded all the same.

"You'll have two roommates, and I would suggest you take your cues from them. They've been here a long time; they can help you stay here a long time, too. Cause trouble, and you won't live to regret it."

He dragged her out of the trailer. The sun was bright, but the air smelled of brine. They were close to the ocean. Which one? She inhaled deeply as she tried to look around for other houses, other people. A shame she couldn't tell which ocean by its smell.

The man opened a door and dragged her in by the arm, not slowing when her feet tangled and she fell. He simply dragged her along like a dog dragging his favorite blanket through the house. He opened another door and yanked her to her feet before shoving her inside.

"In you go. They'll let you loose when they're sure you're going to behave." He looked to the two women standing against the wall and blew them kisses. They pretended to catch them and hold them to their cheeks. The man laughed. "Good girls."

With the door closed, the two women rushed to Jennifer and worked until the zip tie was off. Jennifer hooked her fingers around the collar, found the clasp and undid it.

"What the hell is this place?" she demanded.

The women held their fingers to their lips in a shushing gesture.

The girl on the right moved closer. "We paint for them, and they don't hurt us as much as the others."

"Where are we?" Jennifer looked up to the high, barred windows.

"Near the ocean."

"Well, no kidding. Which one? How far are we from the road?"

The girl shrugged. "Don't try to leave. They'll kill you. We're enter-tainment. As long as we entertain, we survive."

"I'm no man's entertainment." Jennifer pulled a table under a window and jumped onto it. She couldn't get out the window even if she broke it. The bars were on the outside and there was no way to get them loose. She could, however, pull up far enough to peek out. She wasn't super strong, but she held the position long enough to see that there were no houses in sight and no tourists anywhere. "Private beach," she said.

"Stop or you'll get us all in trouble," the girl warned.

"Sister, we're already in trouble."

Sam and Tonya ran into the alley holding hands and laughing. They had outsmarted their parents again and sneaked off for a day of making out and smoking pot. Slowing their pace to a fast walk, they locked lips.

Sam tripped over something large, cursed, and fell sprawling on the pavement. Tonya backed up to the wall and clutched her hands to her chest as she screamed.

Looking back at what he'd tripped over, Sam scrambled to his feet, took two steps, and puked on his shoes.

The body was mutilated. He couldn't tell if it was a man, woman, or child. What looked like a bloody wig dangled from the corner of a dumpster at the other end of the alley. The body's bloody skull showed through parts of the skin. The corpse had been scalped. Some of its ribs stuck out of the skin on its back and the lips had been cut away.

Sam puked again as he reached for his phone to call the cops.

Tonya stopped screaming long enough to alert him to the note in the corpse's hand. He stood over it and tried not to see the ruination of the body. 'My name is Gloria,' the note read.

He giggled at that. He didn't know why, but God help him, he did.

AUTHOR'S NOTE

Dear Reader,

Thank you so much for joining me on this journey and for reading The Librarian! I can't tell you how excited I am to have you here as we dive into a brand-new season with Ava. Writing this book was such a blast, and I have to give a huge shoutout to my amazing editor. Their fresh perspective was invaluable as it helped me catch my bad habits and turn good scenes into great ones. I love working through their feedback because it pushes me to learn and grow with every story. My goal is to keep improving so I can make these books even more exciting for you!

Your support and feedback mean the world to me. Just as my editor's insights help shape the story, your reviews and comments are what truly bring it to life. Knowing what you loved, what surprised you, or even what kept you guessing helps me grow as a writer and keeps me on my toes. If you enjoyed the journey, please consider leaving a review. Your thoughts not only guide me but also help other readers discover Ava's world, and for that, I'm incredibly grateful!

As we wrap up this chapter, I'm excited to give you a sneak peek of what's coming next. In the next installment, Ava is drawn into a perplexing case when a popular artist, Lucia Martinez, mysteriously vanishes from her home in Fairhaven. What starts as a simple missing persons investigation soon spirals into a nightmare that sends shockwaves through the entire community. As more victims go missing, and one is found turned into a gruesome "art piece," Ava realizes she's up against a sinister force that's more twisted and dangerous than anything she's faced before. I can't wait for you to dive into this dark and bewildering adventure with Ava!

And if you're looking for another unputdownable mystery, check out the incredibly well-reviewed latest addition to my Dean Steel series, *Playing with Fire*. Dean is thrown into chaos after a fire devastates a local theme park, and the grand re-opening takes a grim turn. With several deaths, lots of suspects, and an abundance of odd connections, Dean's latest case proves to be his toughest yet...

Thank you for your support and for joining me on this journey. Ava and the team are counting on you, and I can't wait to see where our adventures take us next.

Yours,
A.J. Rivers

P.S. If for some reason you didn't like this book or found typos or other errors, please let me know personally. I do my best to read and respond to every email at mailto:aj@ riversthrillers.com

P.P.S. If you would like to stay up-to-date with me and my latest releases I invite you to visit my Linktree page at *www.linktr.ee/a.j.rivers* to subscribe to my newsletter and receive a free copy of my book, Edge of the Woods. You can also follow me on my social media accounts for behind-the-scenes glimpses and sneak peeks of my upcoming projects, or even sign up for text notifications. I can't wait to connect with you!

ALSO BY

A.J. RIVERS

Emma Griffin FBI Mysteries

Season One

Book One—The Girl in Cabin 13*
Book Two—The Girl Who Vanished*
Book Three—The Girl in the Manor*
Book Four—The Girl Next Door*
Book Five—The Girl and the Deadly Express*
Book Six—The Girl and the Hunt*
Book Seven—The Girl and the Deadly End*

Season Two

Book Eight—The Girl in Dangerous Waters*
Book Nine—The Girl and Secret Society*
Book Ten—The Girl and the Field of Bones*
Book Eleven—The Girl and the Black Christmas*
Book Twelve—The Girl and the Cursed Lake*
Book Thirteen—The Girl and The Unlucky 13*
Book Fourteen—The Girl and the Dragon's Island*

Season Three

Book Fifteen—The Girl in the Woods*
Book Sixteen —The Girl and the Midnight Murder*
Book Seventeen— The Girl and the Silent Night*
Book Eighteen — The Girl and the Last Sleepover*
Book Nineteen — The Girl and the 7 Deadly Sins*
Book Twenty — The Girl in Apartment 9*
Book Twenty-One — The Girl and the Twisted End*

Emma Griffin FBI Mysteries Retro - Limited Series
(Read as standalone or before Emma Griffin book 22)

Book One— *The Girl in the Mist**
Book Two— *The Girl on Hallow's Eve**
Book Three— *The Girl and the Christmas Past**
Book Four— *The Girl and the Winter Bones**
Book Five— *The Girl on the Retreat**

Season Four

Book Twenty-Two — *The Girl and the Deadly Secrets**
Book Twenty-Three — *The Girl on the Road**
Book Twenty-Four —*The Girl and the Unexpected Gifts**
Book Twenty-Five —*The Girl and the Secret Passage**
Book Twenty-Six — *The Girl and the Bride**
Book Twenty-Seven — *The Girl in Her Cabin**
Book Twenty-Eight — *The Girl Who Remembers**

Season Five

Book Twenty-Nine — *The Girl in the Dark**
Book Thirty — *The Girl and the Lies*

Ava James FBI Mysteries

Book One—*The Woman at the Masked Gala**
Book Two—*Ava James and the Forgotten Bones**
Book Three —*The Couple Next Door**
Book Four — *The Cabin on Willow Lake**
Book Five — *The Lake House**
Book Six — *The Ghost of Christmas**
Book Seven — *The Rescue**
Book Eight — *Murder in the Moonlight**
Book Nine — *Behind the Mask**
Book Ten — *The Invitation**
Book Eleven — *The Girl in Hawaii**
Book Twelve — *The Woman in the Window**
Book Thirteen — *The Good Doctor**
Book Fourteen — *The Housewife Killer*
Book Fifteen— *The Librarian*

ALSO BY

A.J. RIVERS & THOMAS YORK